Praise for

The Silent:Chord

"Matthew Kirkpatrick's thrilling *The Silent:Chord* reads something like Kafka writing a Charles Yu story: bleakly hilarious, offering an inescapable claustrophobia of office politics and corporate disaffection, all the while remaining highly attuned to the ways we fail to see each other even as we yearn for connection. A dizzyingly disorienting novel I won't soon forget, from a writer who never fails to surprise and delight."

—**Matt Bell,** author of
Appleseed

"Part satire and part noir, *The Silent:Chord* is a mash-up of Hitchcock's *Psycho* and David Lynch's *Mullholland Drive*. Kirkpatrick's razor-sharp humor and brilliantly executed plot is a synesthetic pleasure in the vein of Paul Auster and Tom McCarthy. But more than that, this is a novel of ideas: about the sanctity of memory, the slippery line between possibility and fantasy, and the threat of literal and figurative erasure. A bold and original novel, *The Silent:Chord* is a deft reminder of the frailty of human consciousness when faced with grief, the brutality of corporate corruption, and the lengths we go to in order to combat perhaps that most haunting of human emotions: loneliness."

—**Lindsey Drager,** author of
The Avian Hourglass

The Silent Chord

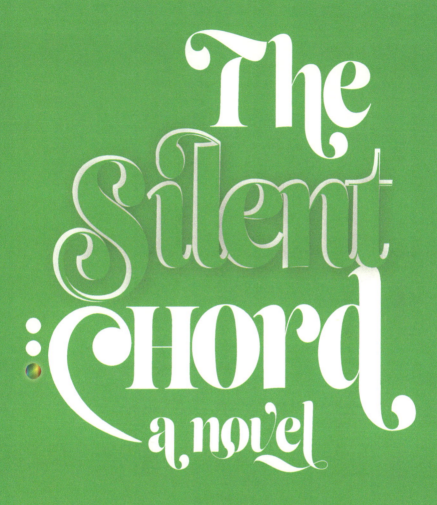

MATTHEW KIRKPATRICK

TRP: The University Press of SHSU

Copyright © 2025 Matthew Kirkpatrick
All Rights Reserved
Library of Congress Cataloging-in-Publication Data

Names: Kirkpatrick, Matthew, author.
Title: The Silent Chord / Matthew Kirkpatrick.
Description: First edition. | Huntsville, Texas : TRP: The University Press of SHSU, [2025]
Identifiers: LCCN 2024028495 (print) | LCCN 2024028496 (ebook) | ISBN 9781680034004 (trade paperback) | ISBN 9781680034011 (ebook)
Subjects: LCSH: Synesthesia—Fiction. | Perfumes, Synthetic—Fiction. | False memory syndrome—Fiction. | LCGFT: Novels.
Classification: LCC PS3611.I764 C66 2025 (print) | LCC PS3611.I764 (ebook) | DDC 813/.6—dc23/eng/20240624
LC record available at https://lccn.loc.gov/2024028495
LC ebook record available at https://lccn.loc.gov/2024028496

FIRST EDITION
Cover & interior design by PJ Carlisle
Printed and bound in the United States of America
First Edition Copyright: 2025
TRP: The University Press of SHSU
Huntsville, Texas 77341
texasreviewpress.org

For Susan

Contents

Part One

1. THE STALE OFFICE AIR AWAKENED, SUDDENLY VIBRANT AND ALIVE 1
2. CHAMPION SAT NAKED ON THE EDGE OF THE CONSULTANT'S BED 3
3. EXITING THE ELEVATOR ON THE 4TH FLOOR, ONE OF THE MEN SOBBED 6
4. SOMEWHERE BETWEEN CONSCIOUSNESS AND SLEEP, CHAMPION STARED 7
5. A SECURITY CAMERA WATCHED BRYCE 10
6. UPSTAIRS, CHAMPION WASHED HIS HANDS 15
7. DENISE SIFTED THROUGH HER INTERNAL MESSAGES 16
8. IT WAS NOT THE SHAPE OF CHAMPION'S HEAD OR HIS DYED WHITE HAIR 20
9. OUTSIDE, THE MAGENTA SKY HUNG LOW 27
10. BRYCE SOMETIMES HEARD THE SMELL OF THE RIVER 30
11. TWO AUTONOMOUS CARS, EMPTY AND DRIVERLESS, IGNORED A RED LIGHT 35
12. I'M TIRED OF THIS, CARL 38
13. BRYCE'S LEGS BURNED FROM THE BRAMBLES' DEEP RED SCRATCHES 41
14. DENISE COULD FIND NOTHING IN BRYCE'S EMAILS 44
15. CHAMPION CRAWLED THROUGH THE PLENUM SPACE 48
16. CHERYL AND TAMMERS WENT TO THE ART MUSEUM 50
17. BRYCE ARRAYED THE FRAGRANCES HE'D ORDERED FROM THE LAB 56
18. CHAMPION STOOD BY THE BAR, UNSURE OF WHY HE'D COME 62
19. CHAMPION DREAMT OF RAGE 64
20. BRYCE'S BODY, STILL AND BLUE, LEANING AGAINST THE WALL OF HIS CUBE 72

Part Two

21. CHAMPION SHOWED SAB HOW TO UNLATCH THE DOORS ... 77
22. THEY EASILY FOUND PARKING AT THE OLD MALL ... 80
23. THE FROTTEURS, WHO RUBBED AGAINST THEM ... 84
24. THE TELEVISION SAID SOMETHING ABOUT RECORD RAIN ... 91
25. MAYBE WE CAN HIDE UP HERE A WHILE ... 98
26. YOU HAVEN'T MADE MUCH PROGRESS ... 99
27. CHAMPION SAT AT HIS DINING ROOM TABLE LOOKING INTO THE SCREEN OF HIS LAPTOP ... 103
28. CARL HAD PROMISED THEM ALL A SPECIAL HOLIDAY PARTY ... 106
29. ON THE SCREEN OF HER PHONE, DENISE SAW BRYCE ... 114
30. CHAMPION AWOKE IN DARKNESS ... 116
31. BRYCE WALKED THE GRID OF CUBICLES ... 117
32. CARL'S LOPS DANCED IN HIS DAYDREAM ... 119
33. DENISE MADE HER WAY ALONG A NARROW PATH IN THE RED LIGHT OF THE NIGHT SKY ... 121
34. THEY GATHERED IN THE DAYTIME DARKNESS ON THE FENCED-IN FIELD ... 125
35. TAMMERS SAT ON A BENCH OUTSIDE THE BON-TON ... 127
36. DENISE FOLLOWED THE CLUES SHE'D FOUND ... 129

Contents

Part Three

37. CHAMPION FELT THE VIAL IN HIS POCKET ... 135
38. STEEL AND GLASS AND A CLEAR BRIGHT SKY ... 141
39. BRYCE AND ANGIE JOINED THE MASSES ... 143
40. CHERYL, GONE FROM THE CONCORDANCE ... 146
41. THE LATE-NIGHT AIR SMELLED LIKE FABRIC SOFTENER ... 148
42. THEY FOLLOWED THE CROWD, THICK WITH WOMEN IN BONNETS AND MEN IN HIGH PANTS ... 153
43. DENISE OPENED THE CLOSET ... 156
44. BRYCE SAT AT A TABLE IN THE FOOD COURT ... 160
45. I'M CALLING THE POLICE ... 163
46. CARL SPUN CIRCLES IN HIS DESK CHAIR ... 165
47. TRASH STEWED IN THE SLOW CURRENT ... 166
48. CHAMPION RECOGNIZED THE SMELL OF INSTITUTION ... 168
49. THE SUN SHIP SWAYED IN THE WIND ... 172
50. THE ROOM WAS LIKE CARL'S BEDROOM AT HOME ... 173
51. TAMMERS IN HER TOWER LOOKED DOWN FROM THE PERCH OF HER PLYWOOD COUCH ... 174
52. AT BREAKFAST, MIKE WAS IN THE MIDDLE OF A STORY ... 180
53. EVEN IF HE WASN'T HOME, IT SEEMED LIKE HOME ... 183
54. SOMETIMES A RINGING, SOMETIMES A WHISPER ... 186
55. CLOUDS COVERED THE SUN ... 188
56. CHAMPION FELT THE NETWORK DEVOURING HIM ... 200
57. THE STALE OFFICE AIR AWAKENED, SUDDENLY VIBRANT ... 202

Acknowledgments ... 205

Part One

1.

THE STALE OFFICE AIR AWAKENED, SUDDENLY VIBRANT AND ALIVE as the technicians opened their morning samples and released the aroma of artificial spearmint, honeysuckle, and rye. In their cubicles, the men bent over their desks and inhaled samples from paper strips or straight from vials and leaned back to look at the ceiling for some hidden answer as they tried to invent new adjectives for what they'd smelled.

The fragrant components coalesced into a kind of chemical white noise, stinging Denise's nose and throat, burning her eyes.

The men broke their concentration and paused to watch her gagging as she stood in the center of their quadrant of cubicles. She hated them and raised her hand to meet their glares, waiting for a sneeze to help expel the amalgamation from her body.

When the burning subsided, she continued toward her cube where she would take refuge while wishing for higher walls, wishing for a door. She took the shortest route—feeling their eyes on her, feeling their silence—and walked by Bryce's cube, even though he was the worst of them. Every morning she dreaded passing him the most, but did so anyway, some part of her hoping he would say something so she could again rebuff him.

Today was different. Something wasn't right with Bryce.

Instead of finding him in his chair, staring into his computer screen or inhaling some new scent, she found him slumped on the floor against the wall with a noose of network cabling wound around his neck.

"Bryce," she whispered into his ear while nudging his shoulder. She loosened the tangle of cables and removed them. "Wake up, Bryce. It's time for work." She pulled a fingernail along the blue bruise arced across his neck and touched her own neck, trying to imagine what had happened. Perhaps he was only sleeping.

Perhaps he'd had too much to drink.

Perhaps it would be difficult—maybe impossible now—to wake him. But he couldn't be. . . . No. Could he be . . . dead? There'd already been three deaths in VisualOptics and two in AudioAural. But none in Olfactory and nobody she'd known. Until now. Until Bryce?

The smell of coffee and the perfume of artificial rose hung over Bryce's skin. Bits of tissue stuck out of his nose and ears. She picked at the nose tissue with her thumb and index finger and unfolded the wad like an accordion, flaking red dry skin with it. She flicked the paper onto the ground, wiped her finger on her skirt, and whispered, "Bryce, it's time to get to work."

When he wouldn't awaken, she stood and leaned against his desk and took a sip of his coffee, still warm, and looked at the ceiling to discern some clue as to Bryce's unconsciousness. She checked the Concordance on her phone—it said Bryce was still alive. Though what was in front of her contradicted what she'd read, it was hard for her to believe what she could clearly see.

"Bryce," she said. "Can you hear me? Bryce?"

At least he could no longer bother her. Maybe he was in a better place; she wished she was in a better place too, and considered the network cabling. Protocol insisted she notify someone first, file a Death report, wait for confirmation. No early lunch for her.

A dozen scent vials were scattered around Bryce's computer screen. She picked one up and examined it, but found no control number or label. Even though it was against Protocol to inhale an unknown sample, she opened the top, held the vial to her nose, pressed her other nostril closed with her finger, and breathed.

What she inhaled was floral and musky, then moldy and foul. The fragrance was like nothing she'd smelled before, but was also familiar to her, and when she took the sample away from her nose the smell spread to the back of her throat.

What gathered there felt less like a fragrance and more like an ache, like a memory of something she could all but describe and grasp, something always just out of reach. Her stomach burned and the tips of her fingers numbed.

Wood and rose bloomed inside something mustardy, like a poison. A cloud of dark urine and sweat contaminated her as each note of the growing chorus emerged and then escaped. Burning leaves turned skunky, then cool, then sharp and camphorous.

The air smelled suddenly like the lingering smoke of melted hair.

2.

CHAMPION SAT NAKED ON THE EDGE OF THE CONSULTANT'S BED and listened to the sound of her saddening.

"I cry for the children and their mother and the dog that died in a fire," she said on her knees, raising her palms to the ceiling. Her lips quivered as she opened her red eyes, not yet wet with tears.

Champion leaned back. "Yes. Please *cry* about them for me," he said.

"Give me a minute. Okay?" She straddled him, sat back on his thighs, closed her eyes again, and showed him her clenched fists. She was trying.

Champion anticipated her authentic sadness. He waited for her eyes to fog with deliberate tears. "That's it. Cry for all those babies on that bus," he said. While he waited, he imagined it again: a yellow bus full of infants, a cliff. "Think of them bouncing around in there, flying through the windows and screaming as the bus falls into icy waters."

She opened her eyes. "That didn't happen."

"Please. I'm paying for this. It happened. It's happening right now in my mind."

"Bullshit," she whispered. She closed her eyes.

As tears began to streak her cheeks, he closed his fingers against his palms and trembled. He could feel his heart. "Yeah. That's good," he said.

She tilted her head back and gasped. The tears fell over her lips and into her mouth and she moaned a little, just enough, before beginning to sob so fully her shoulders and chest heaved in ecstatic wretchedness.

"Like that," he said. "Just like that."

When what came from her eyes seemed to Champion almost exactly like misery, he felt an indescribable release and shuddered. He relaxed with his back against the headboard and looked across the room at the Consultant's stunning paintings of wedding cakes hanging on the bedroom wall. He'd asked her once about the paintings, but she refused to explain. The images made him feel guilty, which he liked feeling, even though he wasn't married or in a relationship anymore. Never waste a Consultant session on guilt; wasn't that what people said?—though he knew he wasn't supposed to enjoy feeling *any* feelings.

"You good to go?" She sat on the edge now, dry-eyed again.

Time wasn't up yet, but he wasn't sure what else he could ask for. He told her about all the dead bodies at work, how the first one, his assistant Dale, had killed himself and when he walked by Dale's body floating in the fountain in front of the office for three days straight, ignoring Dale, leaving him voicemail messages, and reporting him for unexcused absences—even though he knew Dale was dead—he felt a little guilty for that, and for reporting his assistant for bad behavior when Dale had a good excuse for not getting his work done.

Champion told her he liked feeling guilty about Dale. "Fuck Protocol," he said, hoping to shock her.

She looked bored.

"Other than that, I don't really feel anything else I need you to fix for me, I guess. Except that I have to find a new assistant. That bothers me. Having to manage all the details myself. No one to talk to. Dale wasn't very good at much, but sometimes we had fun together—"

"I'm not your Counselor. This isn't therapy."

"—But good assistants, project managers, team players—are hard to find these days. I've tried to get some other guys to step up but all they do is slow me down. I don't really care. But the Boss is always riding me. I just don't want to keep doing those de-sensitivity trainings. It's not like I murdered them. He killed himself."

"Who thinks you murdered him?"

"I don't know; nobody, I guess. He killed himself. They all do—"

"What do *you* do, anyway?"

"—Sometimes I dream about killing people, but doesn't everybody? I've never really killed anybody—"

"Well *I've* never dreamt about murdering people. Maybe you *should* talk to a Counselor, seriously. Somebody. Somebody besides me?"

"—Why did he do it? They took me to the Gentle Hands facility the last time something like this happened. But I'm not violent."

"You've been to Gentle Hands? And they let you out?"

"I'm working on a very important project. I can't tell you about it."

"I didn't ask you about it. Your time's almost up. So you want me to feel guilty for you?"

"Okay."

"I'm not sure what that looks like. No one ever asks for guilt."

"Maybe a little like sadness, but also like despair."

"I can try it."

"Can you shake your fists at the ceiling like you're cursing an angry God?" He showed her, forming his little hands into angry fists, cursing the ceiling with them.

"Got it."

She did.

He asked her if she had time for a little impatience.

She looked at the clock and rolled her eyes.

"Can I have some tea instead, then?" He followed her into the kitchen where she turned on the burner under the teakettle. A black fly landed on the crust of a dirty pan in the sink. Outside, the sky hardened. Thick balls of hail smacked against the window.

"I just have green," she said.

"That's fine. It's good at getting rid of your free radicals. Antioxidants." He handed her an envelope from his inside-jacket pocket. A line of ants marched through a dusting of coffee grounds spilled across the counter. "Maybe on Friday I can get an hour?"

"I'll let you know."

"Did you paint these yourself?" He nodded at one of the kitchen paintings.

"I wish the water would boil," she muttered.

"Me too."

"You need to be out of here in three minutes."

He stood still behind her and waited. Fuck Protocol. On Friday he would ask her to cry for him about the state of their relationship, the space between them, and the love they would never have. They stood there. Maybe then he'd ask her to dinner again, knowing she would refuse everything. The water in the teakettle stood still. He wanted suddenly to put his arms around her, bend her over the counter, pull down her jeans, and fuck her right in her kitchen. He was still behind her. He could put his arm around her shoulder and pull her toward him; he would feel it this time maybe, all of it. But instead he stood still and waited for water that would never boil—his time was up.

⁞

3.

EXITING THE ELEVATOR ON THE 4ᵀᴴ FLOOR, ONE OF THE MEN SOBBED silently into his scarf. He hid his face to avoid a Protocol violation. Filing violations was one of Denise's duties. He bumped passed her as she made it through—the elevator doors closing fast—in time to hit L. Alone inside she poked at her phone with her still-numb fingers, scrolling through Bryce's Concordance record. Her hands were dead cold. Still, his record read: ALIVE.

Outside, she walked among the crowds of workers in black hats and trench coats huddled beneath broken umbrellas. She bought a cup of coffee from a cart and lifted the cup to her nose, inhaling to momentarily suppress the strange perfume still lingering from Bryce's vial.

Bulldozers pushed gnarled cars to the street-sides along with the other recent wreckage. The traffic lights had stopped working again a few days ago when an autonomous backhoe sliced through a major fiber-optic cable below the road. The infrastructure had begun to whither, people suspected corporate sabotage, and because they no longer knew what to do when the lights weren't working, they smashed into each other's cars.

While at first unbearable, the constant honking of horns, the scrape of colliding metal, and the crunch of brittle windshields had become pleasing to Denise who had been without desire or joy for as long as she could remember.

The floral scents in her throat grew like sudden spring and twisted, burrowing into her. She thought she heard a voice, like Bryce's, whisper to her over her shoulder; when she looked, there was no one—only the wet gray faces of the crowd.

A single drone perched atop a utility pole and watched her. The sky had turned an unusual shade of pink over the weekend and had been spitting pebble-sized hailstones since Saturday. Chaos certainly seemed to be on the rise, and as she walked she felt an increasing sense that something awful was about to happen to them all.

4.

SOMEWHERE BETWEEN CONSCIOUSNESS AND SLEEP, CHAMPION STARED at the wall of his office, waiting for the strange visions of a dream to replace his boredom, when he heard the special bell chime from one of the devices attached to his belt. He fumbled to find the right one and switched the notification off, ready to do business.

He uncovered the cart in the corner of his office and headed off to yet another cold cubicle to collect yet another expired body. Though it was important to collect the body quickly, the Boss had warned him never to alarm his subordinates, so as usual he wheeled his cart in a way that would arouse no suspicion; he went casually but quickly and with purpose. Now that they'd already opened their scent samples, the technicians were deeply focused on avoiding work and looking at the Concordance to see what had changed in the moments since they'd last checked.

The body, not yet stiff but not exactly elastic either, was warm, so he checked the wrist for a pulse, then leaned in and waited to feel an escaping breath. He pressed his palm to the forehead and looked at the wall clock. The corpse must have expired sometime in the early morning. If he filed a report with the Concordance this time, or even with Non-Accountance, *this time* he would have a legitimate alibi. Surely the Consultant would remember his name. Her first appointment every Monday morning for the past six months.

He wedged himself behind the body and the wall of the cube, knelt, and pushed his arms beneath the corpse's armpits, then hoisted the body onto the cart as if it were nothing. The body was heavy; they were all heavy, but he'd grown used to lifting the weight of the dead.

He covered the body with a tarp and pushed past the workers getting started on their work avoidance. A familiar tune sang from one of the Non-Accountants's computer speakers and Champion began to whistle, finishing the song long after he could no longer hear it.

The scent samples filled the 4th floor with a complex spray of lavender, musk, and mint. The harmony of fragrance made his job for a moment more pleasurable than usual as he wheeled this particular body away.

He took the corpse to the service elevator and went all the way down to the subbasement. He passed the chemical drums in storage beyond the sample racks and dusty reference library, where an unfamiliar technician stood in front of a book shelf full of file folders, flipping through one of the company logs. The woman looked up from her book and paused, examining Champion and his cart with curiosity. He hoped she had been properly trained and wouldn't ask him what he was doing, but after looking his badge over she seemed adequately impressed and returned to her book.

At the back of the room, he opened the curtain on the wall to reveal a locked metal door. He found the key on a chain around his neck, bent, and unlocked the door to the dark crematorium.

Protocol dictated that he search the body, so he did, uncovering the corpse and then heaving it onto the concrete floor where he first cut free the shirt, traced the bruised collarbone, then kneaded the pale belly with his fingertips, grazed the ribcage, and checked the armpits. Next he sliced open the jeans from belt to cuff and removed them. He massaged the thighs and calves, checked every crevice beneath and beyond the testicles. On a whim he doubled back to the base of the skull, probed the corpse's hair with the eraser end of a pencil, checked the ears and nostrils, then forced his fingers between the stiff lips and into the mouth.

The heat from the incinerator burned Champion's face as he waited for it to increase, the fire inside already red, its tips edging toward violet.

He looked at the body naked on the ground, the bruise around the neck. The six puncture wounds he'd found.

What it must have felt like, what he must have been thinking? What was left inside the body, heatless and still? What the body had been named, and who would miss him? He'd known all the answers to the What and Who questions the moment the notification chimed on his belt. *But Why?* he still wondered.

In the body's pants, he found a wallet and keys and though he had learned the hard way never to look inside, he found it increasingly difficult not to know, so he unfolded the leather wallet. Bryce, the body, now a person again, now a yellowed photograph of a boy holding the hand of a woman with beautiful long hair. Just the two of them facing the camera; safe, as if embraced, not surrounded, by the crowd, the mob, the riot of twisted sign-wielding bodies in the background. An old-fashioned battery-powered megaphone in her other hand. Though he worked hard to forget them all, this particular person had been special once, "a genius," the Boss said; he'd hated this one every day since Bryce started at Scentsate almost a year ago.

"I guess you won't be ordering any more birthday cakes now, Bryce buddy," he said. His face had begun to swell.

He verified the body's address again. They took the same train to work, shopped at the same grocery store, ate in the same restaurants, worked together on the same godforsaken project, yet he had never really seen Bryce before this moment. Champion removed one of the phones from his belt, leaned in to get closer to the corpse's face, and took a photograph of the two of them, together.

He looked at the photo and hovered his finger over the delete button, ready to erase what he'd done impulsively, strangely, without obvious motivation. Instead of deleting the photo, he took another, from a different angle, examined the selfie, then returned his phone to his belt. His own eyes were still puffy from crying before work. Not for them, not for Bryce, not for Dale, but for himself. *Why* did he always do that? He remembered again; the body had been a person once, but now he was simply a corpse. This, the thirteenth body so far this year, was no different than the others: another thing to burn.

5.

A SECURITY CAMERA WATCHED BRYCE from the ceiling of the 6th-floor lobby above a huge aquarium full of eels, more animal than water, writhing and twisting like the gears of some oily machine. A stench hissed from the churning mass, pulsing across the space toward Bryce who was sitting on a couch.

The woman behind the reception desk stood and approached, the room like a movie, the wide window spanning the lobby full of the wide vermilion sky outside.

"The Boss is ready to see you," she said. "I'm Beth."

Bryce straightened his tie and tried to make his smile look like he was really happy to be there.

"Where are you from?" she asked.

"Just across the river. I live in my mother's old house. She's dead. But I've lived other places."

"I almost drowned in the river." She smiled.

"I'm sorry to hear that."

"Do you want something to drink?" Beth pulled her fingers through her tangled hair.

"No, I'm okay. How long have you worked here?"

"Too long."

Bryce laughed.

"I'm serious. I hate it here. After I introduce you to the Boss, I'm going to go home and never coming back—"

Bryce didn't know what to say.

"I'm going to end it all—" she said.

Maybe this was what they meant by "uncomfortable and oppressive working conditions" in the articles he'd read about the company in the Concordance.

"—It's for the best." She smiled again. "The Boss is this way. No matter what, don't call him Carl. Even if he tells you to. Are you sure you don't want something? We have de-ionized water."

"I'd like to try some of that."

She led him down a dim hall behind the reception desk, carpeted with thick burgundy shag, past a number of closed doors, their nameplates removed. Bryce began to smell something like burning paper; he heard something crisp and shrill, then the long, yearning whine of a whale swooping up from beneath a translucent glass door at the end of the hall. The pitch twisted in the air, the turbulent warbling sonics stretching and snapping. Beth opened it and led the way through, then introduced him to "the Boss" and stepped aside.

"We're impressed with your resume. Call me Carl." He nodded Beth off and leaned back in his chair. His face was scratched and purple from old bruises. "We loved you during the phone interview. You have a lovely voice."

"Thank you."

"Please, sit." Carl pointed at the low chaise longue.

"Do you sing, Bryce? Some of the staff gets together to sing."

"No, I'm not very good at that." He looked at the door; he could just walk away, go home, and go back to bed. "I'd love to take lessons though. Singing sounds like a lot of fun."

"It *is* fun, Bryce. It brings the workers a great deal of satisfaction, singing. Brings us all together. All six floors," he gestured widely to the walls of his office as he spoke. The walls were full of bronze and silver plaques: Gustatory, AudioVisual, and Tactile/Touch Awards. Along the ceiling line written in a heavy gold-leaf font was the company's logo and motto; *Scentsated: We're Not Satisfied Until You're Sated*. Between the script and the plaques ran a row of gilded plates, coveted "Olfactory Gold" awards. They'd won the last fifteen years.

"Mouths, ears, eyes, noses, hands—" Carl flourished his own hands and then placed them both over his breast pocket "—and hearts."

"I'm sure it's super great," Bryce said.

"*You're* super great. You're talented. We're on board. We need you here. You could name your price, Bryce."

"Thanks. I'm really excited to be considered, Carl."

Carl started at his name, then smiled and bit his bottom lip.

Bryce looked toward the door for Beth with his water.

"You'll be under me, Bryce. Personally. Your supervisor is my right-hand man on our biggest project. He's weird, but he's mine . . . my protégé of sorts, I guess . . . you'll love the guy. But I'll look out for you myself as soon as I get back. I've got a business trip. Big business. We're making big moves. Lots of meetings with the Big Boys—D.C., the E.U., the Middle East. A working vacation." He was mumbling now. "Gotta save my marriage too, of course." He turned as if to gaze out the window.

It didn't seem possible Carl was still talking to him.

"Can something be saved that has already died?" Carl mused.

"I'm not sure I know what you mean." Bryce looked again for his water.

"Is it better to have never loved at all than to have loved and lost?"

"Is that how it goes?"

Carl turned back to face him. "As far as I'm concerned, you're hired. I'm the Boss, of course, but I've got something you'll need to get started on right away while I'm gone. I know this is going to seem strange to you at first. It's just to satisfy everybody in Human Resources."

Carl hoisted a wooden box the size and shape of a briefcase from the floor and slid it across his desk toward Bryce.

"Let me tell you a story," Carl said. "Do you like stories?"

"Sure," Bryce said. He didn't care for stories.

"When I was your age, I began to feel a kind of emptiness, as if I had once been full of something that was now gone. Have you felt that way before?"

Bryce knew exactly what he was talking about.

"I looked back at all the things I'd done in my life, how I'd risen through the ranks of the fragrance world, raised generations of champion lops with my beautiful and loving wife, golfed as much as I could before the weather began to turn. Still, something felt missing. It was as if the memories of these things had become somebody else's memories, not real things that I had experienced, but things I had seen in the Concordance or heard about from somebody else. I yearned for a deeper relationship to the memories of all that I had done, and this yearning made me very unhappy."

Out the window, beyond Carl, a goose—or a wood duck maybe? Where had Bryce read about wood ducks?—had landed on the balcony and was pecking at what looked like a frozen steak.

"I began too, to yearn for memories of the things I hadn't done, the things I was too old to do. Weird things, Bryce."

Bryce wondered where the goose had gotten the steak, how it had gotten into the air. He'd forgotten waterfowl could fly. They had wings, what else would they have been for? When was the last time anyone had seen a living goose?

"What was the answer to this problem, Bryce?"

The goose tossed the steak into the air, letting it drop on the concrete balcony. Did geese always eat steak? The umber smudge of the sun hung low over the river in a thick haze.

"We're not just fragrances here anymore, Bryce. Scentsate is *all* the senses now. But fragrances are the key. And a man with your special talents has the ability to *turn* that key for me, to do what others cannot.

The Silent Chord

You're going to help me invent what they've all been working toward without knowing it: the smell of memory. The smell of love. The sound and taste and touch of it, the pressure, the temperature, and texture of it. Do you know what I'm talking about?"

Bryce nodded. He remembered the smell of his mother's hair, how it comforted him, how it felt, but also how it was the last silent scent he remembered having before he'd been afflicted with the peculiar synesthesia that made him so valuable to fragrance manufacturers.

Now, with each breath, came noise. With each scent came sound. The memory of her hair, of silence, always escaping.

As a child, Bryce had been diagnosed with a rare airborne form of syphilis. He'd become ill after the disease entered the second stage when every day he awoke with a headache. When multiple trips to the doctor and then a neurologist resulted in an inconclusive diagnosis of stress, the skin behind Bryce's knees broke into a brilliant red rash. The rash spread and covered his legs, his body ached in the mornings, and his appetite rapidly diminished. When finally deep red lesions bloomed on his genitals, his penis afire with clusters of open sores, his doctor diagnosed him with syphilis.

After extensive intense interviews with both his mother and doctor, in which Bryce insisted he hadn't had sex with anyone, his doctor began to research other methods for the transmission of the disease and found research referenced in the Concordance from an obscure Soviet medical journal chronicling three virgin syphilitics, all females, in the former Estonian Soviet Socialist Republic who had, according to the article, contracted the disease through airborne exposure. Bryce's doctor prescribed antibiotics and bed rest and got to work on his own article.

During Bryce's recovery he experienced his first synesthesia, the smell of the pustulating boils on his testicles manifesting to him as the low chanting of Gregorian monks. Ever since, he'd perceived scents as sound, the two coalescing in a peculiar kind of song, both aural and olfactory.

Carl rounded his desk—handed Bryce the box he'd been leaning on—and sat facing him on the chaise.

"Inside are two dozen fragrances. Precious fragrances. Just to start. I need you to test these, to mix them, and write up a full report of what you smell with each, but also what you hear, of course. You know, just do what you do: describe. Use your best metaphors—I want vivid. I want to re-smell these when I read your descriptions. I want to hear what you hear. Feel what you feel.

"Sure, I can do that, I guess."

"Nobody's going to die if we fuck this up, Bryce. But I know what you're capable of. That's why I had to have you. We're doing important things here now. Not just fragrance. The stuff of dreams. Big Dreams. We're about to launch it with the Big Boys—this business trip—they don't know what they're in for."

"I'm happy to hear it."

"But we have secrets here too, Bryce. Big Secrets. Just like they do, everybody does. I can't tell you everything. You'll have to trust me. We know who you've worked for in the past—everybody you've worked for. I've read all your past reports, word-for-word. It's all there. But they didn't see it, didn't see *you*, didn't see what you *really* do. I'm going to show them. Trust me, Bryce, I see you, that's *my* thing. That's how I've gotten where I am. I have a genius for spotting genius. I know things about you that you don't know about yourself. Big things. But trust me, I'm going to show you too. Can I trust you to trust me?"

"I think so."

"That's good enough for me," Carl looked away and spoke to the plaques, "because there's not a lot of joy in this world anymore. The world is dark and miserable. Have you been outside? Everything is shit. We can bring joy into people's lives. If we get this right. You and me."

He smiled at Bryce again. His fingers inched a tiny fan of paper from his breast pocket and he slid it across the top of the box in Bryce's lap. "Your starting salary."

The goose on the balcony had flown away. In its place a small black drone hovered in the window and looked at them.

Carl pointed to the door, and winked.

Bryce could see that Carl was staring plainly and unsettlingly at his lips.

Bryce stood firmly from the chaise, returned the box to Carl's desk and, as an afterthought, sharply spread the fanned scrap open with the blade of his hand against it.

"Oh." Bryce said.

"Be careful with all that," Carl whispered from behind him. He was standing now also. He put his hand on Bryce's shoulder. "It's proprietary."

Bryce lifted the case again and turned to meet the Boss's gaze; it was exactly as heavy as it appeared to be.

6.

UPSTAIRS, CHAMPION WASHED HIS HANDS and returned to his office where he retrieved his other cart, then pushed that cart to the corpse's former cubicle where he disconnected and collected the computer, monitor, keyboard, and mouse. Champion remembered ordering him a laptop when Bryce had first started working there. It was missing.

Champion took what personal items he could find—a coffee mug, a stack of photographs jammed into a desk drawer otherwise full of rubber bands and pencils, a sandwich bag full of hair. He held the photos and examined them front and back. They were curled, their surface smooth and cold, the color washed thin, the woman in the images was the same woman in Bryce's wallet, now surely dead.

He opened one of the samples, lifted it to his nose, and inhaled, coughing from the caustic scent, like something rotting in vinegar. He capped the vial, dropped it into his shirt pocket, and arranged the others like jewels in a padded case that he would deliver directly to the Boss.

He looked up at the ceiling, the frayed network cables cut and dangling from an open panel. As network administrator and the only senior associate left on the project, he'd have to deal with that too, though that required yet another cart, another set of tools.

7.

DENISE SIFTED THROUGH HER INTERNAL MESSAGES, meaningless company announcements—cake memos and brief poorly edited memorials to recently deceased employees—to find requests for updates on the project reports Denise actually collated and created herself, reports that were perpetually late. Which was not her fault.

She'd passed Bryce's cube on her way back from lunch and noticed he'd been collected. She tried to imagine he'd woken and gotten back to work but was taking a long bathroom break, or he'd woken and gone home to sleep off whatever ailment had stricken him, or he'd woken after having passed out while trying to kill himself, had been embarrassed and gone off somewhere quiet to kill himself the right way. But she knew he was already dead and dealt with, however the company dealt with dead employees.

So many of them had killed themselves at the office. Mostly from AudioAural on the first floor. One of them, some senior associate's assistant, had been found floating in the fountain in front of the building.

She filtered her Scentsate email to show only messages from Bryce. Most were memos about the fragrances he'd been working on, full of strange descriptions of their sonic qualities that were meaningless metaphors to her, nothing like the stuff the other men wrote up—*tormented feline screaming, well-oiled hinge on a heavy door, boys' choir, G chord*. He sent status updates too, carbon-copied to long lists of people only marginally concerned with Bryce's projects, it seemed to Denise—and occasional but steady requests for Denise to hang out, to eat lunch, or to drink coffee.

She couldn't stop thinking about him even though she had already thought about him more today than she had since he'd started working there.

Many of his emails to her were morning missives about the conditions of his commute, soliciting sympathy. Nobody cared about other people's commutes. The worst part of everyone's day was facing their own Metro line journey to work. For months people had been jumping onto the tracks in alarming numbers and the bodies twisted between the track and train caused monstrous delays.

She looked for one email in particular, an email she remembered, a wildly inappropriate message, a message she'd read but barely acknowledged and often worked to forget. He'd sent it after last year's holiday party, and she dismissed it—the sentiment of the letter was annoying enough, but even worse, it was indulgent and purple.

Dear Denise:

Despite our awkward drunken fumbling and your apparent desire to never speak to me again, I cannot help but hear your echo still emanating from the patch on the pillow where your head rested that night. I've not disturbed it, in an attempt to preserve you, because the sound of our sweat mixing, our bodies nearly colliding, produces in me profound pleasure and peace. The sound produced was something like silence, something I have not truly experienced in a long time. As the smell of you, of us together, fades, I've been working in the laboratory to preserve the silence by recreating that scent as accurately as possible. I believe I've perfected it, however the silence it produces isn't right: there is still a resonating, a hum. Something is off; it produces only a desire for something, a desire for a feeling, a longing for the absolute silence that only you can bring.

I know it would be strange to say that I love you. Perhaps, though, not so strange to say I *could* love you. I know love is an anachronistic thing, or at least admitting to it has become passé, or dangerously non-conformist, but please, consider this dream. I'm not telling you that I love you, only that something about you, or you and I together, brings me peace. Here is the dream:

We are floating on our backs in a warm pool and the sky is blue again, and not the blue we occasionally see now and try to imagine is a clear sky when in fact the blue is only an aberration of some collision of pollutants. It is the blue of our childhoods.

We kick our legs to move our bodies around the pool for a while and the sun begins to burn my sensitive skin, so we step out of the pool and dry ourselves; we are happy. An aroma of warmth and mild humidity and perpetual spring surrounds us when we are in proximity to one another, and the sound it produces in me is one of harmony and is not so loud that it blocks our conversations; instead, it provides a backdrop for our life together, like a pleasing, neutral drapery. We sit together beneath an umbrella in the sun and sip drinks and read magazines, watching swimmers slowly swimming. The water moves in long, slow ripples. You touch my hand. You point to a daylight owl sitting on a branch above us. We freeze because, as everybody knows, nobody has seen a real live owl in years. The owl widens its wings to fly away, but instead simply spreads and shakes them. The owl whoops, as if to say that the end of this oddly long winter has come and love has returned to the world. In the dream we took it as a sign, and when I awoke, I took the owl as a sign too.

I know this may seem strange to you, but please try to imagine my dream as a scenario, a map for memories we have not yet created. It is not a memory of marriage or children or happily-ever-after, but a memory of, if only for a moment, happiness and peace that I have never felt, and that I suspect you have never felt. I have been having many dreams like this, many dreams in which we are together. Perhaps these are simple fantasies, but I think they are possibilities.

Please respond in the affirmative if you wish to go on another date with me. I feel we have gotten off on the wrong foot and that our next interaction will be more positive. I look forward, too, to hearing your thoughts on my notes about the projections for the quarter, your thoughts on the new silence fragrance we've been attempting to make, your thoughts on the swimming pool, and your thoughts, finally, on the owl.

Best Regards,

Bryce

Denise's reply had been brief and cold. She had read all the approved articles in the Concordance that proved the number one thing all successful people shared was that they sent short emails so she'd only sent short emails since, and what offended her more than anything was that Bryce's message had gone on at length, and was full of feelings he should have been taking to a Consultant rather than feeling them himself, and on a normal day she would have simply deleted it, but it disturbed her just enough that she angrily read the whole thing.

She told him she didn't believe in owls, or love, and that his quarterly numbers were fine and that she didn't care about the silence project. She told him she thought he was lonely like everybody else in the world and that he should, like everybody else, get used to it and leave her alone. Two sentences, 3.5 lines, it was the longest email she'd ever written.

Other men in her life had died or gone away and she never thought about them again, but something was not right when she thought about Bryce. Employees died all the time these days. She'd never cared before, but something about Bryce's death bothered her. Perhaps it was because she didn't really believe he'd killed himself. Perhaps it was something like sadness. Where were all these useless feelings coming from?

The fragrance, burning and ripe, foamed in her throat.

8.

IT WAS NOT THE SHAPE OF CHAMPION'S HEAD OR HIS DYED WHITE HAIR that reminded Carl of his estranged wife. It was the shape of his lips. They were not full lips, but they were pretty lips, and they were most certainly reminiscent of Cheryl's mouth.

"Please sit with me." Carl beckoned Champion to sit on his side of the desk, not across from him far away on the conch-shell chaise—but once Champion rounded it, Carl pointed to the floor.

When Champion sat Carl rotated to face him, suddenly aware of the awkward position this put them both in, as Carl's shoeless feet skimmed Champion's crossed legs.

"How's the project coming, Kid?" Carl refused to call Champion by his name. Champion was a horse's name, or a dog's name, or a superhero's name, or, as Carl often suspected, simply a made-up name. Hadn't his job application sported something more promising? Carl vaguely remembered the interview, all the board members—back when Scentsate had a board—impressed with his surname. Something from the Norman Conquest. Wasn't it Campion? And a given name of course, non-mononymous, something truthful and androgynous. Was it Jain? No. More preppy, like Cheryl's friends: Topper? Skip? Or was it Hap? Yes. Hap Campion. His perfect smile. His lips, like her lips, had always remained perfect replicas in color and substance.

Carl had taken the kid under his wing when he saw what he could do. He'd done a lot for him too.

Carl thought of Cheryl, of the secretive billionaire C___-Mac family, of how he, Carl D___, infamous disowned grandnephew of the Parisian luxury fashion house, had won her from them all. He thought of their upcoming trip, how he might convince her there was still something there. He still loved her, or thought he still loved her, or maybe he just didn't like to lose things. The vacation would be their last chance for a new beginning. His last chance to win her back.

The night she told him she was leaving, Carl had just returned from a business trip, a conference he hadn't wanted to attend but had gone to anyway, because the kid needed to scope out the newest technology, needed inspiration for the project's new network cable, even though there had been something between them for weeks, maybe months, maybe years, something strange that made each day with her feel like he was in somebody else's body, a body he knew, but that had become unfamiliar. He was suddenly unable to feel at home in the living room where even the light coming through the windows was now alien and isolating. Even before she dropped the bomb, he'd known something big was coming; when he left for the conference, he'd said goodbye to her, kissed her lips, and though they were still part of her body, they too felt foreign and cold.

Her Concordance record had changed and he thought he could detect coded messages in her newest connections. She'd always had connections. She was born with connections.

But Cheryl's record still said they were married and though it was an obvious thing, because he knew they were married, this information brought him mild comfort and so he looked at the photographs of them together over the years, smiling, in one another's arms—jetting off to Madrid, London, New York City, sunning on their yacht, Christmas at her family's ranch in Montana—and going way back to their humble beginnings, surrounded by the litters of lops they used to breed and sell at the farmers market when they were young and cared about each other, living hand-to-mouth on a pittance of a trust fund in the cottage upstate, which his uncle let them inhabit before it had to be demolished—for a moment he was able to convince himself nothing was wrong.

But something *was* wrong. The photographs were all just out of focus, incorrectly exposed, or from strange angles, and in most of them he could easily be convinced they were other people. It was as if whoever had taken them had always been trying to screw them up. He didn't remember from where the photographs had come, or how they had even been associated with him and Cheryl. The places were familiar and right, but the people? *Maybe* they were the people in the photographs, maybe they weren't. The photographs were cold and indistinct, affectless. He couldn't remember the exact moment any had been taken with more than a vague recollection, which could have been created by looking at the photographs, rather than memories triggered by them.

What had happened to the yacht? Had they sold it when the weather changed? Even the memories of the champion lops were now suspect; why were they breeding rabbits? He tried to remember how they smelled, how they felt. Had they fed them pellets? Carrots? Nothing; only blurred images.

When he returned from the conference, the night she told him she was leaving him, Cheryl brought Tammers with her to the airport to pick him up in their new autonomous highway yacht, a huge silvery truck-thing with undreamt of legroom. The flight had been tumultuous. The kid was pissed he had to deboard disguised as a mustached pilot to avoid Cheryl's jealousy. When the machine pulled up it went over the curb, narrowly missing his luggage before it hit the Passenger Loading sign. Tammers refused to yield the spacious front seat, gesturing for him to get in back.

He liked Tammers; she was intelligent and attractive and had a pleasant disposition. He liked the way she coordinated colors, and when she was around, he felt like he and Cheryl were at their best. Their smiles were less forced and he stood up straight. They laughed at things that weren't funny because it made them feel good, not because they felt they had to. Tammers made him forget all the things he hated about himself and about Cheryl.

But that night he desperately wanted to talk to Cheryl alone, to confront, to find out what she'd done and what she wanted. He wanted her to tell him that what he thought he'd found was nothing; he wanted her to be angry with him for being so stupid and invasive, but Tammers wouldn't leave. He wanted to talk to her about what they had done together in their marriage, and where they had been, to conjure something tangible from the murk of now-distant events.

Cheryl wanted to cook for Tammers (she never wanted to cook for anybody) and then she wanted to go to the movies. They'd had a spiral ham in the refrigerator since before he left and she claimed it would spoil soon. Carl didn't believe it would ever spoil. He dutifully unwrapped the ham while Cheryl toasted bread for sandwiches. She found the good mustard, and together they ate.

Carl remembered the smell of the mustard summoning a kind of guilty feeling he did not want to talk about at the dinner table, so he ate silently. While it wasn't exactly *cooking*, she made a very good dinner, and Tammers complimented it effusively, claiming it was the best spiral ham she'd ever tasted, even though it was an ordinary ham purchased from the spiral ham stand at the bulk warehouse and was, it turned out, probably on the verge of rotting.

Carl knew he had to work the next day; he was tired, enervated by the trip and work of investigating. Still, he wanted answers, so he agreed to drive them all to the movie theater, since the highway yacht was now on the fritz after pulverizing the Loading sign at the airport.

Toward the end of the movie, in a crucial scene in which the crew of a doomed fishing boat decides to stop battling the mythical storm that had been imperiling them for nearly two hours, sealing their fate and the fate of their record catch, Tammers began to weep.

She whispered to Carl, "my dog is going to die."

Carl wormed his cold hand into hers and said the only thing he could: "We're all going to die."

He didn't believe it, but it was the right thing to say at the time. He still thought so. Even though later, at home alone, Cheryl told him she was leaving.

⁝

He studied Champion's lips; he could see that they were certainly perfect—replicating the tone, the cracks and divots, the same subtle, peculiar spasms. The only way to know for sure they were just like Cheryl's was to kiss him, but he knew if he kissed Champion and Champion did not want to be kissed, somebody would file a complaint. He could make complaints go away, of course, but he wanted to keep things uncomplicated between them.

Champion had been explaining the status of the project all this time. Carl saying things like: "get to the meat of it" even though Champion had already explained the meat of it to him.

Champion dutifully repeated, "I think Olfactory is getting there. We've done lots of focus-group testing. Mainly we're getting positive results. Of course, there are no guarantees with something like this. With fragrances, we can say something smells like strawberries, or we can say a chemical smells like something we can convince people is 'strawberry.' People will believe what they're smelling is a strawberry if we tell them that's what it is, even though it's closer to a blueberry or a banana. But to get from some single smell to people's feelings, to each person's memory of love? And somehow take control of all those feelings and memories? This new project is uncharted water."

"I'm not asking you about *that* project, idiot. You think I'd trust you with feelings? With love? All those morons in Olfactory are just biding time. That's what I pay them to do, look science-y for the corporate walk-throughs. Get the lab ready for production. Place markers until I could get the real thing. It took a lot but I just pulled the last string this morning. I just hired the artistic genius with the research that inspired this whole project. Got him booted by the Feds, black-balled in the fragrance industry, and hired him on with us—took me 90 days. Your new assistant . . . Bryce. Bryce. Bryce. I told you that. Your last assistant wouldn't have lasted a day at Hermès. But this kid could have made them a fortune, he's an artist, all that plus a graduate degree in English. But don't worry, don't mope, kid, he's completely discredited now. He'll never have another job. Knows nothing about business. Better for you and me.

No. What I need from *you* is your report on the new network cables and the Concordance takeover. Don't bullshit me kid, I need to know with complete certainty that everything, and I mean *everything* will work when we do the Onsite testing. That these new network cables can convey anything this kid Bryce comes up with. I'll be meeting with the entertainment world's top CEOs. As far as *they* know, we've got the formula down and it's been in production for a year. Can you tell me the cables are ready at least?"

"I'm installing them in the office as a test. Once they're in, we should be able to send all kinds of stuff."

"Because they're fiber optic."

"It's hard to explain. They're like fiber optic in that they transmit information, but they're more like physical pipes or veins—we can send all kinds of stuff. Smells for now, but maybe more. It all depends on the routers on either end of the connections."

"Routers? We'll be able to send more than scents?"

"You know, sky's the limit?"

Carl had the sense that Champion was fucking with him now, that he didn't know how the cables worked, either, but he was running out of time. "Sky's the limit? Why don't you know how these work?"

"Somebody from Engineering explained it to me, but he could only use metaphors. I admit it all seems a little like magic."

Carl paused and waited, trying to decide whether he was angry at Champion or merely displeased.

"Now get down there and introduce yourself to this kid while I'm gone. Be his friend. Take him under your wing like I did with you. Give him everything he needs. Get that girl in his bed. Get him to trust you. Get him to talk. We need to chart the water. Sound his depths." He thought of the scene in the movie where the whole crew was neck-deep in frigid water, singing a farewell song known only to sailors. He'd forgotten the ending—had they survived by some miracle?

He dismissed Champion, then followed him out to the 6th floor lobby and receptionist area, to make sure the girl had booked the jet. Carl watched Champion disappear into the elevator. The receptionist was gone for the night, he was alone, and with the lights off in the lobby the redness of the long dusk flooded in through the tall windows.

The eels twisted around each other in the tank; it was repellent. Carl opened the lid of the aquarium and hovered his nose over the constantly churning water. The fetid smell revolted him and he recoiled; he let the lid slam down, frightening the eels to the bottom of the tank in a thick, black swarm.

The smell took him back to his first day on the job as the youngest CEO at Scentsate—in a way that was more than memory. He could feel every textured inch of the suit he'd worn that day, a suit he'd later arranged carefully in a bag and stored in the freezer in the basement to memorialize the occasion. He felt his toes in his old most-comfortable power loafers, tight and new back then. He smelled the fresh tiny elvers that—when their crate was pried open—burst from the membrane in which they'd been packed. Lingering on his lips, he could still taste the sugary loops he'd had that morning for breakfast, Cheryl's kiss goodbye before he left for work an hour early to be sure he'd make it there before the delivery. He had the space cleared, center stage in the lobby, and the plaque with his family name mounted, and the giant aquarium filled, before any of the senior executives could object.

From the start, eels were one of his Power Moves, moves that powerful men at powerful companies had shown him how to cultivate. But he'd outdone them all. What but an enormous putrid aquarium surging with eels could simultaneously impress clients and strike fear into his competitors, his enemies, the very men who had once groomed him?

"Who are my enemies now?" he asked the eels.

He spun around to take in the whole view of the sixth floor, the 30-foot cathedral ceiling angling up, the huge triangular windows overlooking the best part of the city, the Herman Miller chairs in the waiting room. All his, now that he'd bought everybody out. Beyond the receptionist's desk, at the end of the dark hallway, he'd left his office's double doors flung open, the room glowing gold as if emanating from all the award-winning work he'd done here. He was especially proud of the Olfactory Gold awards they'd won on his watch, even though Scentsate had actually only won honorable mention from the Fragrance and Taste Society his first year (for a particularly spirited combination of pear and carob flower). He'd been so angry at the slight he withdrew all of the company's work from consideration with the F&TS, and filed a 501C3—recruiting a few equally disgruntled, now-retired CEOs from back in his father's day who were grateful to serve anywhere as board members—under the name "The Taste and Fragrance Society," which had yearly awarded Scentsate all their winning gold plaques, fabricated especially for his office walls. He loved winning.

Eels and plaques—his oldest power moves—they were still working. They'd worked on the Big Wigs from the Concordance just the other day when he'd had them all in for a preliminary discussion.

He needed to celebrate his wins more, both he and Cheryl did. He needed to relax, to clear his mind for the big meeting next week, the bidding war he'd set up with all the CEOs of the Top Five entertainment companies, maybe the biggest in his life, this trip. And she'd be there with him this time, a real vacation, that was important too, starting over, something else to celebrate. But tonight she'd be working late. And the car was on the fritz. He could get back to his roots, walk and ride the Metro line like a regular guy again, come back into his body.

Carl heard something like a human screaming for help and looked out the huge window. In the river, a man flailed in the water.

Carl squinted to get a better look and called out to the receptionist to alert somebody who could do something, forgetting again she was gone. Should he phone the coast guard? The police? A water taxi?

The man disappeared under the water for long enough that Carl thought he'd imagined it all. When the man resurfaced downriver, Carl watched the body gyrate in the current, thrashing his arms to stay afloat.

Soon a tour boat appeared near the distraught man, perhaps to watch him drown, but instead they extended a metal pole and waved it around so he could grab onto it, until the current pulled the man away from the pole, swept him further downriver and out of sight.

⋮

9.

OUTSIDE, THE MAGENTA SKY HUNG LOW above the skronk of car horns, the pounding of constant construction, the buzz of tiny drones flitting though the air like bees. Champion worked his way home through the crowd of happy hour pedestrians with their heads bowed toward their phones.

With his right hand he touched the knuckles of his clenched left hand. It was a lie to say he no longer experienced emotions; in fact, he felt as if most of the time he was full of rage, but rage he compartmentalized, pushed away and suppressed so well that it often felt as if he felt nothing at all even though the truth was that he felt all kinds of feelings. They all did. Everybody lied. That was the secret, the answer. But why?

Even when he didn't visit the Consultant—when it wasn't raining or hailing, too hot or cold—he sometimes walked the city; sometimes the sun shone through the clouds and the sidewalks were oddly empty as people had become so used to bad weather they'd grown suspicious of beautiful days, so afraid of the diseased sun and sky they stayed inside.

He walked toward home, turning away from downtown. The sidewalks became gradually clear of people as the neighborhood transitioned from the business district to one of the old, dead neighborhoods. He passed abandoned office lobbies, boarded or obscured by dusty glass, and storefronts with long shattered windows, the once opulent entrances exposed and littered with broken chairs and empty metal furniture spilling out of the old elevator shafts. He walked over thick overgrowth climbing from inside the crumbling buildings, felt bits of glass snapping beneath his feet.

Humming drones flew high overhead, almost out of sight. The tired faces of the people living in the abandoned structures looked down and followed him. Somebody far behind him seemed to be shouting his name, his real name; he walked with his head low until he could no longer hear it. The clammy day began to release its humidity, a fine mist floating around him and the lonely street.

At the intersection at the end of the block, a team of bulldozers cleared the quadrant of collapses. Many of the buildings had been demolished here, the sidewalks defining the old lots, now prairies infected with thick vines and sick, twisted trees growing along the ground like snakes.

At the edge of a neighborhood of row houses, gardens struggled in the tiny patches of yards marked by old iron fences. His own house was at the end of the block. He'd long abandoned the garden and covered his outdoor space with colorful aquarium gravel he'd bought at the pet warehouse. He took his mail from the box hanging from the fence, and unlatched the front gate.

Champion felt the presence of somebody walking behind him and from over his shoulder he saw two men and two women in dark suits and sunglasses walking across the empty lot next door. They held their phones in front of their faces and, without hiding it, photographed him. He touched his hand, again. His knuckles burned.

"I am gentle," he whispered. After his conversation with Carl, he wasn't sure he could handle an encounter, friendly or not. "Gentle hands. I have gentle hands."

"Excuse me?" The woman behind him spoke. "Excuse me!"

He stopped and turned. The mist began to coalesce into slow, syrupy rain.

"My hands are for hugging!" he shouted at them.

"What?"

"I'm sorry, I didn't mean to say that to you." *My hands are not for hitting*, he thought. *My hands are gentle.*

"We're lost." She scrunched her face and showed him her phone, pointing at the tiny map on the screen. "We can't find the zoo," she said.

"Did you yell my name a minute ago? Back there?"

"No, we don't know your name. We're just looking for the zoo."

"The zoo. That's a long way from here."

"I knew it!" One of the men spoke, vindicated.

"We want to see the baby pandas."

"The baby pandas have all died. There are no pandas there. Or anywhere," Champion said, showing her the Concordance article on his phone.

"Oh."

"—But a few years ago, a female shark gave birth to fifteen baby sharks even though she'd been alone in her tank for a decade," Champion said. "It was a miracle."

He explained to them how to get to the appropriate Metro station. Thinking about the zoo made him feel gentle. "There aren't really any animals left. It's mostly just monkeys and weeds now. And that female shark."

The monkeys were inbred and wild; they'd long ago learned to squeeze through the cracks in their enclosures to roam freely. So far they stayed close to the zoo where they were fed, but everyone knew that one day they would overrun the city.

"Are you from around here?" one of the women asked.

"Nobody's from here."

"Do you live close by?"

"Not far." He took his hand off the front doorknob and slid it slowly into his pocket. "I guess some of the babies are still alive. The zoo sharks, I mean. They're famous."

"They sound fascinating. It's nice to meet such a friendly local. Thanks for your help."

"You're welcome."

As they walked away, one of the men looked back and took another photograph before turning the corner, going in the opposite direction he'd told them to go.

Champion whispered to himself: "*I have gentle hands.*"

Inside, Champion fed the cat and shared a banana with Jellybeans, his parrot, while outside hail began to hit the side of the house like bullets against the brick. He glanced at the mail. He removed a single birthday card from the stack and threw the rest of the stack in the trash. While Jellybeans squawked and flew circles around the kitchen, he jammed the card into the garbage disposal and ran hot water over the labored grinding of the blades until the card, at last, was gone.

He closed the blinds and dimmed the lights, and on the couch he opened his laptop, logged into a series of remote networks, found the Concordance page for Franklin Pierce, 14th U.S. President, and changed the date of his birthday from November 22, 1804 to November 23, 1804.

10.

BRYCE SOMETIMES HEARD THE SMELL OF THE RIVER as music like chimes and today in the wind the water rang like bells. He walked the long way to the train, meandering around the little parks along the river, walking through the damp grass where wrecked cars had been piled on the sidewalks. The wooden case weighed him down.

Occasional hail fell from the rosy sky and bounced like pebbles on the path. Nannies held umbrellas over the heads of children bundled in scarves and plastic coats. While resting against a low iron fence, Bryce accepted a single paper carnation from a red-cheeked clown, and gave it to a little girl thumbing through something on her phone. Now that he was no longer unemployed, he could do things at his leisure. He felt a sense of relief despite the stress of that task at hand—the box—and what Scentsate would expect of him.

The olive river, cold and viscous, heaved in labored breaths, tossing its water onto the spongy grass at the edge of the park. The smell of the river was thick—the bells rang majestically, as if the ringer followed a short distance behind him, striking the bells with a metal mallet.

Bryce held the case beneath one arm, then the other when it became uncomfortable, and finally, he clutched the box awkwardly in front of him with both hands. With each step the glass samples rattled inside.

He took a break on a bench and fell into a deep sleep, waking only to swat away a kid trying to steal his fragrance box. It was dark now—how long had he been asleep?

Bryce took the long escalator down into the Metro station where he saw a man who looked like Carl seated on a bench at the end of the platform. The man looked up and glanced away, hiding his face.

The platform was crowded for late evening and three northbound trains passed before Bryce's southbound train appeared in the tunnel. The hum of body heat and sweat sent Bryce to find a seat on one of the last cars.

At each stop, the train emptied of a few more people. Bryce watched the man from the platform at the other end of the car. A thinning lattice of grey-brown hair barely concealed the man's scalp, the faint line of a healing cut on top of his head. Bryce moved to the front of the car so he could get a better look when he noticed his across-the-street neighbor.

"What's in the box?" She smiled as if she expected the box to be a gift. She looked mischievous.

"I'm not supposed to say." *Proprietary*, Bryce thought. Why would Carl be on the Metro? He had cars, drivers, a car that could drive itself. A private jet, boats.

"Is it for a lady?" The skin of her cheeks had warmth like the red glow of the night sky. Her smile seemed genuine, as if she was really happy to see him.

"It's for work."

"Is it your mother?" she asked. "Are you taking her ashes out on a jaunt?"

"What are you talking about? That's not funny."

"I think something's leaking," she said. She pointed at his pant leg.

"Fuck." Liquid from the box was leaking onto his leg. The smell of butter, creamy and intense, overcame him, as if all the butter in the world had melted into a pool in his lap. Cut grass, sultry and damp, followed. He sneezed and the sounds of the storm rushed from his leg to his ear, a torrent of metal scraping metal.

"I'm a little overwhelmed right now."

They emerged from the tunnel and ascended to elevated track. The sky was dim and thick. Blades of rain snapped against the train's roof. Bryce couldn't remember the last time he'd seen the sky so dark. It seemed as if the sun had, for the last few weeks, only partially set, the nights bathed in a deep red glow.

A sharp pain surged through his temples. The man a few seats ahead looked up from his phone, turned just enough that Bryce could see that he was Carl for sure. But Carl definitely didn't live all the way out here. Wasn't he leaving on a trip? A vacation with his wife?

"Are you okay?" Angie moved to the seat in front of Bryce. She put her hand on his arm. "Are you okay?"

Bryce wasn't sure if it was his neighbor Angie that spoke or if the scent on his leg was rendering the words. The scents rarely spoke to him, but the butter-grass was so intense he could not be sure.

"Bryce. Bryce. Bryce."

"Are you speaking to me? Is that you Angie?" He shook out his pant leg and said again, "Is that you?"

The train approached the airport. A one-legged man on the bicycle path below the train tracks pedaled furiously up the steep hill where the path rose over the highway below. The man's foot was locked into the bike pedal and his lopsided cadence as he alternately pushed and pulled looked like an accelerating steam locomotive chugging up the hill through the storm.

Bryce watched as Carl pressed his face against the glass, rapt by the one-legged man's determined race with the commuter train.

"Are you okay?" Angie asked. "Bryce, what's wrong?"

Bright and blurred light gathered over his eyes wherever Bryce attempted to focus.

"I'm sorry, my head hurts."

"You look terrible. Like shit. Your suit's all wrinkled."

"Our stop's coming up. I've looked like this all day."

"We should have coffee some time. We haven't seen each other in such a long time."

"Yes."

As the train slowed, both Carl and Bryce stood and glanced at one another in a way that Bryce expected would finally lead to some physical signal of acknowledgment, but instead Carl just stared—eyes glazed over, it seemed. When the door opened, Carl sat unmoved until Bryce exited, and then just stood on the platform while Bryce passed him to go down the escalator.

At street level, Bryce set the case on the a bench and fumbled with his umbrella. When no Carl appeared, Bryce began to walk home with the wooden box. His arms ached. As he crossed the parking lot, he watched Angie get into her car and despite the rain and her request to have coffee, she didn't offer him a ride, instead waving to him and smiling from behind her windshield wipers.

The rain and wind cleared Bryce's head and dulled the roar to a soft, persistent thrum. He crossed the abandoned tracks of the miniature railroad that used to run tourists through the neighborhood. A makeshift shed had been thrown together where some people were working to restore the track so they could run the train again for some reason. He cut across the park where his neighbors sometimes gathered, his back seizing. The gravel paths had eroded from so much rain and the long, wet grass soaked his feet.

He glanced over his shoulder and felt Carl's presence somewhere behind him.

At home, Bryce pushed aside the mail and a wooden bowl full of film canisters to make space for the case of scents on the cluttered kitchen table. The liquid fragrance had stained the pine box dark around the seams and the butter and grass inside filled the room.

Bryce found the plastic bag of his mother's hair in the freezer, opened it, and held the bag to his face. He inhaled and remembered again his childhood illness: the smell of his mother's hair, his body nearly recovered, his sores evaporating, his appetite returning. The smell of her hair, the perfume of shampoo all but faded, penetrated his nose and his throat and quieted the sounds of the scents on the table. The silence wasn't perfect—a residue of sound still pulsed with each breath. It was better than nothing.

Something tapped at the glass.

He saw his reflection in the window, then someone else on the other side of the glass masked behind the reflection of his own face. He stepped back and bumped the kitchen table enough to shake the case of fragrances. Lemon filled the room with a sick violin. The smell rose from the box like fog, drifted over the edge of the table and crept along the floor, curled around his ankles, and then evaporated into a piercing screech.

Gunpowder and grapefruit smothered the lemon and together they collapsed around one another. Still more howled from the box.

The oily resin of scent seeped down his throat. Insistent rose petals numbed his tongue. Long, low howls echoed inside of him, each voice joining the other from his stomach, his liver, his nerves, and his veins. The rumble felt like it could vibrate his body to pieces.

If he could just get rid of the box, give it back to Carl, he would be okay, but he couldn't. Who else would hire him?

He ran from the house. His skin wept the rank mixture, intense and deafening.

He cut through the vacant lot near the end of the block, and ran through the backyards of his neighbors' houses until he reached the dirt road, where he went up the hill into the woods.

The clouds, still red and light, blushed the full moon. When he found the trail he followed it into the dark canopy of pines. Needles soft beneath his feet. A river somewhere. Roiling water, out of sight.

The smell of the forest was quieting—distant rambling water and the buzzing of distant drones covered the melancholy. He felt as if he might drop onto the soft ground, fold into the bed of pine needles, and disappear.

He fell asleep on the forest floor.

He forced himself forward against sleep.

He heard feet falling behind him, someone following. He imagined dogs, desperate and hungry, tracking him.

He began to dream: Carl looming behind him, his dead mother, the scents evaporating into a fine mist, not making a sound.

Angie pouring thick, black, coffee.

When he looked over his shoulder, there was nothing and no one.

11. TWO AUTONOMOUS CARS, EMPTY AND DRIVERLESS, IGNORED A RED LIGHT to crush a third car—full of a family—between them. They'd hoped to kill everybody inside, but were happy to teach them a lesson even if they didn't die.

Through the smoke and debris a flock of drones coalesced, floating and diving, photographing the wreckage while the passengers and drivers worked to squeeze their broken bodies as best they could from the grip of the metal.

Two drones began to chase one another, grabbing and poking with their beaks and claws until one of them yielded, the blade of its rotor broken, and fell into the automobile remains.

Cars backed up at the intersection. Driver or driverless, they honked and yelled out of their windows at the dying cars and the people climbing out of them.

One of the cars set itself on fire. The gathered onlookers breathed a long, collective *oh*. They couldn't wait to see what would happen next.

Denise had been about to step into the intersection and was both relieved and a little sad she hadn't, because if she had, her death would have been fast. She looked over her body and clothes for blood, a broken bone, a tear in her dress. She noticed a coffee stain across her chest, probably there all day. Maybe it could pass for a wound of some kind. She'd file an insurance claim.

She felt fuzzy, certainly from the horror of what she'd witnessed, all the metal and broken bodies upsetting her equilibrium; she could smell the gasoline, felt her lungs fill with smoke, everything fighting with the feeling of the fragrance she'd inhaled still burning in her throat. A tire had flown through the air and smashed the window of one of the shops across the street, crushing a mannequin and her children, setting off alarms inside the store.

The crowd joined the drones in photographing the mess, moving a little closer as the fire grew. A tepid siren sounded a few blocks away, a sign that an emergency vehicle was unenthusiastically on its way to the scene.

She looked through the broken glass at the scattered mannequins and then inside the store, the workers in shock, yelling into their phones. The mother mannequin had been wearing a bow in her hair and a long bag of a house dress. She'd held a can of wasp spray aimed at a couple of kids in little bear costumes crawling around on the ground. Now their arms were twisted, their heads on wrong, the wig and bow struck from the mother.

Such a pretty display, Denise thought, *ruined*.

The few customers who had been inside held their heads, pretending to have been hit by the tire or broken glass. They moaned for effect and supported one another as they limped out of the store to report their woe to the authorities.

The tire had rolled across the store, sullied a round of jumpers, and knocked over a table of neatly folded sweaters before finally coming to rest in front of the register. A bit of smoke lifted from the still-wobbling tire and filled the store with the smell of burnt rubber.

Denise looked at the jumpers, not sure if she was really a jumper person, picked one out in her size and held it up in front of her to scrutinize in the mirror. She'd like to try one on, she thought, but nobody in the store seemed to want to help her.

One of the cars exploded and silenced the crowd for a moment. The drones scattered, rose to a safer altitude, and then alighted on the edge of a building to watch.

She carried the jumper through the store, stopping to try on a pair of shoes she found on the clearance rack. She rooted through a pastel pile on the floor for a sweater, tossing each aside until she found one she liked, one that hadn't been ruined in the accident. She looked at watches, jeans, blouses, another style of jumper, put on a pair of earrings and left them in, and selected a leather bag from a hook on the wall. She liked the look of the bag hanging from her shoulder; she stuffed her old bag, the shoes, the sweater, and the jumper in the new bag, and walked back and forth in front of the mirror. She took a picture of herself with the bag, looked at the picture, held the bag to her nose and savored the scent.

Nobody asked to help her; nobody asked if she wanted to try something on. Instead, the clerks were behind the register, one of them on a landline, all of them crying even though the shop was far from destroyed. All it needed was a new window, a little attention to the display.

Denise stepped over the broken glass and exited through the frame onto the sidewalk. She tried to fit in with the crowds to look horrified, but was privately disgusted by the way the barely ablaze bystanders acted, circling and screaming with their arms in the air, waiting for the fire fighters to arm their hoses to extinguish them.

"Would you like to make a statement?" a slow-approaching officer asked Denise. The officer looked like she really didn't want to take a statement. "Did you see anything?"

Denise clutched her new bag close to her body. "Oh god," she said. She did not want to make a statement. "Did I see what?"

The officer pointed over her shoulder with her thumb. "This shit."

"No, I didn't see a thing. I was just shopping. I think my leg might be broken."

The officer rolled her eyes.

"From the tire. A tire rolled through the store."

"Thanks, I'll make a note of it. Do you want to give me your name and number?"

Denise looked up at the drones, their thin necks craned downward, scanning.

"No, that's fine," she said. "I hope nobody was hurt."

"A lot of people were hurt," the officer said. Behind her, the fire fighters hosed down the bystanders. "A lot of people."

"Did anybody die?"

"Just the cars," she said. The officer looked at Denise's bag, the security tag and price clearly still attached. "They were really nice cars."

Denise could only process so much death. She tried to look concerned, bending her face into something like sadness and horror. She looked back at the store and thought about the shoes and watches. She'd forgotten to look at the scarves, would need a new hat if the sun ever came out again.

⋮

12.

"I'M TIRED OF THIS, CARL, I'm not a violent person naturally."

"Everybody's violent; you've just been suppressing it."

"That's not true." The Consultant stood over him, ready, but not ready.

She'd grown used to a lifestyle that she surely couldn't maintain without Carl. Yes, she had her regulars, the regulars who wanted her to cry, to yell at them in anger, to spank them with wooden spoons until they bled so they wouldn't spank their kids. She'd started cooking for one of her clients only because he promised her he wouldn't eat any of her food—he only wanted to watch her feel domestic for him. But Carl was so loaded and paid her so much she could thrive on him alone.

Carl stood in her kitchen, naked, with his hand and forearm thrust into the garbage disposal. She stood by the power switch holding a leather bat.

"Hasn't it been getting easier? You seemed pretty okay with it last time."

"I guess that's true, but that doesn't mean I like it."

She was lying; it was getting easier, and maybe she liked it. At first she hesitated when slapping him, but now she genuinely felt hatred; she hated him in a way she had never hated anybody before. She enjoyed slapping him, punching him, enjoyed watching him recoil, enjoyed hearing him begging her to stop. But she wouldn't stop; that's what he paid her for.

She hit him with the bat, then hit him again, gestured toward the power switch as if she was about to turn it on.

There was no safe word. The tears that would gather in his eyes were less about the physical pain than they were about watching *her* give in to her anger. He hated someone—his mother or father?—and wanted her to hate him too.

He told her he'd hit somebody's little dog with his big expensive car and that he'd just kept driving. He said he'd parked his car across two parking spots—one a handicapped spot. He said he'd kicked the walker away from an elderly woman in the parking lot.

"And then I pushed her," he said.

"Seriously?" she asked. "That's what you did?"

"I did it," he said. "And I felt nothing. But if I did, I'd say *I hate old people and dogs and the infirm. I hate them.*"

She hit him on the back of the neck, then again: the side of his head, shoulders, his ass, his legs. With every few blows, she lunged toward the switch, watched his horror.

"That's not good enough. You need to hit the hate out of me. You need to make me feel it, hear it, smell it."

And so she did: she dropped the bat and slapped his face, tore at his chest hair and punched his ribs, his face, his ear. A small cut opened on the back of his head.

"Please," he said. "I've had enough. You did it."

"You haven't had enough," she said. She put her hand on the power switch. "I'm just getting started."

"Really, I'm serious. I'm done. I don't want you to do what you're about to do."

"Yes," she said. "You do."

She smiled, knowing exactly what he wanted her to do.

In the hall Carl paused outside the door of the Consultant's condo and adjusted the blood-soaked bandages wrapped around his hand. By the elevator he looked at himself in the hall mirror and wiped the blood from his forehead with the gauze on his palm, his stomach in delicious knotted pain.

With his phone he took a photograph of himself and filed it in a private folder. No amount of make-up would cover his clearly beaten face and there was no hiding his gnarled hand. He didn't care. The rules had never applied to him. He liked the look of his swollen eyes and mouth, the bloody wad of cotton wrapped around his hand.

The elevator door opened and out came Champion. Carl cleared his throat.

"Hello there, young man," he said. This wasn't the first time he'd run into one of his employees in the hall outside the Consultant's condo, but it was no less awkward than the first time. He looked at the arrangement of plastic plants in a brass display between the elevator doors, a tuft of animal fur stuck in the branches of the fern. "Are you following me?" he teased.

"Oh," Champion said. His face reddened. "Are you okay, Boss?"

"Carl," he said. "Please, you're practically my right-hand man.

Call me Carl."

Champion's lips twisted into a puzzled frown. His clothes were clean and pressed and he'd tucked his shirt into his pants.

Carl picked the fur out of the plant, showed it to Champion, and dropped it on the ground. "Cat fur," he said. Carl held his bandaged fist out and waited for Champion to bump it with his.

"I have gentle hands," Champion whispered.

Carl was watching, reading his lips. "Well, it was good to see you."

Champion nodded and pushed past him as Carl stepped between the closing doors of the elevator.

13.

BRYCE'S LEGS BURNED FROM THE BRAMBLES' DEEP RED SCRATCHES even though he'd been in long sleeves and pants. Mud caked his shoes and he'd tracked a path across the living room, upstairs to the bathroom, and then downstairs where he'd fallen asleep curled on the couch in the quilted blanket his mother had patched together.

He remembered walking home from the Metro with somebody. He thought of Angie, but remembered she'd left without him. He remembered the snarl of dogs and the whisper of pine trees in the wind.

He felt beaten, as if he'd been attacked.

He lit incense and put it on the mantle next to the photograph of his mother. She was standing behind a microphone on the Capitol building steps—back when DC had a Capitol building. It was his favorite photo of her. The incense was a very mild jasmine, a jasmine he'd invented, a scent he'd designed when he worked in government fragrances that had been copied again and again. The jasmine most often produced wafts of something low and distant, like a far-away cello. He sank into the couch.

Somebody knocked. He opened the door an inch and looked.

"Huckleberry pie?" Angie had one in her hands.

She pushed inside before he could speak. "You look terrible."

"I'm not sure what happened."

"You woke me up at three last night and made me take your box. It's drenched and smells terrible. I put it in my backyard."

"Shit. Yeah, I forgot about that. Thanks. I'm sure it's ruined."

Together they walked from the living room to the kitchen. Bryce hoped she wouldn't notice the bag of hair on the coffee table.

He served them pie and coffee and they ate. She smiled too much—her given name was *Anger*, he remembered. She went by Angie instead, now that *anger* was against Protocol. Bryce tried to make small talk. He asked her how her job was going. He knew she was an engineer. The fog of his head and fatigue kept him from thinking of anything else to say.

"Are you kidding? Can we talk about something else? Work is boring." She picked up a film canister from the bowl on the table.

"Be careful with that." He took the canister from her hand and put it back with the others.

"What is it?"

"It's film. Photos my mother took." He picked up the bowl and put it on top of the refrigerator.

"What are you going to do with them?"

"There's a place at the mall to get them developed."

"The mall? I thought they closed that place down years ago."

"Yeah, I know, but that's where I have to take them. The old mall. Not the new one with the Bon-Ton. So tell me about your job. I'm curious."

"Can't we talk about the tourist train, instead? It's going to be amazing." She looked at the ceiling, imagining how amazing it would be. "It's going to bring everybody together. You'll see."

"I don't care about the train. I really don't," Bryce said.

"You're kind of a drag." She sipped her coffee and shrugged.

He knew it was true. "I'm just curious about your job," he said. "I'm trying to get to know you better."

"You want to know how much money I make to see if we should get married. I'm not going to marry you, Bryce."

"I don't want to get married. I don't care how much money you make."

"That's because you love your job. You just keep getting fired. Mine's just a job."

"Sometimes I feel like it's what I'm designed to do, like those dogs that are bred to climb through tunnels. I don't love it, but I don't know what else I would do."

"Why would they do that, climb through tunnels?"

"Everybody needs a job, I guess. They ferret out rats."

"I thought they used ferrets for that."

He had no response.

"Why does this new place need you? *Scentsate?* To hear the sound of smells, I get that. But who cares?"

"It's because there aren't enough adjectives for smells," he lied.

"But you're the only one who hears the smells."

"That's true. That's not really what these guys want me to do. They want me to reproduce the smell of memory."

"I don't get it."

"I don't either. Some kind of universal scent. So people can imagine something, inhale the fragrance, and then what they imagined becomes a memory."

"That's stupid."

"It's a job."

"Okay, well I design rigid airships. For the government."

"What?"

"Sun ships. Technically, I'm working for a company that fills contracts for the government. They want to hang sunlamps on them and fly them over parks to make it look like it's nice out and to encourage plants. Have you been in a park lately? They're terrible. We're hoping the heat from the lights will dissolve some of the hail, so it'll feel like a sun shower. Remember those?"

"What?" He'd been distracted by his phone buzzing in his pants pocket.

"The zeppelins will simulate pleasant weather."

"Won't they explode?"

"Only if you fill them with hydrogen."

"You won't use hydrogen?"

She ignored his question.

"Will it take a lot of them to feel like sunshine? Won't it be sunny again someday, anyway?"

"Why would it get sunny again?"

"I don't know, I thought the weather was just a phase."

"When's the last time it was sunny?"

"I don't remember. I was just hoping. Why hasn't it been dark lately, if there's no sun?"

"Zonal waves in the upper atmosphere. Airglow. Ultraviolet light breaks it down."

"Zonal waves?"

"We're doomed."

"I hope that's not true."

"Maybe if we hope hard enough, it'll happen. Real sunshine for Mr. Cheery-pants. In the meantime, we'll have some fake sunlight to make people happy. The lights are very bright—they'll certainly blind you if you stare at them, and give you cancer if you let it touch your skin for too long."

He offered her more coffee, but she said no; she needed to go research pies in the Concordance and run errands. She'd be back later and if he was in the mood, he could come to pick up his box and maybe stay for dinner. He walked her to the door.

On his computer, he looked at the Concordance and noticed he had a new entry in his employment history. He'd gotten the job, amazingly, but was already late for his first day.

14.

DENISE COULD FIND NOTHING IN BRYCE'S EMAILS to explain his sudden death; she began instead to look at his project spreadsheets, comparing the time he allotted to projects in his records to the list of approved projects in hers.

She saw he'd worked on "compost" for a few days, and that he'd worked on a skunkworks project to simulate the smell of the inside of a person's mouth. He'd spent a few weeks working on a big project they'd eventually abandoned to capture the complexities of a dying forest. He'd worked on rot, moss, fungus, lichen, and beaver. He'd tested almost everything, so his spreadsheets were long, full of project numbers.

Much of Bryce's time, if not all, was cross-coded to an unspecified project number, a code for which no record existed.

She scanned the list of chemicals he'd ordered associated with the project. Mostly the usual, though he'd made a special request for six liters of thioglycolic acid and an unspecified amount of :CH—methylidyne radical. She had no idea what he could have used it for; the Concordance noted that thioglycolic acid had an unusually unpleasant odor, and the other one—the radical—was highly reactive and was common in space.

"Hi Denise." One of the men stood at the opening to her cube. She refused to call it a door, because there was no door there, just a space from which she could escape, or could be blocked, as was the case with this man.

"Can I help you?" She turned to look at him only to confirm he was somebody she knew and was not likely to attack her. It was late in the day and many of them had gone home.

"There's something on your jumper." He pointed.

Shit, she thought, looking down at her chest.

"Made you look," he said. He wasn't laughing.

"Please, leave me alone."

"Will I see you at happy hour?"

"No."

She returned to her investigation.

Carl had them all working on all kinds of secret projects. She'd heard the rumors about the mustard fragrance and she wasn't stupid; she knew they were working on more than perfume. Bryce's main project number was assigned only to him and somebody named Champion, who she'd always disliked, mostly because of his stupid name. He acted like a big shot but his office was on the 4th floor, not the 6th.

"Excuse me, Denise?" Another man's voice from behind. She turned.

"Can I help you?" She had seen this one before, one of the lab managers, possibly from another floor. His skin was brittle and red, flaking off of his face and arms.

"Can you show me how to fix an error I'm getting in Excel?" He was carrying a laptop. "I heard you're really good at Excel."

"It's a little late."

"I think it'll only take a second. I like your jumper." He smiled, pointed. "Are you going to happy hour?"

She sighed, closed her own laptop to hide what she hadn't been working on, and made space on her desk for his computer. He leaned down, his head too close to hers; she could smell his foul, hot breath, burnt and dark.

"See, I'm trying to figure out this one." He pointed at the screen.

"Hmm," she said. She looked at the error, fixed it, and pushed the laptop back to him. "Fixed."

"You're amazing," he said. "Pretty and smart. Can you show me what you did?"

"I have work to do, so no, sorry. Simple error, though."

"Did you change your hair? I really like it."

"I don't do anything to my hair."

"Hey, did you see that movie about the blizzard? The one where the snow's so deep people have to live in snow tunnels, but sometimes the tunnels collapse?"

"Is it called *The Blizzard?* I've seen it."

"*Snow Tunnel.* I hear it's really great."

"*Snow Tunnel!*" she said. "It's terrible."

The man, a little round in the face and body, looked rejected, as if learning to fix Excel errors was all he'd ever wanted from life, all he could possibly want from Denise.

"So, will I see you at happy hour?"

"Most definitely not."

"Okay, well then, maybe tomorrow you can show me some more Excel stuff?"

"I have my own job to do, so no."

"Okay, then." He stood silently behind her for a moment too long. He scratched his arm.

She returned to her investigation. As a Non-Accountant she had access to all the sub-basement stuff, including internal files that Carl requested.

Bryce's was a pet project, something known only to him and Carl and possibly Champion. She thought of Bryce's email. He had mentioned his personal project to recreate the smell of silence, or whatever it was he was talking about, and wondered if this was an official project, something sanctioned. She cross-referenced all the known project numbers with personnel and was able to use that data to compile a time sheet for everybody on the floor, including Bryce, to see how much of their time was allocated to what projects. What she found was that most of Champion's time was going toward the secret project assigned to Bryce on his first day on the job.

What were they all working on? What did they know?

"Excuse me, are you Denise?"

She had *had* it. She spun around. It was Champion. He had beautiful, sensuous lips, but the rest of his head and face were oblong and strange, his long white hair thin and brittle from so bleach and dye.

"Yes," she said. "I'm Denise." She tapped her mouse to close the record on her screen.

She waited for whatever bullshit thing he was going to tell her so he could linger in her cube.

"I know it's late, so not asking you to help me now, but I'm curious if you kept records of employees' timesheets after they've left the company." His lips twitched as he spoke.

"Are you fucking kidding me, that's what you want to know?" She could no longer hold back her hatred for these men who came to her cube every fifteen minutes to chat, to ask her made-up questions, to invite her to nonexistent company happy hours where only that one guy showed up frothing at the mouth, moist with body spray. "That's what you came to waste my time with? Go fuck yourself."

He stood behind her and whispered. "Gentle hands," he said. "My hands are gentle."

She vaguely remembered a man crying into a scarf a few days earlier—hadn't he said the same thing? "I'm sorry," she said. "It's been a very long day."

"Hands are for hugging. Hands are for holding."

"Relax, I'm sorry, I don't want to hug you or hold hands." She stood and peered over the edge of her cubicle to see if anybody was left in the office to help her. "I didn't mean to snap," she said. She hated this bullshit. Apologizing to some guy about to boil over in tears.

"No, I'm sorry," he said. "I have a problem. I didn't mean to bother you."

"The answer's yes," she said.

"Yes?"

"Yes, we keep records on the expired employees. If they were fired, or quit, or you know. Whatever happened to them. They're collected and filed down in the Reference Library."

"Thanks," he said. "I'm sorry to bother you."

He walked away and she felt a great sense of relief, but could hear him repeating: "My hands are gentle."

15.

CHAMPION CRAWLED THROUGH THE PLENUM SPACE, dragging a braid of new network cable behind him.

When he wasn't burning bodies or working on his main project, Champion retreated to the metal shafts in the ceiling, wide enough for him to crawl through and tall enough for him to wedge into a sitting position with his feet against one side of the shaft and his back against the other. Here he could escape his coworkers while still hearing them murmuring below. Here he could still feel the buzz of his phone. From here, he could slip down into his office undetected when necessary and then retreat back into the blue light of the ceiling maze where he could be alone with the pulse of the new data drumming through the bright wiring. He was hardly done, but already he could feel the new capacity.

He crawled forward some more, dragging the cable toward the trunk line that ran down to the fiber network below them, beneath the street. Where the cable connected to the trunk was where he liked to sit, wedged comfortably into the womb of the tunnel where it opened into the wide shaft full of cable tied together in bundles from the upper floors of the office building.

When he approached the shaft, he could hear the charge of data—he could feel the usual digital traffic, but also now the new sensory data beginning to flow alive through the network.

He'd replaced far more cabling than he'd needed, the project now a long one requiring multiple visits to the ceiling tunnels. He cut an old cable, unwound the twisted pairs of wire inside, and crimped them into new plugs. He checked the connection with his tester, and repeated for everything Bryce had cut. He rebundled and zip-tied and when he was done, he folded himself into the tunnel, careful not to disturb the cable path, and admired the neatly aligned and color-coded lines. He peered down the shaft full of the building's trunk wiring, on its way to the backbone below, then closed his eyes and listened to the music of it all, a kind of harmony, equal parts sound and magic.

The sample he'd inhaled from Bryce's desk lingered in the back of his throat, aching like illness about to erupt. He cleared his throat and coughed, but the feeling expanded, a corrosive taste sliding down into his stomach. He felt as if his throat might close and he began to panic, feeling for the first time claustrophobic as the tunnel walls collapsed around him.

The Silent Chord

He tried to disengage from his crouched position to crawl back toward his office, but something had taken over. He could no longer control his body. The more he tried to free himself, the more he pushed against the sheet metal walls, the more stuck he became. He sucked air into his mouth and through his narrowing throat and gagged.

16.

CHERYL AND TAMMERS WENT TO THE ART MUSEUM because of another fire at the mall. The fire had been started by a loose zoo monkey in Sears, but all Tammers cared about was Bon-Ton. Instead of going to Bon-Ton, which was closed because of the fire, they decided to go to the museum.

Cheryl hated the mall, and had told Tammers this, but Tammers never quite heard or didn't want to hear her because she loved everything about the mall—the smell of new clothing, the sound of the fountains, the taste of food court food. She loved the mall even when they weren't shopping, even when they were just sitting on a bench, splitting an Orange Julius, talking about all the great stuff at the mall.

"I love to watch all the people!" Tammers would say. "Doing things and going places!"

They'd had to pay for parking in a garage three blocks away and the rain came down so hard their rain slickers had failed them as thick streams of water formed rivers in the creases of their jackets and directed them onto their jeans and shoes. Their feet and legs were soaked, and here, in front of this painting, Cheryl contemplated the meaning of it all.

They'd started in the basement near the restrooms and coat check where the museum put the contemporary art. Had they found a convenient parking space, and had it not been raining, she might have been more invested in what she saw: a naked man with no genitals, the height of a giant, surrounded by dismembered jaws, ears, and eyeballs. The figure of the man, like a doll, was scarred with wounds—precise, bloody slashes across his entire body.

Like Carl, she thought.

She knew the body and the eyeballs surrounding it were not real because the card next to the painting confirmed that, though realistic, what was on display was still only a painting. *I'm no idiot*, she thought. Was she supposed to *think* it was real? She hadn't seen another painting quite like this one, so had no model from which to judge it. Her instinct was that the painting was very bad, but here it was in the museum; what did she know?

The card told her the painting was a comment on gender. The wounded man had no genitals, so in a sense, his gender was muted both by the lack of a penis, the wounds on his body, the lack of clothing or other indicators. Desexualized. The body parts surrounding him, the card said, were the detritus of abject bodies, senses (taste, hearing, seeing, touch, smelling) separate and discarded. Inputs without a central processor, according to the description.

"To what do they bear witness?" asked the card. Cheryl did not know. All she could fathom for herself was that the composition of the painting was symmetrical, and despite the unsettling image, she felt comfort in symmetry. She was more interested in the idea of a *real* wounded man, one who would pay somebody to mutilate him rather than ask his wife to do it. She would have been happy to hit Carl, if he'd only told her that's what he'd wanted. She'd reluctantly agreed to a trip, "somewhere romantic." He'd already booked the jet. She knew she would regret it, but he had been so insistent, promised it would be the last thing, really. He'd try to talk her into staying with him and she would refuse. She'd probably have to refuse twice, maybe three times. She knew splitting with him wouldn't be easy.

Cheryl took a photo of herself in front of the painting. Her face appeared in the photograph next to the man's sculpted torso and doll-crotch.

She followed Tammers, winding through a small crowd of others who, with their cameras and sticks, took photographs of themselves in front of the paintings, sculpture, and an installation replicating an office space.

They navigated the maze of soft blue cubicle walls, looking into each one of the roped-off enclosures to gaze at the dusty desks and their contents: typewriters, old computers with CRT monitors, blurry photographs of families and pets. Effigies of workers slumped over their computer keyboards seemed to be the focus of the installation. Realistic pools of red-black blood from unseen head wounds oozed from the corpses across the surface of the desks.

The fake blood, like rich pudding, reminded Cheryl they'd have to find something to eat.

The installation suggested that work made people's faces bleed. Cheryl liked work—she was the CEO of a non-governmental-government public/private consultancy which did many amazing things, but most recently had taken over the management of a beleaguered project to engineer artificial light to alleviate environmental gloom. She was good at her job, though to somebody who didn't understand how things worked, it would seem that all she did was create inefficiency and delay, but when her company took on a project, that project was done *right* and safely. Now the project was no longer beleaguered.

And who doesn't love light? "I'm glowing just thinking about it!" She'd worked hard on that punchline, tested it on Tammers who was just the right kind of smart for Cheryl. Not like Carl, who she'd loved because of his ambition but had proven himself to be mostly a fool, like all the well-bred Ivy-leaguers she'd met as a youngster just out of B school shopping as much for a look as a partner. She pushed these thoughts away, because here she was on this day with Tammers. Tammers! Her name was always on the tip of her tongue. And here, in this mostly okay museum, looking at this terrible art wasn't a chore at all because they were there together.

Cheryl didn't believe that cubicles killed people, didn't make their faces bleed. *These people were already dead,* she thought, *before they'd even gotten into the elevator.* Each corpse in the installation had desk photographs of miserable-looking toddlers throwing balls, climbing on furniture, or torturing pets. Children were the real killers, not work. If only these people had gotten to make light, or some other thing that brought people joy.

Once through the exhibit, they retreated to the quiet second floor, vaulted and church-like, and lost themselves in the galleries. They walked aimlessly among the endless portraits with placards identifying only the artist and date of the painting. Here, they looked at each enormous, brown portrait or landscape, and pondered it for three to four seconds before moving on without the pressure of feeling like they had to learn something. Cheryl liked not being told what to think, though here she could use some help: was this all they had to offer them, these dark halls of excess? She felt like they were browsing the vault of a bank.

The museum reminded her of Tammers' apartment. Tammers had made a small fortune after college when she'd invented an app that allowed users to make anonymous three-second videos of themselves that were added to a collage of other, randomly selected, three-second user videos. The application was a huge sensation for those looking to create real connections with people all around the world. She'd sold low, but it was still enough, and she thought at the time of the sale she'd become briefly famous, the toast of the tech world. The app had since been absorbed, rebranded, and replaced by some more exciting app.

With her new money, Tammers retired and moved into a cavernous condo near the top floor of an architecturally significant building designed as a holding place for the storage of excess capital. What Tammers had purchased was unfinished space with concrete walls, rough floors, and plywood furniture. She liked the coldness of the space and its simulated furniture.

In the corner of a dim corridor, Tammers stopped them in front of a small oil-on-wood panel of a girl and her dog, a sort of primitive, proto-cocker spaniel. Tammers' dog had been a cocker spaniel too, and Cheryl thought the dog was a dead-ringer for Mr. Slippers, though wider and wild. Tammers looked at the painting longer than any other painting in the museum, but didn't reach for her phone. Instead, it looked as if she was trying to conjure the kind of sadness she thought should have been provoked by suddenly seeing the image of her beloved dog emerge in the darkness of a museum hallway from the ethereal light of a small, minor oil painting.

The eyes, Cheryl thought. *The dog's eyes.*

She understood exactly what Tammers was going through. Cheryl slid her hand into Tammers' hand. She was in the process of realizing in a new way that her best friend was gone and Cheryl wanted to be supportive.

Tammers shrugged. She looked at her phone.

"I'm thirsty for a Julius," she said. "I wish the mall hadn't burnt."

They decided to drive to Tammers' condo, where Tammers felt she might be able to make them Orange Juliuses from scratch, though Cheryl was skeptical because Tammers had neither a refrigerator nor a blender. Tammers promised her, so she agreed.

They walked back through the contemporary gallery on their way to retrieve their coats and paused again to try to find something in the art they'd come to see. Cheryl thought of the mall, the things on display, and the desire she sometimes felt in the Bon-Ton, watching Tammers try on tracksuits or a marked-down dress. She could have those things, could understand them.

Cheryl stopped in front of a small painting, barely larger than a notebook page, a landscape of a dead farm with a feeble, purple horse grazing in a sterile field. Something about the purple horse activated a kind of feeling in Cheryl's stomach, a feeling like hunger and pain, a longing for something she had not known she wanted. She tried to conjure an articulation of this new feeling, like an awareness of something long lost.

Next to her, an unattended child stood in front of a large landscape, a smudge of purple and yellow and bright green at the foot of majestic slate-gray mountains. The child had pushed his entire hand into his mouth and saliva drooled out around the perimeter of the boy's wrist.

She looked back at the painting in front of her and waited to feel the new feeling she had felt, but now, the painting was just a painting.

A crack sounded somewhere in the wall of the gallery.

The child pulled his hand out of his mouth and pressed his sopping palm against the canvas, then moved his hand like a brush in a broad sweep across the painting. He smiled. The painting, at last, was finished.

"Hey, step back!" A guard yelled, running toward the child.

Another crack, louder, from above them.

The guard grabbed the child's arms, pulled them behind the child's body, and secured them with zip ties. The guard, having touched the boy's hands, thick with saliva, looked as if he might vomit.

"Cheryl, I'm ready to go." Tammers hovered behind her.

"Just another minute," Cheryl said. "I'm feeling something."

Tammers snorted.

The boy began to scream. A rasping, like the bending of metal, echoed through the gallery. The museum visitors paused, looking away from the art on the walls and to the ceiling and floor, looking for the source of the sound.

Someone shrieked as a pool of brown water surged across the museum floor. The foul water, like sewage, covered the bottoms of their still-wet feet, and quickly reached their ankles, soaking into their shoes and socks and the bottom of their jeans. An alarm howled, and a voice on the intercom, hard to hear over the noise, said something about evacuating.

"This is not a test," came through clearly.

The guard who had been struggling to take the child somewhere, perhaps to an undisclosed interrogation room, left him alone with his arms zip-tied behind his back, and ran toward the door, dropping his badge on the ground behind him.

The visitors moved like they were stuck in a chaotic current, bouncing around each other with no idea where to go. Some of them pointed to a glowing exit sign leading them away from the filthy, wet floor, and together they swarmed forward, pushing into one another as if their lives were in danger.

"Please move carefully to the nearest exit," the voice said over the intercom. "This is not a test."

Cheryl took Tammers by the hand and together they joined the river of people trying to get out, pausing to help a toddler who had stumbled, a toddler whose mother had pushed ahead of her, leaving her to fend for herself.

"Do not use the revolving doors," the voice said. "Do not trample one another."

Years ago, during a horrific high-rise fire, people evacuating the building were crushed in the revolving doors as too many pushed forward despite others trying to exit. The door became jammed with bodies and the survivors inside waited nearly two hours, bodies piled upon bodies, while rescuers freed them.

"I can't leave without my raincoat." Tammers pointed to the coat check.

Volunteers helped the suddenly swamped attendant find people's coats and bags, repeating "we need to get out of here," but still dutifully attending to people's outerwear.

"I'm not going down with the ship," the attendant said, jumping over the counter and rushing toward the door.

A security guard told them to leave their belongings; the water was coming in fast and they didn't know if the ceiling would hold, but there they waited, the water rising.

The smell of the museum's shit engulfed them. Tammers began to cry. She whispered to Cheryl that she missed her dog, that she could feel him still, in her arms, and that she did not really believe he had died, but was instead taken away from her. At night, she could hear his claws scratching on the cold concrete floors. She begged to no one for his return, her pleas echoing through her enormous, empty apartment.

Cheryl put her arm around Tammers. "You need to get a new dog."

Together they pushed through the crowd to the front of the coat check line. Tammers sobbed, convulsive and gulping, into her arm. "Please, we need our coats," she said to nobody in particular. "It's an emergency."

17.

BRYCE ARRAYED THE FRAGRANCES HE'D ORDERED FROM THE LAB across his cubicle desk and listened to their notes. He marked on a sheet of musical staff paper: oil of sweet pea, clear and bold, the sound of a low G; orris a messy E, an eighth note, a long and wobbly flag; and the flower of the stitchwort, a fuzzy quarter B, sketchy and light. He closed his eyes and with the hum of the air conditioning system, the buzz of the fluorescent lights above, the fragrances created a sonorous coarse sorrow that swelled over the din of his coworkers.

He thought of his mother, focusing on the details of her face, appearing as fragments that could not be put together; he saw her wrinkled chin, her lower lip, her swollen eye the time she had fallen down the basement stairs. He could see a blue dress she'd worn: Italian wool, he remembered, a special dress. He saw her body in it, her hands, the skin still smooth, the indentation around her ring finger where she'd worn a band before her husband, his father, had gone away.

He put on his headphones, waved his hand over the vials of fragrance and inhaled the swell of the low note blending with the slow piano of Chopin's Nocturne in E minor, drawing the song as he went.

He stared at his cubicle wall, pressed his nose against the fabric and could smell his old job, his old government cube, the sounds of the scents he made there: the utterances of complicated rain, the vocalizations of drowning earthworms amplified and distorted, their dying cries.

He inhaled again, and heard only a tremulous, high D, the sound of almond; he drew the shape of a whole note at the top of the treble clef.

He imagined his mother's fragmented face. He could see her sitting in front of a table in her bedroom, looking at a mirrored tray in front of her full of decorative glass perfume bottles shaped like birds, an elephant, delicate glass fruit. He could see the spray of mist surrounding her, could hear the orotund fragrance, resonant, baritone, and rich.

"When are you going to move in?"

"I'm all moved in." Bryce turned.

The technician wore a lab coat even though they were not real scientists. His name, Terry, was monogrammed in jovial script across the lapel above a pocket full of pens and a glass thermometer. "Where's your stuff?" Terry asked.

The first thing Bryce had learned as a junior analyst was not to bother putting up office decorations because he could be fired at any moment. His boss had given him this advice as if it was the most important thing he could learn, not just because he was dispensable, but to show everybody he *knew* he was dispensable and did not care. So he never cared, never decorated, even though he sat in that same cubicle, his first cubicle, working for the Bureau of Fragrance and Taste for nearly ten years before the agency was finally shut down. When he looked at his coworkers' cubes, made to look like miniature rooms with colorful throw rugs, toys, plants, and framed portraits of beloved dogs, he wasn't sure what he would do with his anyway. He had no family, no pets. He hated action figures, did not care for plants.

He remembered what his boss had told him, how humiliating it would be to fill a box with his belongings and carry them to the elevator after being fired. The worst thing would be to have to make two or three trips, or to need to ask somebody to help him.

He'd sat in his bland government cube for years formulating and testing scents with vague instructions and no disclosed purpose, creating secret fragrances used for all the covert operations and wars that never made it into the Concordance. When he was laid off, he was able to slip away.

"I don't care." He didn't know what else to say. He had work to do. He looked at the ceiling panels, the air conditioning duct overhead. "I don't have anything."

"What are you working on?"

"I'm not really sure. Something for Carl."

"One of his secret projects?"

"I don't think I can say so if that's what I was doing. That's what 'secret' means."

"But we're friends."

"Are we?"

"Sure, we're work friends."

"I don't think that matters."

"Are you on the mind control thing?"

"Mind control?"

Terry reddened. "I'm just joking."

"What kind of mind control?"

"I shouldn't have said that. It was just a joke."

Bryce returned to his work. The buzz of the chord felt less like sound and more like a migraine forming, bright dashes of light skittering across his eyes, blocking his vision. The buzz began to increase in volume; Bryce grabbed the edge of his desk to steady himself, feeling faint even though he was sitting. He looked behind him to make sure he was alone in his cubicle, opened his top desk drawer, and removed a sandwich bag of his mother's hair, held the hair to his face and inhaled three times, sucking in the scent and holding it in his lungs as long as he could.

His vision returned and the pain eased as the volume decreased. He shoved the bag into the back of the drawer, moved a folder over it, and closed his desk.

He opened a sample of the oil of plumeria, a deep G so pure it was nearly without modulation. He darkened the bold head of the whole note, looked at the melody emerging on the paper.

With a thin glass rod, he dropped a sample of the oil onto a card, then added clove and a bit of vanilla to create a rich, resonant, baritone D major. He leaned back in his chair, closed his eyes, and listened to the billow of sound and fragrance.

"Hey." Another voice from behind him. "Thank God it's Friday!"

He opened his eyes. Bryce was certain it was not Friday. A guy with a cone-shaped head, dyed-white hair, and strange pretty lips stood behind a cart overflowing with colorful cables.

"Hey buddy," the man said. "Everything cool? You need anything?"

"Yes, I'm good, thank you."

"I'm Champion," he said. "I'm your supervisor." He held out his hand.

"Great, thanks."

"I'm the one who invented the new network cable." He chuckled. "I ordered you a new laptop."

"Really?"

"Yeah, you emailed me and said yours was slow."

"I don't think I emailed you that. My computer's fine. I just use it to send emails and fill out forms."

"Then why would you ask me for a faster computer?"

"I didn't."

Champion shook his head. "Hey, can I ask you something?"

Bryce didn't reply. He thought to take off his headphones, but felt that by doing so he was tacitly agreeing to a long conversation.

"Do you like cakes?"

"Not really, no. What kind of cakes?"

"Chocolate, vanilla. All kinds. They're really good."

Byce looked at his sheet music, began to draw the notes of the D chord with his pencil.

"How about steaks?"

"I'm not that into food."

"My partner and I had a little side business. Steaks and Cakes."

"That sounds like a great idea."

"Raymond made the cakes, but I ran the steak side of the business. Grass fed, organic. Beautiful, marbled meat. Cruelty free."

"How is it cruelty free? Do you not kill the cows?"

"I don't, no. Somebody else kills them, thank god. They kill them while they're asleep. That way they're not scared, because it's night and they're not awake. It's like a bad dream to them."

"Then you slaughter them? In the night?"

"Well, I don't. But somebody does. I just cooked the meat afterwards and Raymond sold it. He still does. It's delicious. The marbling is so good, you have to get a look at one sometime."

"I'm kind of in the middle of something, if you don't mind."

"Oh, you're not bothering me. I'm just trying to drum up a little interest in Raymond's side gig. I had to let him go off on his own. The Boss needs me to focus. And you and me need to get to know each other—since I'm your supervisor and all."

"I'll let you know if I ever need a steak."

"Or a cake?"

"Yes, or a cake."

"People around here, they'll pay almost anything for non-toxic meat. They're wild for it."

"Excuse me, are you Bryce?" A woman squeezed between the wall of his cube and the IT cart. "I'm looking for the new guy."

"I'll have your new laptop set up in a few weeks."

"I don't need a laptop."

Champion shrugged, pushed his cart away. "Well, I'll leave you two alone. I'll be back to check on your progress tomorrow."

The woman who had taken Champion's place was strikingly plain, somewhere between beautiful and hideous, the ideal office worker, the immutable form to which they all aspired. Her hair was long and unruly, tangled and thick.

Bryce worked hard to achieve plainness—he bought the right shirts, the right pants, combed his hair. He worried about whether he should wear short sleeves or long, whether he should tuck in his shirt, if flip-flops were okay to wear in public. He always fell short, his office pants too tight, his white shirts stained and too wide at his chest and too tight around his stomach.

Though she was abnormally typical, the woman's hair, however, was special. He could not smell her from across the cube through the fog of E minor, but still, the back of his neck tingled; he detected a subtle, significant chemical thing happening in the air between them. He squirmed, wishing he'd worn his other shirt.

"I'm Denise," she said, loudly. "You're the new guy, right?"

He took off his headphones. "Yes, I'm new. What do you do?"

"I don't know."

"Oh, okay."

"Sometimes I'll send you emails. You should read those emails and then reply to them, because your reply indicates to me that what I've said in my email is correct. Does that make sense?"

"What are the emails about?"

"Don't worry, they'll be short. I'm really good at email. You send all your reports to me."

"How long have you worked here?"

She sighed and rolled her eyes, threw her head back. "It feels like I've been here all my life. It's not a good place to work. But we get to go home at the end of the day most of the time. Can I go now? I just wanted to make sure we met this one time, that you know that I'll send you emails, and that you're not to ignore them. Cool?"

"Sure, sure."

Bryce put his headphones back on and turned away from her, though he could feel her standing behind him for a moment longer than necessary. The longer she stayed, the more he could feel the chemistry between them—the muted scent of her hair, the E minor fragrances, the office hum, the Nocturne, all of it coalescing and muting inside him. The sounds became softer, fading away. The effect lingered after she left and his head cleared in the sudden near-silence.

He closed the vials of orris, pea, and stitchwort, the clove, plumeria, and vanilla, and opened another chord from the gamut of fragrance, selecting scents from the treble clef: the C of jasmine, the E of the Oil of Portugal—the essence of orange. He opened the G of the orange flower, dabbed a drop on a card and waved it in front of his face.

The Silent Chord

He turned to a new sheet of staff and sketched a song: together the fragrances sang a bold, citrusy C major. The sound crested and subsided, muffled by the lingering presence of Denise's hair.

The grand chord sent him back to a walk in the low mountains a few hours' drive to the north.

He'd been told long ago that it was good for people to enjoy nature, and when he felt his health was being compromised by spending so much time in a cubicle, he took this to heart and on Saturday mornings he would put on the shoes he'd purchased specifically for walking outdoors, drive north, park at a trailhead, and set off with his water bottle and walking stick. He remembered the steep inclines, looking down at his feet, careful not to slip on a rock, how his calves ached, how after the light started to fade and the air cooled he would fear getting lost before returning to his car. He remembered the nearly constant mist and how through it, everything seemed a little out of focus. He remembered the slight rain coating his rain jacket like fuzz. The mist changed to rain and then to hail, shifting violently from innocuous to aggressive.

As he walked, he counted the drilling towers, like mile markers, extracting natural gas from the ground. In the distance, he heard explosions across the valley where miners were using dynamite to blow the last of the mountain to dust from which they could extract the last crumbs of coal. Though there were more birds then, they were almost always silent, hiding away from the hail in the remaining trees, waiting for the silence of night to sing.

18. CHAMPION STOOD BY THE BAR, UNSURE OF WHY HE'D COME.

He scanned the dark room, full of coworkers lifting drinks to their faces, illuminated by the glow of their phones. The new guy wasn't there, and neither was the girl—how could he get them goether if neither of them ever left their cubes?

A familiar figure stood at the end of the bar and raised his drink to him. He couldn't place where he'd seen him, but nodded anyway, and turned to order a drink. He asked for a White Russian. The bartender rolled his eyes and gave him a beer instead, which he accepted, perhaps because it's what he'd really wanted.

"You're Champion, right?"

One of his coworkers was suddenly next to him, his eyes glassy and red.

"Yes. Soon I'll be Lord Champion."

"Lord Champion? That's impressive."

"Well, I've earned it. Who are you?"

"Paul. My name is Paul. We've met at least three times. I'm the assistant lab manager of Olfactory."

"I'm sorry, I didn't realize we'd met."

"From down the hall."

"Nice to meet you, Paul."

"Like I said, we've met. I'm on your floor all the time."

"What do you do again?"

"I just told you, I'm the assistant lab manager. Or the assistant to the lab manager. Something like that."

"Cool." Champion looked around for anything to take him away from the conversation. The man he'd seen at the end of the bar was still there, watching. He wasn't sure where he'd seen him before; he was sure they'd spoken.

"I hear you're working on something big. Something you can't talk about."

"I can't talk about that."

"Is it the mustard project? The cow manure project?"

"I don't know what that is."

"So what is it? You're Carl's little helper, right? You're always meeting with him."

"Believe me, I'd rather not meet with him at all."

"You don't like Carl? After all he's done for us?" Paul was gulping his beer, belching, almost choking. When he'd finished his drink, he slammed his glass on the bar and twirled his finger in the air at the bartender, who ignored him, disappearing into the kitchen.

"Look, I'm in a bad mood. Why don't you stop by my office tomorrow and we can talk some more about this."

"What, you're too good to talk to me now?"

"I have gentle hands. My hands are for hugging."

"I don't want to hug you. I just asked you a question."

"I'm not feeling very gentle right now. You're going to have to excuse me."

Champion stood and turned away from Paul. He thought of Dale, his old assistant, and began to feel a familiar rage. Outside, he stood for a moment in the rain, watching the streetlights flicker on and off, when a windowless van pulled up to the curb.

The man from the end of the bar was suddenly beside him.

"We're taking you back," the man said.

19.

CHAMPION DREAMT OF RAGE. He dreamt of humiliating his assistant Dale at meetings, dreamt of firing him without cause, or demoting him, or sending him off on some meaningless, eternal errand. He dreamt of grabbing Dale by the back of the head and punching him squarely in the throat until Dale lay lifeless on the floor. He dreamt of dragging Dale's dead dream-body into the office elevator to the fountain where he would leave him floating face down for days.

But this was only a dream; he was not a violent person.

Dale had killed himself. Each time he imagined punching Dale, he checked the Concordance and confirmed: Dale had committed suicide, seemingly by floating in a shallow pool of water until gentle death overcame him. It must have been a peaceful death, a good death.

Champion's hands were gentle; he'd suppressed his rage like they'd taught him at Gentle Hands. He'd grown inside, and used his hands only for hugging, petting, and stroking. Gentle Hands had cured him. Bad feelings transformed into bland actions.

He was not surprised when he awakened in a concrete cell with a headache and a chalky mouth. The first time he'd been spirited away to the facility, when he'd been shouting too much in meetings, they'd taken him by surprise. The counselors from Gentle Hands had broken into his apartment at night, administered tranquilizers, and covered his head with a black bag. He hazily remembered being thrown into the back of a van, being beaten mildly, waking up in a cold cell, and beginning his rehabilitation. He didn't think shouting in meetings was something that required rehabilitation, but they'd revealed his latent feelings of violence to him.

When he woke in a cell after difficult dreams, he was not surprised to have returned, though he had no recollection of being taken. He remembered a fight, maybe with a coworker.

He thought of the people he'd seen outside his house, asking for directions to the zoo, taking his pictures. He'd failed some kind of test. It was a situation he could accept, an unplanned vacation, a chance to reassess and recommit himself to peaceful thoughts.

"Where are we?" He heard a meek voice from the bunk next to his. "Who are you?"

The man next to him reminded him of Dale, small and fuzzy and confused.

"I'm Champion. We're in a place called Gentle Hands."

"My name's Sab. I was just out in the park, picking up litter, and then these people in wet suits crawled out of the river."

"They crawled out of the river?"

"Yeah, they put a bag over my head, and then dragged me back into the water with them. I thought I was dying. That's all I remember."

"That's pretty cool." Champion wished he'd been taken that way.

"What is this place?"

"We're not in jail, really, though we're not free to go."

Champion thought for a moment. "It's sort of a camp. Like rehab. My employer makes me go sometimes. At least I think that's who sends me. I'm not really sure. Once I stayed for so long I lost count of the days. I dreamt of the wind and the sky, and of the soft felt walls at work and long leisurely lunches."

When Sab told Champion he didn't know why he'd been sent, either, that he could think of *nothing* violent, Champion asked him if he'd been feeling depressed, if perhaps he'd been feeling badly toward himself, and that maybe this was, in some imperceptible way, causing him to think violent thoughts. Maybe he, in fact, *did not know what he was feeling at all.*

"They'll explain it to you here. Sometimes when we don't think we've been feeling violent thoughts, it turns out all we've been thinking are violent thoughts."

Sab looked puzzled. "Maybe," he said. He paused as if he was going to scratch his head. "You know, maybe. Maybe I've been a little down lately."

"Do you think about killing yourself sometimes?"

"Doesn't everybody?" Sab grinned and when he laughed, Champion laughed, too.

"Yeah, they do. I think about it almost constantly, but not consciously. It's something I push into the back part of my mind."

"How do you know you're thinking about it, then?"

"Because I think about having pushed it to the back of my mind. It reminds me it's there, somewhere." Champion began to feel his anger percolating. He didn't like to think about everything he worked hard not to think about and feel.

"I should try that."

"You won't be here long. Sometimes they make a mistake. Who knows? I learned a lot about myself and my hands the first time I was here. I didn't think shouting at meetings was that big of a deal. I always thought of myself as mild-mannered, but after my first and third visits, Jesus, I realized how enraged I was. For a little while I thought I was going to go to prison. I kept having these dreams, and then I'd react poorly in them, and then I'd wake and my knuckles would be bloody or my shoulder would be sore, and I'd know, I'd know I'd blacked out after not being gentle."

"When do they serve breakfast?"

"Soon. We get dry toast and water, and then group therapy."

Sab looked as if he was concentrating on keeping something inside and finally said, "Toast makes me so angry."

In group therapy, they sat on chairs in a circle. Champion had been there before and felt that as a guide to Sab, he should just sit close by and be supportive. He took Sab's hand and nodded at him when he looked up. Sab was obviously afraid of Champion. His gentle hand signaled that things would be okay, no matter what.

Sab whispered. "I don't remember what I did."

"You should get used to not remembering things."

"I miss my cell phone."

"We've only been awake for an hour."

"I miss the Concordance."

"You need to elevate your mind: you must free yourself from things if you're to know yourself."

"What?"

A man in an orange jumper and slippers stood. They all wore orange jumpers and slippers and mostly they used fake names, so it didn't matter who stood up, except that it was someone who was neither Sab nor Champion.

"My hands are angry. I didn't know, then. I'm not sure who sent me here the first time, but I'm thankful. Maybe it was my wife, maybe it was work. They fired me. I'm unemployed now because I can't shake the violence. And divorced, after my second visit. I came back on my own, this time."

The man's hands, arms, and face were covered with old scars and new scabs; it was clear he needed Gentle Hands more than most of them.

A counselor put his arm around the man. He told him it would be okay, to take a deep breath. "Relax, brother," he said. "Relax."

"I'm so filled with rage right now."

"You have gentle hands," the counselor said. "Your hands are *so* gentle."

"I have gentle hands." He formed his gentle hands into hard little balls. The skin of his knuckles reddened. "Hands are for hugging. Hands are for hugging. Hands are not for hitting or hurting, but hugging and petting and drawing gentle circles in my sketchbook."

"That's right. What else are your hands for? Why don't you tell us a story?"

He took a deep breath and unlocked his fists. He stared at his hands as if they didn't belong to his body, as if he could only barely communicate with them.

"I hate my hands. My hands are horrible. I wish I'd been born without them."

"Your hands are just a metaphor, Mike. The problem isn't your hands."

"I hurt people with my hands. My hands have to go."

"Tell us a story, Mike. A gentle story. Maybe a new story? Or an old story with a different ending?"

"Okay, I'll tell you a gentle story. My gentle story is that I was never a violent person until I woke up in this shit hole."

A Counselor put his arms around Mike and tried to guide him back to his chair, but he wouldn't move.

"Sometimes we don't *know* we're violent until we come here," the Counselor said.

"My hands were perfectly gentle until I spent a month here. Now I'm fucked. Brainwashed."

"That's enough, Mike."

A few more counselors entered the room and surrounded Mike who had re-clenched his gentle hands into fists and was swatting them around like he was trying to knock flies out of the air.

"Okay, okay. I'm sorry. My hands are gentle. I can tell a story. Who wants to hear a story?"

They clapped. They wanted to hear a story.

"Okay. I used to be an engineer, a controls engineer. I programmed machines that made cookies. The kind of cookies that are hard and come out of machines in rows of plastic. The kind of cookies you like to dunk in milk. Crispy, delicious little cookies."

Champion drifted away from the story, focusing instead on the patients gathering in activity area on the other side of the room. He watched them pulling the chairs away, folding them, and stacking them neatly against the wall before arranging themselves into rows. Two counselors in black tights walked to the front of the room and clapped a few times.

"Let's go, everybody!"

They began to jog in place. The patients followed, limbering up, jogging.

"If I fucked up my job, the company I worked for lost millions of dollars, and the price of cookies would go up, though nobody would notice if it did, because people love this company's cookies so much they would pay anything for them. And the price never did go up, because I was really good."

They leaned forward in their chairs. Champion tried to pay attention, but he was transfixed by the gathering on the other side of the room. He watched as the counselors stood in front of the room; they stretched their arms, pointed their fingers to the ceiling, then bent down to the floor. He watched how they moved fluidly from standing to kneeling on their mats, like great mechanical birds, and how the patients mirrored the movements of the counselors so closely it was hard to tell if they were following them or moving with them to a memorized routine.

"Good job, everybody! You have gentle hands, gentle bodies, gentle mouths!"

The Counselors began to dance slowly, lifting their feet high, moving their arms like serpents; they moved to embrace each other, whispering to one another, but never touching.

The patients in front of them followed, partnering off, making the dance their own.

"The software's so sophisticated I wondered why they didn't just program it to do the work for us. Anyway, as easy as it was, there are a lot of idiots in the world and I was better and faster than anybody."

Champion felt the loose sinews in his arms, his muscles always on the verge of falling away from his bones to hang useless in the bags of his skin. He inventoried his organs, cataloged each dull ache; with each breath he felt a burning in the lower lobes of his lungs, which felt to him like heavy sacks of mucus.

"Anyway, I didn't think too much of it, except that Nut Jobs are one of our most popular cookies, and though I knew our whole product and manufacturing ecosystem, among other things, I could never figure out how Nut Jobs fit in, where they were made, even, and it drove me crazy."

Sab whispered to Champion. Champion nodded. They would have to sit through the whole story.

"So we work out the logistics. I'll be staying on a compound near the factory, a walled-in place where foreign workers can stay and be spared from seeing anything that might upset them."

The group in the activity room began to look to Champion like the eels in Carl's tank as they shed their orange jumpers to reveal black leotards, pressing in close to one another, contorting their bodies into the space around their leaders, reaching for them, grasping toward them, but never touching. He unfastened the top buttons of his jumper, excited by what he might find there, quickly disappointed to find his bare chest.

"The first weekend, me and the other workers go on a bus trip and see all kind of animals running around. We get to see a lion eat her cubs. It's great."

No matter how long Champion stayed in Gentle Hands, his parrot was never dead when he returned. In fact, Jellybeans always seemed a little disappointed when he returned home, even from work, but was never so sullen as when he showed up after a week or two of rehab. He imagined they had a team, a team in a van full of food for all kinds of pets; they'd break into their homes to feed their animals, to give them a run in the yard.

"They ask me to make sure 'the machines are shaking hands'—whatever that means."

The group in the activity room had formed their bodies into a sort of quivering ball around the counselors, each shaking body held in an awkward puzzle around the other bodies.

One of the counselors called out from within, her voice muffled but audible: "Gentle, gentle, gentle!"

"What most people don't know is that at the end of almost any manufacturing process where food is involved—whether it's breakfast cereal, bread, or cookies—one of the final steps is for the food to be sprayed down and washed in formaldehyde. It's mostly harmless to the consumer, but the shit is nasty in relatively small quantities and repeated occupational exposure is serious."

The cluster broke, each body falling away, hands in the air, legs spread, tumbling onto the floor. Each lay still while the Counselors stretched and then jogged in pace as if shaking away something particularly intense.

"The workers were doing the washing by hand. There were workers in coveralls—no eye protection, no respirators, not even gloves—standing next to the conveyor belts holding hoses, spraying down the Nut Jobs."

The group slithered along the ground, found their jumpers and wiggled into them, still on the floor.

"Good job gang, good job," one of the counselors said. He put his hand on the counselors lower back and began to tap a rhythm, his fingers crawling down like a spider.

"One guy's face looked like it was melting like it was going to slide off of his skull. Another guy's eyeballs had fallen out and were just hanging from his face. I'm not exaggerating. He had to pick them up and point them in the direction he wanted to see."

Champion ran his gentle hands through his hair, thin and oily and pulled a few strands out with his fingers. He looked at Sab, fixed on Mike with awful eyes.

"One guy showed me how the stuff had scarred his tongue. He couldn't taste a thing. Can you believe that?"

Another counselor had entered the room and was waiting to interrupt Mike. "Okay Mike, that's great. Let's all clap for Mike. Who asked Mike to tell a story?"

The patients pointed to the counselor.

"And what do you think I did? Did I sit by and watch those poor workers suffer? That's exactly what I did, at least for a few weeks."

Everybody clapped.

"That's okay, Mike, we all know what happens next." The counselor tried to lead Mike to his seat.

They clapped more loudly.

"At the time it all made sense. I thought I was doing the right thing. It was..."

"The worst thing you've ever done," the Counselor said. "We know, Mike. We know what you did. And that's how you ended up here again. Why did you let him talk? Don't you read their files?"

"Telling stories is good for them," another Counselor said.

"You don't believe me."

"It doesn't matter if I believe you or not, Mike. You believe it. That's what's fucked up. You shouldn't let Mike tell stories."

"I should have gone to prison for the rest of my life, that's what should have happened. But nothing happened. Nobody did anything."

The lunch bell rang and the smell of a hot meal wafted into the room. Most everybody was very hungry while at Gentle Hands and nothing could keep them from a meal.

Champion and Sab sat with Mike. Champion knew how important the fourteenth step was to their recovery, so they sat with him as a sign of their support.

"Hello, comrade," Sab said. He smiled at Champion, looking for his approval for adopting the Gentle Hands lingo. "Are you gentle?"

"Yes, I'm gentle from my head to my hands, from my foot to my heart. My hands are gentle. Are you gentle, comrade?"

"Yes, I'm gentle from my head to my hands, from my foot to my heart. My hands are gentle. I use them for hugging and high-fives."

They high-fived gently.

"Me and Champion wanted to know if you wanted to tell us the rest of your story? About the chemical burns and the snack cookies?"

"I'm not proud of what I did. I'm not in the mood anymore."

"Whatever it was, it wasn't gentle," Champion said.

"Do you guys like to party?" Mike asked.

Champion knew what he meant by "party"; he did not like to party.

"I love to party," Sab said. He put an avocado slice into his mouth.

"Well, I've got a bunch of schnapps. Little bottles. Every flavor you can imagine."

"Yeah?"

"Yeah. If you can get out of your cell tonight, and meet in mine, we can drink them. I probably have close to a thousand bottles. We'll get ourselves good and blotto."

"Blotto?"

"That means drunk," Champion said.

"Good and blotto. You in, Champ?"

20.

BRYCE'S BODY, STILL AND BLUE, LEANING AGAINST THE WALL OF HIS CUBE with the bright cables noosed tightly around his neck. Denise remembered how much he annoyed her, how persistent he had become, how he was like all the other terrible people, always coming to her cube, always wanting something, but there, dead or almost dead, he was something else entirely. If only for the time she'd stood watching him that morning, she could feel every inch of her own body, each constituent part, each thing broken and aching.

Each thing she'd swallowed to expunge his experiment—mouthwash, vodka, coffee—had only strengthened its presence.

Bryce had kept his cubicle spare. Without the minuscule signs of his presence—his mug, his samples, the scraps of notes scrawled on index cards—the desk was just a desk. Someone else would soon come to claim it.

The network cabling she'd found wrapped around his neck had disappeared, seemingly retracted into the open panel in the ceiling, from which a strange, dim light now glowed. She'd seen Champion go up into the ceiling, something he seemed to do regularly; maybe he was still there.

She climbed onto the desk and stood on her toes, balancing herself in the opening with her hands. Inside she saw the soft light from somewhere far inside the metal duct. New network cabling lay next to a thick bundle of data cables secured with ties.

"Hello?" she called into the shaft. When she heard nothing in reply, she climbed down.

She opened each of Bryce's desk drawers and searched for something amid the office supplies, pushing aside the pens, bags of rubber bands, and paper clips. She found a bottle of rubber cement and opened it; he'd used about half the bottle for some reason. In the bottom desk drawer, she found files for old projects with wrinkled printouts of spreadsheets, emails, handwritten project notes she could not decipher. She saw a few words scribbled on a scrap of paper, something part formula and part recipe: thioglycolic acid and :CH, heat and hair. She folded it and stuffed it into her work bag.

Beneath the folders, she found a hairbrush like the one she'd kept in her own desk. She lifted it to the light from the opening in the ceiling and extracted a single, long, brown strand of hair, her hair, she was sure, and when she returned to her own desk and looked, she confirmed: her hairbrush had been missing.

Part Two

21.

CHAMPION SHOWED SAB HOW TO UNLATCH THE DOORS from inside at night; it wasn't difficult, as if they were free to go if only they tried.

Champion had heard of a patient who just walked away. But that was rare. He figured it was because at Gentle Hands they were reminded daily of their vulnerable position in the world; few of them really wanted to go outside before they were ready. And, because they were brought to Gentle Hands with bags over their heads, most of them were afraid that if they *did* escape they wouldn't know how to find their way home. Many simply didn't want to leave their phones behind. For Champion, Gentle Hands was an easy place to be, and for that he was grateful.

In Mike's cell, he showed them a cardboard box full of hundreds—perhaps thousands—of tiny schnapps bottles in every flavor, just as he'd said. Mike tossed Sab a root beer, and Champion a lemongrass. Like many evenings in which the guests of Gentle Hands snuck out of their cells to get wasted together, tonight they went too far. Hours later, Champion estimated they'd each had around fifty airline bottles of schnapps, enough to kill most people. Though that seemed an excessive number, there were a lot of bottles on the ground and he could no longer think clearly. He alternately longed for the Consultant and focused on keeping the room from spinning. He couldn't remember if Mike offered up a krabkake pipe or not, but when questioned later, after the suggestion had been planted, he couldn't stop remembering a particular smell, followed by a decided change in Sab and Mike.

Mike began to curse his hands. Champion told him to calm down, that his hands were gentle, and that he was as likely to be brainwashed by this place as cured, something he would never admit sober. Champion suggested they try to escape; he was drunk enough, he thought, to just walk away.

Mike continued to curse his hands, pausing only to take little hits from his krabkake pipe. After he inhaled, Mike would be silent for a moment, teeter, and then begin to look down at his hands, telling them to go fuck themselves. "It's time to go hands, it's time to go." Mike dropped the pipe and from beneath the bed slid a large, green metal board, a paper cutter.

"Where'd you get that?" Sab asked. Mike picked up the pipe from the floor, took a hit, and exhaled blue-green smoke. Sab stumbled backward onto Champion who had reclined on the bed. Champion passed out and awakened. Sab was standing again and inhaling from the pipe.

"I snuck it out of the office. It's the solution to everything."

"What is it?" Sab asked. He sounded like he was purposely talking in slow motion.

"A paper cutter. It's our way out of here."

"We're going to leave?"

"No, I'm talking about a cure. A real cure."

A cure, Champion thought. "A cure for what?"

The room swam above him and he imagined being free, free from the sickness of anger. He believed Mike—they could be free. But then, even in drunkenness, he began to wonder again why he'd been sent there, as if Carl was playing a cruel joke on him, or programming him, for some reason, to believe he was constantly controlling his anger, when in reality, he was rarely angry at all. They told them not to think about that here— they *were* violent, they said, even if they didn't feel it.

What he saw when he tilted his head to see what Sab and Mike were doing was the paper cutter on the card table, Mike sitting with his arms outstretched across the green metal plane of the cutter, his wrists in the line of the blade.

"Are you sure?" Sab was already screaming.

"Do it. Just fucking do it," Mike shouted. "And do it hard. Harder than you imagine. You've got to crack through all my arm bones to pull this off. I think there are at least three. You understand? You're going to have to give in to your anger."

Sab held the krabkake pipe to Mike's lips and let him inhale, and inhaled himself, and then as if he meant it, he slammed the paper cutter blade down onto Mike's wrists. The blades made it into Mike's arms, though not quite through them. He screamed and bled and screamed again. "Do it again. Do it again!"

Sab brought the blade down again, and again, unable to break through Mike's bones. Champion thought he heard a crack; perhaps he had at least broken a bone or two. Champion couldn't believe Mike had it in him to sit there, clearly in agony, with his arms hacked and bloody still resting on the paper cutter while Sab chopped at him with the blade.

"I'll be cured," Mike screamed. "I'll be cured."

The sight of so much blood both frightened and sobered Champion. Rather than wait for the counselors to show up, he waited for the room to steady and attempted to guide Sab away from his task using logic. Both Mike and Sab sobbed. Sab had not succeeded in cutting Mike's hands from his arms.

"You're not going to cut through his arms with this. Not tonight. He might die, but you're not going to crack his bones."

Sab hacked at Mike's arms with half-strength. His energy was gone.

"You think he'll bleed to death?"

"Maybe the two of you should have thought of that."

"Can we just leave him?"

"They're going to be here soon. They'll stitch him up, bandage him, take him to the hospital. Whatever it takes, okay? We have to leave."

And so they left, but they were blocked from going back to their rooms by what sounded like counselors coming down the hall, so instead they went into the stairwell and climbed to the top floor where they found the door to the roof unlocked.

22.

THEY EASILY FOUND PARKING AT THE OLD MALL among the cars they'd long ago paved over, the black bumps of sedans and station wagons entombed in asphalt, ghosts among the trees and weeds growing through the cracks.

"I don't feel safe here," Bryce said.

Near the mall entrance, a bonfire burned despite the rain. Teenagers drank from bottles of cough syrup and tossed tires and broken chairs and table legs onto the fire.

"We'll be okay," Angie said. She reached her hand into his and guided him around the fire party, giving the teenagers as much space as they could.

One of them shouted something, smashed a bottle against the pavement.

Bryce put his head down. In his free hand, he carried a bag full of film canisters.

Inside, the mall howled mold and thick humidity. They passed a boarded steakhouse and stores covered with long-faded "coming soon" panels. A banner, smeared and stained with what looked like blood, hung across the wide corridor: "The Future of Indoor Shopping."

Water spurted from fountains, full and clean, in the center of the thoroughfare. An elderly man sat smoking on a bench, tapping his cigarette into a round ash can filled with fine white sand.

Mall music played softly from speakers above; somewhere deep inside, somebody played an organ over the recorded soundtrack.

They felt the threat of dim lighting and dark corners. A side corridor that used to lead to an exit led instead to barricades blocking the flooded floor where the roof had collapsed.

At the central atrium of the mall, a ramp spiraled up to the second floor around a lush plastic garden and grand fountains squirting streams of water overhead. At the top, a boy pushed a bowling ball to the edge of the ramp and released it. While the ball rolled down the spiral, the boy rode the glass elevator to the bottom to meet the ball. When he saw Bryce and Angie watching, he abandoned his project and ran away, disappearing into the ruins of the old arcade, overgrown with lush ferns and spiraling tendrils.

As they got closer to the camera store, the organ music grew louder. The benches were clean, the ashtrays full of sand, and the water sprayed, illuminated from below by colored lights from the fountains. The overhead lights were on and bright and they passed the first open store, a Hickory Farms, full of plastic-wrapped gift meats. A happy employee approached them with a tray full of samples.

"Would you care for a treat?" the young woman asked. She wore a maroon apron and her hair was pulled back beneath a paper hat. She smiled.

Whoever was playing the organ began to play "The Entertainer." The dark notes came, painful and slow.

"Cured meat is bad for you," Angie said.

The sample woman snarled, pulled the tray away from Bryce's hand. "Everything's bad for you," she said. "Look around."

Beyond the Hickory Farms, they came to the gaping mouth of Sears surrounded by a ring of retail brilliance: DEB, Chess King, the Piano Player, and an open and apparently functioning camera store, The Film Center.

"I don't believe any of this."

"I wish we'd tried samples."

"That stuff is terrible for you. I wouldn't let you put something that toxic into your body."

Bryce looked behind them; the sample woman had gone away, into the store full of orange and red and the song of salty meat drifting in the air.

They browsed in the DEB and then in the Chess King, walking around the round racks of clothes that seemed to them to be from another era, but perhaps were contemporary versions of some style inspired by the past, facsimile fashions that neither he nor Angie understood.

Angie picked a men's leather jacket from the rack and ran a finger over the leather fringe hanging above a false chest pocket. She held the jacket up to Bryce.

"Maybe time for an update?" Angie asked. "You're always wearing the same thing."

A stone-washed teenager approached them.

"Can I help you find anything? Those jackets. They're not real."

"What's wrong with this place?" Bryce asked.

"I don't know what you're talking about."

"Where are all the stores?" Angie asked. "The real stores. The ones that aren't out of business."

"These are retro," said the employee.

"It's great they've recreated Chess King and DEB, and I can tell you I wouldn't be sad if they brought back Merry-go-Round. I'd kill for a true Julius. But where's the rest of the mall? Stores that sell stuff we might actually want?"

"Recuperating."

"Chess King has been out of business for thirty years."

"Yes, that's true."

"So how is it a thing?"

"Rebuilding. Bring Back the Mall, but with modern stuff like pop-ups and collabs. You know, stuff kids like? We got a Federal Mall Revitalization grant, and we're doing some crowdfunding. Do you want to try on that jacket? I have to unlock it."

"Unlock it? It's not even real." Angie examined the jacket. A thin metal ring threaded through the sleeve of the jacket was attached to a long chain locked to the rack. "No, that's okay."

"Jesus, 'The Piano Man.'" The organ player sang them a song from across the concourse.

"He does that all day," the sales clerk whispered. "It's really great."

The thrum of the Chess King, the whining lullaby of new clothes, brought Bryce back to the edge of a memory. The organ and the bright lights, the high-contrast colors, so much black and red—he remembered hiding in the racks, back-to-school shopping, the shame of not knowing what clothes to wear.

"Are you sure you don't want to try it?" The salesperson looked Bryce up and down. "Maybe time for an update?"

"That's exactly what I was thinking." Angie stood next to the salesperson in solidarity, both of them scrutinizing Bryce's lackluster look. "That fringe is sick."

"No, that's okay." He *was* fond of the jacket.

The smell of the fake leather from the jacket and the air in the store bubbled already in him; tiny explosions, like half-inflated balloons popping, began to interrupt their dialogue.

Outside, the organ player sat at an electric organ in front of the piano store and played medleys of songs that Bryce recognized but couldn't name. Angie bobbed on her feet and watched, and for a moment looked like she might like to dance, but there it was, the Film Center.

The store was nearly empty as if going out of business, a hodge-podge of old and new cameras dusty with paper tags.

"We're looking for film," Bryce said to the old man sitting on a stool behind the counter.

"This is a good place to buy film," the man said slowly, as if it might be the last thing he would ever say. He looked like a shrew. "We have that here."

"Can you develop film? Make prints?"

"This is a good place to print film," he said. "We have a man who knows how to do that. And a machine." He raised a frail arm and pointed past the sparse aisles of cameras, camera bags, and empty shelves toward the back room, where through an open door, they saw another man, younger, sitting behind a desk examining something mechanical with a screwdriver under a desk lamp. "What kind of film do you want?"

"I'd like to print these." He held up the bag with the film canisters.

The man took the bag and peered inside. "We can print these. I just have to fill out this form."

From below the counter he found a pad and filled it out with a pencil, carefully printing Bryce's name and address.

"It's going to take some time," he said. "There's lots of film to print before we can get to yours."

"How long?"

"We're very busy, and the machine is very slow. After the holidays some time? We'll call you."

23.

THE FROTTEURS, WHO RUBBED AGAINST THEM whenever the tram hit a rough bit of track, were unusually attractive, especially by Florida standards. The woman in front of Carl, a leggy brunette with too many teeth, for the fourth time pushed her ass against Carl's crotch where, despite his best efforts, his penis twitched a twitch that momentarily invigorated him in ways he'd long forgotten. He wanted to push Cheryl up against the glass tram door, lift her skirt, and take her right there, but as if by design a robotic voice announced their arrival and asked them to exit expediently and walk in an orderly fashion toward the park, which, the voice reminded them, was a steamy adventure where it's always a party at 3:00 AM after you've had too much to drink.

He told Cheryl she looked fantastic and he meant it. She looked amazing. Her lips were full and red and vibrant. One of Scentsate's old fragrances, a deep, earthy musk with overtones of sweetness and lavender, emanated from her body in waves so thick he could almost see them. He too had walked through a cloud of mist at the office that morning by mistake and now reeked of a caustic pine used in furniture polish.

The problem was they were no longer in love, even though their therapist had told them love was something people had made up. The word, she told them, was empty. The scientific proof that love did not exist, that it was an imaginary feeling, made it no longer adequate, no longer enough, and Carl and Cheryl's problems could be solved simply through the realization that though they missed being in love, they had never really been in love in the first place. She suggested that instead of worrying about imaginary feelings, they find a new hobby together they had not done before, like sailing or a model railroad. Cheryl suggested that they get divorced instead, which seemed easier than trying to find a new hobby, and it would solve all their problems.

Carl wasn't so sure. Divorce seemed like losing, and he did not like to lose.

Cheryl had not expected Adult Disney, imagining some place far more interesting—London, Paris, Bali—almost anywhere. But Carl insisted, talking her out of ditching him at the airport when they arrived at the gate for Orlando. "It'll be fun," he'd said, "like a joke." What he hadn't told her was that he'd spend the whole day in meetings trying to sell Disney on Scentsate's new research. So far, she'd apparently had little fun, choosing to spend the day in their suite working. She did not like the joke, she'd said, but still she'd agreed to go. That was something.

As they walked toward the park entrance from the tram, fireworks exploded periodically around them. Whips cracked against the sidewalk, held by characters like Cinderella, Prince Charming, and the Little Mermaid. They dressed in tight leather costumes with hanging chains or revealing shreds of cloth draped suggestively over their bodies. The characters wore elaborate feathery headpieces and whipped familiar costumed characters: a diapered Mickey Mouse and a Donald Duck wearing metal clamps where one imagined his nipples might be.

Carl started to point out to Cheryl he was pretty sure ducks didn't have nipples when she surprised him by reaching her hand into his. Perhaps she was having a good time. Perhaps it was because the magic Disney characters they both knew and loved had joined hands in a chain and were dancing across the promenade while fireworks whistled overhead.

She whispered into his ear: "This is the stupidest thing I've ever done."

A giant dark dome with artificial stars glowing from above enclosed the park, the always-descending sun illuminating the orange western edge where the distant roof met the horizon.

The artificial weather was nearly perfect: not too cold, and not too warm, with a breeze that smelled of wood-smoke and fried food always pleasantly blowing. Faces passed them, sullen and hollow, as if the trick of light had kept them from sleep for days.

They joined the crowd around Cinderella's Castle and watched nearly nude dancers twirling and singing about how everywhere was Fantasy Land, which was true inside the park; Frontier Land and the rest had been bulldozed. The castle had been renovated into a simulated porn palace with leather-clad men and women waving from the windows while cautiously delighted patrons looked on.

The park was particularly seedy, even though it had only been open for a year. Perhaps that was the appeal of it, the crumbling plaster, the rampant weeds in the planters, the peeling paint, the trash everywhere. The park felt like it was on the edge of a bad neighborhood, both a little bit dangerous but also a place where anything could happen, a place where dark secret dreams could come true around any corner. Another firecracker exploded above their heads. A bottle broke somewhere in the vicinity and Carl realized they'd been hearing this sound since they'd arrived: breaking glass always somewhere in the distance.

"All this trip is doing is reminding me how much I dislike you," she said, standing in line for *It's a Small Adult World.*

"Can we give it a chance?" Carl asked. "You're here, that's something."

"I'm here because I thought we were going somewhere better. *Florida*, Carl, really?"

Maybe he'd already won; she was standing here, in the park, agreeing to spend time with him.

"I think some part of me thought that yes, we could try again, but this is just reaffirming to me that this is a bad idea," she said. She looked at her phone.

Carl looked up into the dome and could just make out the lattice of air ducts above, imagining Scentsate pumping this place full of fragrance.

People they recognized from the tram rubbed against the patrons. He felt a bulge against his buttocks. "Do you work here?" he asked the guy behind him.

"Work here? I'm just having a good time. Are you having a good time?" The man with the bulge loosened Carl's tie, twirled around him, and reached his hand into Cheryl's hair. He threw a handful of glitter into the air above their heads.

Carl thought he was making fun of him for wearing a tie to the park. He'd only brought "park-casual" clothes with him. He was, however, wearing short sleeves and he'd moisturized his elbows, and for that he felt he deserved praise.

As the man pulled Carl close, he asked if Cheryl was with him.

Carl nodded.

Holding his tie in one hand, the man put his free hand around Cheryl's neck and brought the two of them together. "Fun vacation? Lover's weekend?"

"A little of both," Carl said.

"It's a business trip," Cheryl said. "I just booked a flight out of here."

Carl stammered when the man asked him how long it took him to get to the park, and if he had to pay for parking.

"Why wouldn't I have to pay for parking? I'm just like everybody else."

"Sure, you are. You're just a regular fella enjoying Disney."

He leaned in and whispered. "I know who you are."

"Who *I* am? Who are *you*?" Carl asked.

"I'm just here to have a good time. Do you guys like to party?"

The last time somebody asked Carl if he liked to party he'd been just out of college, living in his first apartment with four roommates he'd met on the Internet. A neighbor, a woman, knocked on his door and asked, "Do you party?" She handed him an uncorked bottle of wine. The same feeling of nervousness had come over him. When he told her he *did* like to party, she asked him if he knew where she could score some krabkake, and while Carl was not a prude—he'd smoked his share of krabkake in college—he had no idea where to score some. When he divulged this to his neighbor, who was standing too close to him too, she backed away and took the wine. He'd never been much of a ladies' man. She bade him goodnight.

"Sure, we like to party."

Carl knew for a fact she did not like to party.

"That's what I like to hear. Where are you from?"

Carl told him where they were from and asked him the same.

He whispered in his ear. "I'm from wherever you want me to be from."

"Come on, that's ridiculous."

Cheryl played along, still looking at her phone. "Could you be from Marbella? Portofino?"

"Hot. I'm totally from Boca."

"I said Portofino," Cheryl said in a way that made Carl fear for the man's safety. "What's hot about Boca?"

The man pulled Cheryl close and their lips touched. He growled a little, and then licked Cheryl's nose.

"Don't touch me," she said, pushing him away. "What the fuck?"

Carl wasn't sure what to do but, while this was happening, they'd been inching forward in line and were now at the ride entrance being beckoned by employees toward a sign that read: "Get Loaded!"

The man waved a hotel key-card in front of them. "Meet me on the roof! In the Hot Tub! We can dress up like ducks or mice—anything you want!—" he wiggled his fingers at them, kissed the air, then turned, "If you'd like to watch a thirty-minute presentation on an in-park timeshare, that would score you some coupons—" he said over his shoulder and walked toward the back of the line.

Inside, they were guided to a gondola in a shallow canal. The black water shimmered in the dim light, and though they could see that the water was less than a foot deep it did almost seem like they were boarding a boat. A safety bar lowered over them and with a lurch they floated into a dark tunnel where a Theremin wobbled an otherworldly melody.

Carl touched the glossy key card in his breast pocket as they emerged from the first tunnel into a wondrous room full of mechanical mannequins: Elvin women in red lingerie and men in leather pants.

Cheryl looked either mesmerized or bored by the dirty Victorian Christmas village. As fake snow fell over the artificial landscape, the heathens wandering the streets seemed especially childlike wearing only underwear despite the cold.

They continued their slow ride through porn clichés from around the world recreated by childlike mannequins: a baby-faced man in coveralls coming to fix a lonely housewife's plumbing, Turkish prison shower scenes, and run-down roadside adult bookstores. Thailand Ladyboys. Naïve tourists lost in a Dutch red-light district. Pants-less Germans spinning high on a carnival swing ride. In one room, fanged Elven Helpers pinned a frightened Santa to the ground and tore at his and each other's clothes while biting each other's flesh.

After, they followed the crowd slowly out of the darkness and together they walked across the park. A line ringed Pleasure Mountain, and though tired, Carl insisted it would be worth the wait. The reviews had promised it would be the highlight of the trip. Mostly he wanted to be able to tell the Disney execs about everything he'd done.

The sun still hung on the western edge of the park. Another single white light exploded above their heads, and then another, and it began to rain.

Pleasure Mountain had been transformed on the outside into a pinkish, flesh-colored mound. *A little like an enormous clay tit or clitoris,* Carl thought, *but also a little like somebody's first attempt at throwing pottery.*

Inside, they were guided by sexy futuristic flight attendants to a pair of empty seats in Flesh Rockets. Once seated, employees in short-shorts and tank-tops offered them drinks in hand-blown glasses with tiny bubbles and colored ice cubes like planets.

"Please hold onto your drinks," a voice echoed inside the mound. And with that they were off, accelerating until it became difficult to sip their cocktails, so much so that Cheryl spilled most of hers on her blouse. It reminded Carl of the flight earlier—what had she expected? Transatlantic flights were few and far between since the weather shifted.

They were lucky to have gotten as far as Florida.

Through the flesh they rocketed into a tunnel—illuminated red, then orange, then yellow—the car lurched rhythmically like simulated thrusting. It went on for a little while until in sudden darkness they spun around a loop where Carl sprayed his drink and all the change in his pockets into the void, and though he could not see or feel it exactly, he could tell he was out—no longer in the tunnel with her. Fireworks exploded around them like wasted galaxies, exposing him to glimpses of the strange rafters and dimpled ceiling above, and the rocket limped to a stop in what smelled like a cloud of burnt gunpowder.

Waiting there for something else to happen, Carl remembered the old haunted-house rides back when they were kids and wondered again, *What a rush it must have been for those lucky boys who had girls to be stuck inside?*—but back then he was not one of those boys. Now he leaned over to Cheryl and searched for her lips with his. She was facing away from him; so instead he found the back of her head and buried his nose deep in her hair. *Was she afraid?*

"Something's wrong. We should be moving." She sounded less frightened and more annoyed as she pushed him away, like it was all his fault.

He reached out of the car and groped stupidly in the dark to see if he could feel what was below them. His arm was too short. "I'm sorry," he said, "I think we'll just have to wait."

"I want to get the fuck out of here."

"I'm sure they have a plan."

"I smell smoke. I should have known. Oh God, Pleasure Mountain's on fire."

"I'm pretty sure that's not real smoke," Carl said, he knew artificial fragrances and was almost certain the smell was simulated, or at least intentional—all a part of the ride. "Don't over-react. I'm sure somebody will do something soon."

Somebody screamed behind them, something snapped, something that sounded like heavy metal tearing; whatever it was, it was not insignificant. Their rocket vibrated and lunged forward a few feet. Carl's eyes stung as the mound filled with smoke. A thump like a body hitting the ground echoed far below them. A muddled voice on the P.A. crackled somewhere in the dome.

Somebody yelled "Help!"

Somebody else, "We're going to die here!"

Carl imagined Cheryl's arms crossed against her chest like a teenager. If they were going to die, they should at least try to make out, he thought. *It might help us get back on track.*

A dim red emergency light flashed on and off, and then another, and soon the entire ride was exposed in flashes: Through the smoke filling the vast warehouse space, they could see the track snaking around what looked like a complex system of screens, cameras, spotlights, and cables hanging from the ceiling over the expanse of the interior. On the top track a fire was burning a hole through the roof, like papier-mâché. Inside Flesh Rockets on other tracks, riders stood and looked down from three or four stories in the air, also assessing the situation.

Carl pried up the safety bar, stood, and stepped out of their rocket onto the walkway now exposed in the light. He and Cheryl walked toward the blinking exit sign at the end of the catwalk. Water poured from the hole in the roof.

Outside, a fire brigade of furry-headed Disney characters—bare-chested under transparent raincoats—fought the fire from a life-sized fire truck. Patrons spiraled down an enclosed "emergency" ramp that wound to the ground. Beyond the hoses' deluge, it was still just sprinkling, still dusk, the sun (still visible) still setting to the west.

At the perimeter they were greeted, again, by porny park employees, whose wet T-shirts and cutoffs were re-hosed periodically. They apologized for the inconvenience and handed Carl complimentary tickets to the Live Sextravaganza at the castle, which was about to start; if they hurried, they wouldn't miss a thing.

The tickets promised "Live Sex Acts" right on stage.

Carol shook her head. "Are you fucking kidding me?"

"Isn't that why we came?"

"You can do what you want. The jet's waiting for me. I'm going home."

24.

THE TELEVISION SAID SOMETHING ABOUT RECORD RAIN over the bay and the overflowing river, but Denise didn't care; she looked instead at the Concordance. She looked at Bryce, now officially DEAD; her mind sometimes wandered to other things as she scrolled, but always returned to him.

When she realized she was again thumbing absently through his photographs, she put down the phone, tried to focus on the television, and picked up her phone again a moment later.

She threw her phone onto the floor and kicked it away with her foot. She looked for something to eat and put water and rice on the stove to go with old chicken she found in a zipper bag in the refrigerator. While the rice simmered, she found her phone and looked, again, at Bryce.

She turned her phone off and tried to think about work, about what she could do besides what she did, something that would take her away from the office, away from her coworkers. They were all damaged, obtuse in ways that baffled her. They were monstrosities of their own making. Bryce was not even the worst of them.

She turned on her phone and scrolled through job descriptions for museum curators, pastry chefs, and life coaches. Everybody had life coaches and those who didn't were life coaches. She could be a life coach for life coaches. Her own life coach had said she should just give up because they were all going to die anyway. Maybe somebody would pay her for the same advice: *Do nothing, wait, it will all be over soon.* She kept looking. She would work almost anywhere.

Maybe she was insecure. Maybe she was more marketable and more valuable than she thought. Maybe she had good references, coworkers who saw the good work she did for them, despite her bad attitude. She was smart. She was so good at spreadsheets; she was practically an accountant. She had good business-casual outfits and knew how to send a brief email.

She thought she would have made a good veterinarian because she hated people and liked the look of white coats. The thought of people crying while she euthanized their pets brought her deep satisfaction. Once when she was little, her parents had taken her to a petting zoo where she remembered being scared by a horse. She remembered its massive teeth, its grotesque face, the way it formed a sinister grin when she approached it. When she cried, her father told her to "shut up and smile," while her mother held her firmly on top of the horse so her father could take a picture. Her parents were always kind to her. They told her she could do whatever she wanted if she'd only try to do *something*, or that she could get married if she turned out to be pretty enough. She didn't want to be pretty and she couldn't set her mind on anything, so here she was, her mind a cold, quivering jelly.

The fragrance was still growing like a disease, tightening her throat.

She looked again at her phone, at Bryce. She checked her email for something, anything , that might explain his death. She kept coming back to the long email he'd sent, how he was working on something *"to preserve the silence."*

She returned to the Concordance and paused on a photo of Bryce sitting on an empty bench on what appeared to be the edge of a windswept field, the long grass flattened and wet. Bryce seemed to be off-guard and was un-posed. The angle of the photograph suggested it had been taken from the hip, perhaps without Bryce's knowledge, and whoever had taken it had applied a sepia filter that evoked old, real photographs, the kind that none of them had seen in a long time. Maybe the photograph had been taken by a sick drone, hovering only feet above the ground, its algorithms confused by its own imminent death, the machine afflicted by whatever strange disease had been spreading through the network.

Bryce held a thin hardbound book at arm's length, his other arm draped over the back of the green bench. A child ran across the field in the background, chasing an out-of-focus dog.

Maybe the photo wasn't Bryce at all and she'd been making the same mistake the facial recognition software had made, but it didn't matter really, because there it was in the Concordance, with his name on it, forever Bryce.

The photo produced in her the beginning of a fantasy somewhere between the love expressed by Bryce for her in his dream of rippling water and simple togetherness and the loneliness of the spectral image of Bryce sitting on the edge of a field.

She imagined she was the one taking the photo; instead of Bryce asking her out in the coffee room, instead of going home with him after the Holiday Party, she imagined she'd become interested in him and walked by him along the edge of the field. She imagined she'd known him a long time, perhaps their whole lives. She was beginning to hate him a little less.

He'd been asking her out almost once a week since becoming comfortable enough around the 4th floor to regularly harass her. She finally agreed so that he would see clearly how much she disliked him. Or she'd asked him, knowing the date would be terrible, knowing it would end in disaster. She would send a message to the whole floor.

He'd driven them to her favorite restaurant, a restaurant she could only imagine, a restaurant so grand it could only have existed years ago. She'd wanted to try it, but it was too expensive, the kind of place one didn't go to alone. The kind of place reserved for special occasions and business decisions.

But that's not where they'd actually gone. In real life, he'd driven them to the Golden Fountain, famous for its repellent buffet with food piled in terrible heaps on a very long steam table.

She tried to remember a time when there were restaurants that weren't buffets, a time when people loved to be served at their seats. She tried to remember the kind of place she'd first imagined, elegant and expensive, the kind of place where they could enjoy their meal slowly and get to know one another. But she didn't want to get to know him; this was only a way to prove to him how much she wasn't interested.

She couldn't remember the last time she'd gone on an actual date, or to a restaurant with menus. She remembered as a child selecting items from the pictures on a placemat. She remembered four waxy crayons, drawing monsters on the paper, following the dots of an easy maze. Most of her meals came in a bag.

Together they stepped up to the buffet and selected brown Salisbury steaks, mashed potatoes, and vegetables the color of the mashed potatoes. They went back for pools of yellow pudding, cadaverous lengths of fried boneless chicken, and salads drenched in French dressing. Denise overdid it on crabsticks.

She was ravenous, gluttonous, and used far too many napkins, crumpling and discarding each next to her plate. She gulped soda with no ice from a huge mug still warm from the dishwasher.

Bryce had worn nose-plugs to keep the smell from overwhelming him.

She found this oddly attractive in the same way she occasionally felt pangs of what she thought might be love when she saw two-legged dogs with wheels attached to their hindquarters.

She worked through the pile of brown food on her plate, lifting mounds of food with an oversized fork to push more food than she could handle into her mouth, each bite like progress toward an ending.

Bryce was not unattractive. He was dull, and maybe a little crazy, which she liked. He was attentive and funny, unsure of himself, bumbling his way through his own pile of food.

"Tell me, how are you feeling?" he asked.

"Jesus." Her mouth was full of pudding and shreds of some meat—turkey? Chicken?

"What?" he asked.

"Just, not that question. I'll tell you what I'm thinking instead: This is not very good food."

"I can't really handle flavors so well. Maybe dinner was a bad idea."

"Why does everybody keep asking me how I'm feeling?" She remembered a woman who had spoken to her at a party. The lights had been flickering on and off and finally she heard silence from the silver stereo system as the power went off, then a deep thump, and then a crackle before the music, some sort of slow jam, resumed.

"What are you thinking about?" the woman had asked her.

"I'm a life coach." Denise hoped she would go away. She didn't know how to respond. She had at least six canned responses to "What do you do?"

The homeowner's husband came by in a big sweater and fiddled with the stereo knobs, worrying over them as if he were trying to defuse a bomb about to explode.

"I asked you what you're thinking about, not what you do."

"What?"

"What are you thinking about? Tell me how you're feeling." The woman put her hand on Denise's shoulder and gave it a little squeeze.

"I think you should kill yourself," Denise said.

"I'm Crystal," the woman said. She looked concerned. "So, why are you frightened?"

The husband had a screwdriver out and was removing the front of the stereo. He held a tiny flashlight between his teeth, the beam shining into Denise's eyes.

"I feel nothing," Denise finally said. She held her hand up to block the light. "I'm not a very good life coach," she admitted.

Crystal smiled and leaned closer. One of her teeth was on the verge of falling out, hanging loose in her mouth.

"That's not what I asked."

Crystal's necklace was made from wooden beads and she wore sandals despite the weather. She was not dirty, but she was wearing a troubling skirt and, as she leaned closer, Denise detected an earthen scent.

"I shoot guns and then I eat what I kill," Denise said.

"What?"

"Have you ever tasted a cat, Crystal?" Denise showed Crystal her teeth. Denise's teeth were perfect; she wanted Crystal to be jealous.

The man was pounding at the stereo components, pulling wires out and tossing them over his shoulder.

Crystal stepped back. She frowned in a way that seemed to exaggerate her disgust, to be clear to Denise she no longer wished to interact with her.

Denise picked up a chicken plank, dipped it in a mysterious sauce, and sucked the sauce from the tip of the chicken. Bryce bounced his spoon on a crabstick.

"I don't know, I just thought since we already know what we do for a living, that it was the only thing left to talk about. That or all this weather we're having," Bryce said.

"We certainly are having a lot of weather," Denise said.

"Yes, for sure."

"Why do people eat here?"

"Textures," Bryce said.

Next to them, a girl older than a baby but younger than a real girl, a girl old enough that it would no longer be right to call her a baby, but still a long time before it would be right to call her a young woman, began to gag, and then choke. Alone with her father, she looked at him helplessly, pointing at her throat, as if she knew he would be helpless to assist her, and that this final moment of breathless discomfort would be her last. The father looked at her as if he was pretending not to notice.

"I'm sorry. Maybe next time we can go somewhere better, or you could come over to my house. We could look at photos. My mother had tons. Real photos printed on paper."

"That sounds amazing." Denise looked at the time on her cell phone. The numbers were illegible, garbled, like foreign glyphs. She glanced momentarily at the girl in distress beside them and touched her throat. She looked at Bryce. He'd have no idea what to do.

The girl's father, instead of standing to perform the Heimlich on her, began to yell at her.

"They have soft serve." Bryce looked longingly toward the ice cream machine. "What are you working on at work?"

"Same shit as you. Project budgets for new smells. P&L for new smells. I look at the spreadsheets you send me and I send them to the 6th floor. Or send them back when I can't approve them. Same thing I tell you every day when you ask me."

"Sorry. I don't know what to ask you. This isn't easy."

She didn't reply and there was a silence while they chewed.

"Did you really masturbate before your job interview? In reception?"

"No, why would you think that? Who told you that?"

"Beth. That was her last day."

"I remember her. It sounded like she was going to quit."

"She killed herself. I think somebody needs to help that girl."

"Maybe it was for the best."

The young little girl climbed out of her chair and began to beat her own chest. The piece of food obstructing her windpipe fell out of her mouth and onto the floor. She climbed back into her chair, took a deep breath, and began, again, to eat.

"There aren't many people out there like you. You're suited to the fragrance business." Denise smiled at him for the first time. "Why do you keep asking me out?"

"I don't know, I think maybe there's something between us."

"There's not. I'm sure of it."

"We have chemistry. There's something chemical between us."

"I'm certain there's no chemistry."

"No, I'm serious. I can tell when there's chemistry. There's an actual chemical reaction happening right now. I can feel it. I'm very sensitive about these things."

"I don't care what you feel."

"There's something different about you."

An explosion had sounded above them, followed by a rumble, followed by a scream from the kitchen. They felt the weight of the building above them as the restaurant shook. The lights went black, then on again, and Bryce and Denise and the other diners stood and looked around as if waiting for somebody to tell them what to do.

The buildings collapsing, the cars crashing, the weather; they were nearing the end, she was sure.

The girl next to them looked up at the ceiling and shook her head, as if to say she'd had enough. She led her father by the hand toward the door.

The building shook again and the plaster ceiling, layered with decades of paint, splintered. Customers filled their mouths and handbags from the buffet. Some untucked their shirts and made pouches and filled the pouches with mashed potatoes and fish nuggets.

Denise took Bryce by the arm and led him toward the door, funneling into the crowd of bewildered eaters who'd also made the reluctant decision to abandon their meals, skipping the soft-serve to get to safety. A siren sounded.

Outside, they watched the fire trucks pull hoses and erect their ladder to investigate a smoke plume rising out of the top of the building.

Bryce slid his hand into Denise's, as if in the confusion of the disaster she would realize how lucky she was to be alive. His hand was cold and damp, but together, as they watched the building erupt in flame, there was a strange absence of scent, as if the burning building was something on a television screen. The strange smell of flowering pear trees came from within her, rising from her stomach into her throat and mouth.

Maybe this was chemistry.

She looked up from her phone. She could hear the dog that lived in the apartment upstairs running in circles, and then something like a bowling ball rolled across the floor. She walked to the kitchen, scraped the burnt rice from the bottom of the pan into a bowl, and took a bite. She looked out the window to the window of her neighbor; he was looking back at her. She closed the blinds, looked back into her empty apartment, and again found herself looking into her phone.

25.

"MAYBE WE CAN HIDE UP HERE A WHILE."

They propped the metal door to the roof and walked out. The air was cold and wet and when they didn't see what they'd expected to see—a cold, black desert night—they were silent; they were in the city and the landscape was a familiar one: uniform lights illuminating empty office cubicles in window after window on nearly vacant, homogenous office buildings, gray, steel, and silent.

"I think that's Scentsate," Champion said. "That's the fifth-floor sky bridge."

"I think that's my apartment building," Sab said.

"The first time I came here, I felt like I was in the back of that van for days," Champion said. He was sure he *had* been in it for days. He looked at Sab and the blood on Sab's face and clothes reminded him why they were there. "I can't believe you did that. Hacked his arm up like that."

Sab looked at his hands as if trying to figure out what had happened. "I can't either. I feel like Mike cast a spell on me."

"You were super fucked up."

"I guess so."

"Maybe it's good you're here, then. Get your gentle hands back."

"I think I'm already hung over."

"Maybe we can just leave. We could walk to the Metro from here, I think. I'd like to go home." He did want to go home, but there was also work: the work he should have been doing on the Project. The Boss would be furious. Unless he was the one who'd sent Champion there. But still, he would blame him. He didn't want to be sent up to the 5th floor, the tactile floor, the *hands* floor.

"Won't they just bring us back?"

"Maybe. You mangled Mike's arms pretty badly, so yeah, maybe."

"I want to go home, but they have my phone."

"You can just get a new phone."

"I don't want a new phone. I want my phone."

26.

"YOU HAVEN'T MADE MUCH PROGRESS, have you?" Even though it sounded like it could have been a question, Bryce knew it was not. Carl's desk was covered with paper—project spreadsheets, Bryce's reports, emails, estimates.

"That's not true," Bryce said. "I'm still new. I'm learning. I'm getting closer." He wasn't any closer than when he'd started, agreeing to do this thing he couldn't do, this thing he barely understood—the smell of memory, the smell of nostalgia.

"I've tried the prototypes myself," Carl said. "Inhaled a whole vial. I can't say that they're working, although I can't say that they're not."

Bryce thought of his mother's photographs, the process they would go through at the mall to be turned from old film to printed photographs, ghosts emerging from some dark past. He had been in a dark room once, helping a friend develop black-and-white photos they'd taken with his father's old camera. The smell of the fixer sibilating from the tray, the images appearing before them out of nothing.

"Just because they don't work for you doesn't mean they're not doing something. We're closer."

"I can say that maybe there is something like the glimmer of new memories," Carl said. "A spark, perhaps. But nothing more."

"These things take time."

"You haven't even started to look at touch or sight. And your reports are vague. I need to know more about your memories. More about your dreams."

Bryce looked over his shoulder at the closed metal door; he looked at the glass windows, the sliding door that led to the concrete balcony overlooking the river. He could leave the hard way if he had to. He fidgeted in his seat, thinking about what it would be like, how it would feel to take a dive. "I'm ordering some chemicals to synthesize some unconventional materials."

Carl smiled. "Unconventional materials? Should we be running this by legal?"

"No, I don't think so. We should be fine."

Carl leaned in. "Does this involve flesh, Bryce? Human flesh?"

Carl was not far from the truth, but it wasn't flesh he was interested in dissolving. "No, it's not flesh. It's nothing. I'll tell you all about it if it works."

Carl laughed and wagged his finger at Bryce. "You really know how to turn things around. I had you in here, all ready to fire you, and here you are, telling me you're ordering chemicals to dissolve people's bones. Great stuff."

"Not their bones, it's not that big of a deal."

"Well, you wait and tell me when you've got something, a breakthrough. I can feel it. You're on to something big. I get it, Bryce, and I'm excited."

"You know what you're asking, it's like you're asking me to bottle nostalgia. Or a dream. What you want, it's not a science."

"What's science? This is magic."

"A lot goes into magic," Bryce said.

"I'm not sure what the big deal is. I just want results. Do you need more money? Is it a budget problem?"

"No, thank you." Bryce stood. "You've been very generous."

Carl guided Bryce to the door. "You know I love you, Bryce. You're our biggest brain. You're our star."

Bryce looked for something in his pockets. . . .

"I wouldn't ever do anything to hurt you, you know that, right? I just want to see some results. Is that too much to ask?"

Carl put his hand on Bryce's shoulder.

Yes, it was too much to ask. "No, it's not too much."

"Good, good," Carl said, pushing Bryce into the hallway, closing the door behind him.

⋮

At his desk, Bryce sent an email to requisition six liters of thioglycolic acid, probably an enormous amount, but he had no idea what he would need. He explained how much he'd need and tried to explain why he'd need it, careful to word the email in such a way as not to be explicit about exactly how he was going to use it. If he was vague, they wouldn't ask any questions.

On a whim, he ordered compressed methylidyne gas—$:$CH. He'd been researching the organic compound, found in the tail of comets, one of the first interstellar molecules, and it had developed a kind of mythic quality in his mind, so much so that he knew it would be key to what he was doing even if he didn't understand exactly how.

He'd researched the process as best he could using the Concordance and hoped that what he was going to do wasn't dangerous. He had no qualifications or real knowledge of these chemicals, but like Carl said, what they were doing was more akin to magic.

⋮

Far away from the vials on his desk, he walked and listened to the subtle sounds pulsing from the houses, surges of slow songs, plodding notes squeezing from beneath doors and open windows, released into the cool air like tiny clouds of sound so subtle he had to focus to hear them.

The louder sounds and smells: garbage pounding out of the back of trucks grinding by, the backed up sewers spewing cthonic chords so putrid and loud he had to hold his breath. The weeping and whining of the pathetic trees, still trying to blossom after fighting the threat of death in the cold and wet of another stunted spring.

He walked along the historic canal, down the old stairways between the old buildings, the swollen river visible below. He watched the living-history demonstrations along the waterway: a team of men sawing a log, a family taking turns churning butter, children pulling taffy.

An elderly woman sucking on the tip of an electronic cigarette stood before a group of three men holding a struggling lamb to the ground while she sharpened a knife on a stone. She began to chant, a sort of prayer he guessed, then pressed the knife against the throat of the lamb and cut. When she opened the lamb's throat, blood came as if from a cracked pipe, spattering the woman and men red, then slowing into rivulets of ooze covering the woman's hands. They threw the severed head into an orange bucket and hoisted the headless body into the air to hang from a tree, the blood draining onto the ground and into the canal. The smell of death sang a ghostly carol.

The song followed him even as the scent faded.

At the canal lock, men in colonial costumes guided horses to position an old boat full of glass-eyed tourists into the lock. The passengers bent their necks over the railing of the boat to see what was happening to them as the water drained to lower the boat so it could pass to the next section of canal where they continued their bygone journey. The glassine water, fetid and still, whistled and rang and he remembered the feeling of his mother's hand in his as they walked the path when he was a child.

Farther up the towpath, Bryce watched a three-legged turtle drag a soda can into the stagnant canal, rippling the green syrupy water.

He sat on a bench to eat his lunch, a wet sandwich he'd found in the department refrigerator. He felt Denise's hand curling around his; he remembered her rough skin, the empty look in her eyes.

Above the buildings on the other side of the canal, the sad sun shone through a crack in the ruby clouds. The song of the sacrificed lamb stayed even as he inhaled the moist meat and bread of his lunch, the song bouncing around in his head like a catchy melody he could not shake. He tried humming, then whistling, to expel it, but the repetition only strengthened the song, modulating between actual and imagined space.

Bryce walked back to the office in the rain, and when he arrived, his jacket and pants were heavy with water. He hung his jacket over the wall of his cube and shivered, waiting to dry.

He had four hours to kill before he could go home, and so opened an array of samples next to his desk and tried to recreate the sounds and smells he'd just experienced. It would take at least another week for the acid and ⁞CH he'd ordered to arrive.

27.

CHAMPION SAT AT HIS DINING ROOM TABLE LOOKING INTO THE SCREEN OF HIS LAPTOP, absently feeding walnuts to Jellybeans. The parrot had been bothering him more lately, bothering him so much that he cursed the colorful bird and said things he couldn't take back. The bird had warned him to *be nice*, repeating the words over and over again as Champion yelled about his gentle hands. Jellybeans reminded him that parrots lived for decades—they'd be together for a very long time—so it was probably easier if they could just get along.

While Jellybeans followed him, begging for peanuts or crackers or to go for a walk or for Champion to throw its toy for it to chase, he had not seen the cat for days. When he remembered the cat, he dutifully checked to make sure its food was full—wherever it had gone, it was still eating its meals there—and to clean its litter, but the cat itself had become a bit of a ghost. He suspected the parrot.

The wind knocked against the side of the house so hard Champion thought it might collapse the wall. These houses hadn't been designed for so much weather; he could hear the wall creaking from the pressure of the gales, the shingles pulling away from the roof, the wind whistling through the gaps in the old windows.

Champion followed the orders the Boss had given him and worked his way through the Concordance, changing the facts as he saw fit as he worked through his list of targets. He turned off the overhead lights, preferring the ambiance and allure of the desk lamp next to his laptop, which made him feel even more like a spy, like somebody doing something he wasn't supposed to be doing.

It *felt* like he was doing something wrong, but it also didn't feel like that. He was following orders, making minor changes. He didn't think anybody would care about what he could do except for Carl who had bigger plans, he knew, but he could not fathom a profitable use for this "genius" he had—that's what Carl had called him.

He changed Franklin Pierce's birthday again, from November 23, 1804 to November 25, 1804. He added a few lines to Pierce's page that said his son had been decapitated by a train.

The bit about Pierce's son was pure flourish—something to amuse Champion in his dim dining room, the wind tearing at his house, his parrot driving him absolutely crazy with its incessant demands.

"Pretty bird pretty bird pretty bird." The parrot talked, but sounded lifeless, dull, affectless. "I'm a pretty bird. Pretty bird pretty bird pretty bird."

He fed the thing another walnut, which seemed to make it happy, if only for a moment.

He changed the death toll of the Hindenburg explosion from 121 to 97. He changed the scientific name of the African wild dog to Lycaon pictus, and he removed Alan Alda's date and cause of death.

All of the changes stayed. In the past, these falsehoods would have been caught in a matter of seconds by the millions of people looking at the Concordance, waiting to revert strange edits, but Dale had figured it out, figured out how to roll out changes undetected and without an audit trail; Champion could control the Concordance and could do with it as he wanted.

Champion wondered what kind of world they lived in that didn't care whether Alan Alda was alive or dead.

Champion added a line to Alda's page to say the long dead actor had burned himself in the 1980s freebasing krabkake.

He edited a giant baked goods conglomerate's page to explain how formaldehyde was used to wash cookies, which was true, though it was something he thought the company would want to keep a secret.

"Pretty flowers for the lady pretty flowers for the lady pretty flowers for the lady," the parrot shrieked, dancing around the table. He gave it another walnut.

Champion felt himself reaching through the computer and through the network, his tentacles altering the very record of their lives with little effort. He was an octopus, he thought, and imagined himself growing very tall with power. He checked his hair with his hand to see if it had thickened, but it hadn't. Instead, he yanked a few strands, let them fall to the floor.

Jellybeans chewed at Champion's sleeve and made a clucking noise.

Carl would want an update soon and so Champion wished for his death, yearning for a kind of real power untethered from recourse. He imagined pushing Carl in front of a Metro car, of seeing his dead and bloody body twisted between the train and tracks. He could hear him screaming—something brief but piercing, could hear him stuck there, pinned to the platform, his torso severed, about to die, whispering his last words.

"I love you I love you I love you."

He gave Jellybeans the last walnut, squeezed his ball of stress clay, and thought gentle thoughts.

⋮

28.

CARL HAD PROMISED THEM ALL A SPECIAL HOLIDAY PARTY; he'd promised a rented restaurant and baubles hanging from the ceiling, a tree *and* a menorah, and cake for everybody. He'd promised them a kind of light decadence in which the employees could celebrate all the small accomplishments of the year—Bryce had come a long way in the year since he'd started. Scentsate had come a long way. They expected a big bash where they'd drink heavily and touch each other without fear of reprisal.

Instead, he'd fired everybody from the first floor and cleared it, covering as much of the carpet and empty cube walls with blue plastic tarps and vaporized enough artificial pine fragrance into the air to choke them. He'd sent an email telling them *not* to touch each other, and that they should throttle their drinking appropriately to avoid scenarios in which touching each other might seem like a good idea.

The air smelled so much like floor cleaner they couldn't help but feel festive despite the gagging, as they'd invented the award-winning scent, and it had earned them small bonuses they spent with care not on gifts for their families, but on gifts for themselves: liquor, mostly, but also lamps that generated light similar to the light of the sun's light. They installed these in their cubes, because that's where they spent most of their time, but also in their tiny beige apartments next to the worn chairs where they spent the rest of their time in front of computer screens looking at the Concordance, promising themselves over and over again they would log off and do something productive and interesting.

They looked at the evidence of other people's lives, better lives, they thought, and then felt terrible and worthless. They wished for things to appear about themselves so their friends would envy them in the hopes that *they* would feel terrible, and they did.

While the pine choked them, they'd created it, and that brought them small joy.

At the far end of the room, behind the tarped cubes and decorative holiday balls spinning and shimmering from the dropped ceiling, a crowd gathered around the liquor table. They were all in their holiday best—poofed-out dresses with cotton ball sleeves, shimmering tuxedoes cut from the latest glassine fabric, finally available to the masses, and the big hit this year for all—spaced out jumpsuits dripping with showy baubles and shine.

Bryce walked toward the liquor, knowing it wouldn't last long. Though he was ignorant of trend and immune from most of the fun of a party, he had tried, and though he didn't own a jumpsuit, he had tried his best with a glittered tie, festive and bright.

"Hey, are you ready to rub?" one of his colleagues had clearly gotten there early, their jumper already drenched with spilled booze.

Bryce smiled and nodded, his best defense, and negotiated the small groups of employees, most with as many as four drinks each. They'd crowded into the narrow corridors between the cubes. When they finished their drinks they dropped their cups on the ground and with their free hands photographed one another taking photographs.

Bryce overheard their conversations.

"How long do we have to stay?"

"I think the holidays are starting earlier this year than they used to."

"I'm really into coloring books, lately, but not the kind for adults."

A tiny helicopter, festive red and green, buzzed by and flashed a light onto him from above, pausing to capture a photograph before flitting away.

"Everything tastes like Pine-Sol."

"What are we celebrating?"

He squeezed between them, barely interrupting as they continued to talk around his body as it moved among them.

"Why would he wear that?"

"I want to go home."

"What would it look like if my cheek bones were higher?"

"I'm tired of your jargon. I'm leaving."

"I've been thinking a lot about children."

The pine hid the soft murmuring of mild body odor, perfume, garlic, and onion.

He pushed his way between his coworkers.

"They've got us working on Benzene; I have no idea why."

"Sometimes I just sit in the park and gaze into the distance."

Bryce could see the matrix of employees at the liquor table beginning to thin.

"He told me he'd spilled something on himself, but I don't believe him. It wasn't that kind of stain."

He worried they'd run out of alcohol.

"What do you think of all the weather?"

"But then I realize I've been sitting on my couch the whole time!"

He saw Denise at the edge of the crowd waiting at the bar.

"I don't think I'm supposed to talk about that."

He remembered her in his cube, the promise of silence.

"I can't right now, I'm saving up for some new lights."

"Fragrances are just what I do for work; pies are my passion."

"I live across from the playground."

"We've *got* to get rid of those owls. I don't know what to do anymore."

"I think we're making mustard gas. I'm not even kidding."

"It's a little bigger than a bread box. But just a little."

"Bryce? Bryce?"

The fragrances spoke. While he listened to the sound and their songs, sometimes he would hear his name. They whispered intimacies, or scraped like rust against rust. He heard white noise and cold, dead water.

"Bryce?" The voice spoke again.

A person was speaking to him.

"Hello," he said. "Happy holidays."

He knew that he'd seen this man before, but all the men in the office looked more or less the same to him.

"Are you going anywhere for the holiday?" the man asked.

"No, I'm not going anywhere." He knew he should say something else, return the question, but instead, he nodded nonchalantly and walked away.

"Hey, I'm talking to you," the man said, following.

"Sorry, I don't have time," Bryce said. He paused, turned, saw his face redden.

"But it's the holidays. I'm just trying to be nice," he said. He whispered, "My hands are only for hugging."

"I'm sorry," he said, waving him away.

"It's me, Champion," he said. "I'm your supervisor."

A heat took over Bryce's face. His supervisor? Bryce answered only to Carl.

"I'll be back in a moment," he said, not knowing what else to do, and wove himself into the crowd.

The people at the bar had dispersed into cubes or hallways between cubes or the dance floor, a small area cleared of walls and desks where the IT guy had set up a public address system and was joylessly DJing from a laptop.

They danced alone but drifted drunkenly toward each other and into each other's arms before stumbling away. They danced on the blue tarps that protected the carpet and sometimes they fell, but when they fell, somebody still standing helped them to their feet.

Bryce asked for a beer and they gave him two vodkas and soda and he tipped them a dollar. He drank the first quickly so he didn't have to carry two drinks as he moved back through the party.

"Hey guy, how's it going? Happy holidays." Carl swayed when he spoke.

"How's everything? You're doing a great job. You're brilliant." Carl slurred. "Your work? It's brilliant."

Carl took Bryce into his arms and hugged him. Carl felt more solid than he looked. When Carl pulled away, Bryce could see what looked like smudged make-up. Beneath the smear, his skin was splotched black and purple.

"Are you happy, Bryce?"

Bryce didn't know what to say. He looked over Carl's shoulder for some reason to escape.

"I'm happy."

Carl leaned in close to Bryce. "Business," he said, "is great. This was a very good year."

"That's great, right?"

"Oh, we've done better. We could always do better. We're really counting on you. All we've talked about. I have a master plan."

"A plan?"

"Yes. A plan. I can't tell you about it. The Concordance. The fragrance. I can't tell you any more."

"The Concordance?"

"Yes. I can't talk about it. We figured out how to change it."

"Anybody can change it."

"Look, you can't share this with anybody. See that guy over there?"

Carl tipped his cup in the direction of the man who'd tried to talk to him earlier.

"Him? He thinks he's my boss."

"His name is Champion. That guy's figuring it all out. We'll be able to edit Concordance entries. Delete people, even."

"Why would we do that? What good is it?"

"What good? It's going to revolutionize the company. That and some government contracts we've got."

"What are you talking about?"

"I can't say any more right now. Have a great holiday. Things are going to be great this year. It'll be our best year yet."

Carl touched him again: first he put his hands on Bryce's shoulders, then he moved them to his ribcage; he pulled him close, Carl's skin, a smoky whisper.

"We're going to create new memories for people, Bryce. New memories people create themselves. It's going to be magical."

Bryce could only nod. What Carl said was impossible, but he wanted to believe it.

"What I've shared with you? I would kill to keep that a secret. I don't know why the fuck I told you. I'm drunk. You have to keep your mouth shut."

Carl pulled him closer, so close their lips touched before Carl gently pushed him away. It wasn't a kiss, but it was also a kiss. Bryce looked around for Carl's wife—he'd been married, he was certain. But only Champion was watching them from behind the turntables.

Bryce found Denise standing in a corner with a ring of empty cups around her on the floor like rose petals. She poured something from a flask over the melting ice in her red plastic cup and offered him what was left in the flask. He drank it and winced, handed the flask back to her, and drank from his vodka and soda instead.

"Do you need me for something?" Denise asked.

"I just thought I'd say hello. I don't know too many people here."

"What's in your nose?" she asked.

"I'm an analyst. We work together."

"I know who you are. I asked what was in your nose."

"Nose plugs. I like your eyes," he said. Bryce was the worst, and he knew it.

"Please," she said. "Where are you from?"

He wanted to tell her where he was from, that he had grown up across the river when normal people could afford to live across the river, actually near the river, when the river was still brown, how he'd moved away from home when he worked for the government and lived in a tiny apartment complex near the highway, the kind of apartment complex with a sign that read "If you lived here you'd be home by now" and how the sign had made him really think: *if I lived here, I would be home.* The apartment was covered with dismal carpet and he could tell by the sounds the carpet made the people who lived there before him hadn't been attentive to the needs of their dog. Worse was the lingering sound of semen emanating from the floor and walls, the origin of which Bryce could not imagine. Despite repeated steam cleaning, something still stayed, the specter of a family with whom he'd never grown comfortable. He wanted to tell her how after his mother had become sick, he was excited to move back to the house in which he'd grown up, that the distant scent of his absent father and the smell of his mother's hair were much better than a stranger's semen and dog shit, and how by then he'd been laid off by the government, perhaps the only person *ever* to be laid off by the government.

The government had gotten out of fragrances so they were closing entire divisions at the Bureau of Fragrance and Taste. The classified stuff he'd been working on for years just wasn't that interesting to anyone and had never had a real use they could think of, anyway. He wanted to tell her that after his mother died, he just stayed, even though the neighborhood was strange.

"From across the river," he finally said, but he could not bear the silence, so he said whatever came to mind. "I know what poisonous gases smell like. Mustard gas smells like mustard, but crackles, and phosgene smells like hay and cut grass, but sounds like bees buzzing with a whine like a far-away siren always approaching."

"I'm sorry, what?" she asked.

"Sorry, I didn't mean to say all that. People have been talking about mustard gas for some reason." He was a little drunk. "Where are you from?"

"Pennsylvania, but not the interesting part."

He followed her through the crowd to the bar and realized he'd finished both his drinks, and after she ordered two martinis, he ordered two more vodkas and soda. The woman behind the table told him they were out of soda, so why not just try two vodkas without any soda. The bartender told them both to drink their drinks fast because the plastic cups were cheap and it wouldn't take long for the liquor to eat through the bottoms.

Denise finished her drinks while they stood at the liquor table and asked for two more.

"Do you live close by?"

"No. I have to take the train."

"Fine."

"I'm sorry, what?" He didn't know exactly what she meant.

"Let's go to your place. You seem nice. I'm not picky. I just don't want things to get weird. Can you be cool? Bryce, is that your name?"

"You want to go home with me?"

"It's not like I'm asking you to go to Adult Disney. It's the holidays. Lighten up. Can you be cool?"

"I can try to be cool."

"Be cool, Bryce."

He wanted to assure her it was just to have another drink, since they were out of liquor at the party. It was still early, before Carl would get up in front of them all and give one of his famous "state of the fragrance" addresses in which he would compare himself to Jesus and announce the cutting of the cakes. Carl seemed to put weight in the idea that a savior would one day sweep them to some better place when at this point they all knew, or at least suspected. He was disappointed to miss the speech and cake cutting, but going home with Denise seemed much better.

The rain and wind blew through the valley of office buildings on the way to the Metro station. She huddled against him. When he put his arm around her, she removed it, then put her arm around him and pulled him closer. She stumbled and steadied herself against his body. He could not remember feeling such warmth.

In the darkness of the Metro station, they stood alone on the edge of the platform in a shallow pool and listened to the echo of water spilling from a broken pipe somewhere above them. Denise rocked gently.

The intense odor of hot, agitated people waiting for afternoon trains was gone; tonight, the station, almost empty, was tolerable.

The longer they stood, the greater the chance Denise would come to her senses. But then, maybe she would go home with him and nothing would happen, a greater insult than abandoning him on the train platform. He turned away from her and removed his nose plugs and heard the smell of the Metro platform, the smell of transportation and the lingering smell of commuters.

He asked her if there was anything left in her flask and this reinvigorated her. She found it in her purse and handed it to Bryce and then took a long drink herself before closing her eyes.

When the train arrived, he guided Denise into one of the last cars.

"Wake me up when we get somewhere," she said.

In between stations, the train stopped in the tunnel, lurched forward a few inches, and the lights flickered. If they died there, how long would it take for their bodies to be discovered and what would the discoverers do with them? Days could go by with them hunched over in their seats, the eyes of the commuters and late night drunks not even noticing the early stages of decay.

The conductor announced that, due to track repair, they were dealing with one track in both directions. He apologized for the inconvenience and told them to settle in, because they might be there a while.

He slid his hand into Denise's to recapture something; she recoiled and swatted at the air, but relaxed, resting her head on his shoulder. He leaned over, inhaled, the scent of her hair, a mix of cheap conditioner and some unknown styling product. He inhaled the silence, absolute and pure, the first complete relief from sound he could remember since his childhood. He pushed his nose further into her hair and she, asleep, nestled into his shoulder and together, they waited.

29.

ON THE SCREEN OF HER PHONE, DENISE SAW BRYCE in his wool coat reading a book, or writing in a notebook. He sat on a bench at the edge of a park, the book in his gloveless hands, despite the cold day.

She watched. She was there with him.

Across the field a child chased a dog and when the child yelled, both she and Bryce looked. The child had stumbled and fallen, but jumped back up and limped after the dog, a brown longhaired shepherd retriever thing, maybe the most beautiful dog she'd ever seen. Bryce looked up from his book and instead of smiling or speaking to Denise, simply nodded. They watched each other. He glanced back at his book, and she took his picture with her digital camera, shooting from her hip, capturing him while a gust of wind whipped a sheet of leaves between them. She walked a few feet more and looked back. He was still reading his book.

She knew it was Bryce, but he was no longer the Bryce she thought she'd known. He was taller, a little thinner, and had more hair.

The boy had caught up to the dog and held on tight to the leash.

The river-water flooded over the bank, covering the grass to the edge of the asphalt path. Tarp-covered sailboats bobbed in the marina on the other side of the river and a skiff, free from its mooring, tossed in the waves. The boy struggled to hold onto the dog, pulling them closer to the edge of the water.

She walked back toward the city blocks where she would find a cup of coffee and the Metro. Instead of passing Bryce again, she took a fork in the path through a boulder garden. Rain fell. Ahead of her, a man in a black trench coat walked against the wind and rain.

The photograph took root, the image like a disease. Sage and lemon bloomed and burned in her throat; she coughed.

She found herself at the edge of the memory, the scene she imagined ending at the invisible edge of the extended photograph. The street became an expanse of whiteness where the vivid color of the dream faded to nothingness. She wanted to keep walking.

She looked up from her screen. She was standing in her living room, staring through the window.

She distracted herself by taking selfies with her phone. Particles of dirt lodged inside the camera lens scarred her face in the image and she wished she hadn't taken them. Now, they were out of her hands.

She tried to read a book, the same book she'd been reading for almost a year. She read each word aloud, slowly and clearly, but with each new word, she couldn't remember what she'd just read.

The sound of her voice sounded like another voice. She looked again at her phone, then her laptop, and then again at the book. She tried to remember what she'd read—something about an art forger and a lesson about the true meaning of art, she thought. Maybe it was the true meaning of Christmas? She examined the image on the cover. "Knitting With Dog Hair."

She looked out: the parking lot, the playground full of rusty cages, the new high-rise on the corner glowing and blue. Some kids cut free a bike locked to the playground fence and heaved it into the intersection.

The sky was bruised crimson, the clouds a low pall. She stood on the strip of grass between the sidewalk and the parking lot and looked up at the glow of her laptop screen in her dark apartment. She felt a phantom vibration, touched her hand to her pants pocket where the phone had been, and momentarily panicked even though she knew exactly where she'd left it, upstairs on the kitchen counter.

A couple walked by with their dog and she knelt to pet its head. The dog didn't want to be touched, pulled away from her, and barked a high, shrill yap.

She could smell somebody grilling a distant dinner. The smell reminded her of another time.

As she breathed, the night air diluted the poison fragrance. She thought she could smell the parking lot and the cars and the dog walking away from her. The taste in the back of her throat still lingered, nearly dormant, though mostly gone.

A truck ran over the bike in the road and kept driving, dragging the gnarled frame beneath it.

30.

CHAMPION AWOKE IN DARKNESS—not the darkness of the tunnels above the office, but some other narrow darkness, devoid of light and space, not a tunnel, but a tube. He could feel his eyelids open but the walls of wherever he found himself were just as close, a thick membrane cocooning his body. He worked to breathe and felt thick, hot air tinged with collisions of melting plastic, the toxic sting of chemical lemon, the weight of must and skunk. So heavy were the smells he could feel them inside his lungs seeping thick into his bloodstream, infecting him and pushing outward, stretching the walls of his enclosure.

He remembered the heat of the furnace in the basement, inhaling something from a vial, crawling into the ceiling, but the new constrictions devoured his memories. When those images were gone, there was only the moment as much as he struggled to think of the things that mattered to him in this, what felt like his last moments—his home, his partner, anything he'd done in the moments before he'd awoken and all the moments before that. He saw Raymond hovering over a steaming cake pan, smiling at what he'd created, his face then blurry, contorted and impenetrable, finally dissolving into the steam.

When he felt as if all the adrenaline his body could conjure had gathered in his chest for distribution to his arms and legs to make an attempt to free himself, he felt a pulse move glacially from the bottom of his feet, through his muscles, bone, and blood, up his legs, through every organ in his chest, penetrating every membrane and cell, into his neck, brain and skull, bursting outward from the bald spot on the back of his head in slow waves. The pulse changed him, shifted his cellular structure, and moved him away from himself toward the walls of that which enclosed him.

Something crawled up his leg, a tendril entwining him. He felt another pulse like light or current move through him. The tentacles grew up his legs, twisted around his body like wire, the rhythm of the pulses beating through and around him quickening as if the cadence of time was speeding around him.

⋮

31.

BRYCE WALKED THE GRID OF CUBICLES, checking each to make sure its occupant had gone home for the night, making sure he would not be seen.

He entered Denise's cubicle and with tweezers he swept the back of her chair, plucking what he could when he found a stray strand, adding it to a growing collection he kept sealed in a specimen bag.

Tonight he opened a desk drawer, and then another, pushing aside old boxes of tea and empty file folders, finally finding what he'd been looking for: a hair brush, the bristles thick with tangled and knotted strands.

"What are you doing?" A voice from behind him shattered his excitement, his spine tracked with chills.

"Looking for a stapler." He should have dropped the brush; instead he stood and turned, palming the head of the brush to hide it.

"It's on her desk," he said. "You weren't very nice to me."

Champion. Something about his haircut reminded Bryce of folding paper into birds.

"I'm sorry, I didn't mean to be rude."

"My hands," he said, his hands balled and tight. "My hands are gentle. I have gentle hands."

"You have gentle hands? What?"

The man reddened. "What do you have in *your* hands?"

"It's a hair brush. It's mine. I was brushing my hair."

Bryce looked at him, blankly, puffing air into his cheeks to make himself look more childlike. He held the brush behind his back. He needed to get back to his desk where he'd been dissolving his own hair in thyoglycolic acid, trying to find the right dilution and time to properly liquefy hair. If he waited too long, he'd have to start again tomorrow.

"You never came to find me. You said you'd come talk to me. I supposed to be your boss."

The man's face was glazed and empty, his skin gray and beaded with thick, almost gelatinous sweat. He blocked the exit with his body. Bryce stepped forward.

"Well, I have to go home now, going to be late for dinner."

"You're not late for dinner. I just checked the Concordance."

"I'm hungry."

"I need to know what you're working on," he said. "I'm your boss.

You can tell me." The tension in Champion's voice relaxed, but still he blocked Bryce's exit.

"The smell of memory?" Bryce asked. He didn't know why he kept insisting he was his boss.

"I'm working on fake memories. False information. In the Concordance."

"Do you have any hard candy?" Bryce asked. "My blood sugar's low."

Champion gave him a few cough drops from deep within his jacket pocket, stepped aside, and beckoned for Bryce to exit.

32.

CARL'S LOPS DANCED IN HIS DAYDREAM, the floppy rabbits a memory of happier times with Cheryl when their days were filled with creatures and bliss; now his life was dull anger and a tank full of eels. Now, his life was darkness and the vastness of their house, no longer warm, no longer a home at all but an empty expanse of difficult memories and the residue of fractured and incomplete feelings poorly articulated.

He opened the eel tank, dropped a scoop of their food into the morass of thrashing bodies. How sad that their lives revolved only around mealtime.

He didn't know what to have for dinner and had forgotten what had transpired since lunchtime when he'd eaten a thick piece of lasagna at the Italian place down the block. He'd eaten alone, and would eat alone again tonight. His stomach rumbled as he watched the eels fight over the curled pellets he fed them every morning and every night.

Champion stood in the darkness of the lobby; Carl could sense him there, hiding in the shadows to avoid delivering another bad report.

Bryce was dead; the project would fail. In his desk he had what Bryce had left—a few vials of what Carl believed was the unfinished product of Bryce's research. He'd produced so little, the culmination of his shoddy work a few drops of liquid secured in tiny vials.

Carl's legacy would not be fragrance and flavor; he would not die alone, a broken man whose greatest contribution was the marketing of pungent, chemical pine.

"You can come out now," Carl said. The slapping eels at the surface of the water like thick, wet lips.

"Why do you keep these things?" Champion emerged in a trench coat and sunglasses. Carl liked his style. Carl wished they'd met on a foggy pier or in a parking garage instead of the lobby. Though he despised Champion, he felt something unusual in his presence, a kind of chemistry he both looked forward to and feared.

"It's your final lesson," Carl said. He closed the lid of the aquarium, took a step back. He needed to cull the population, make more room for these sad creatures. He'd never killed an eel before, wasn't even sure if he could do it, even if it was for the best.

"Where are we? You've been working on this for how long now? All you had to do was test."

"It's working, I think. I want to do more testing."

"Can you delete people? Erase them?"

"I don't think we should do that. We'll get caught."

"I want you to try."

"The whole thing will be off. They'll trace our requests, cut us off."

"Who will?"

"Everybody. Everybody will notice. I delete somebody, people will see that."

"But there's no way to re-add them. They're just gone. Poof."

"Why do you want to do this? I don't even understand why—"

"Nothing's going to happen. Nobody will notice."

"Delete people. That's like killing them. Murder."

"It's not even close to that. Erase somebody who's already dead—Bryce, Dale, whoever. Nobody will care."

"I don't think this is right."

"Really? Maybe you should think about your job. You're what, 43? Nobody will hire you if I fire you. You're ancient in the tech business."

Champion nodded.

"You might as well be dead."

Carl looked back into the aquarium, and thought of the rabbits, how beautiful and soft, how they chewed holes in their shoes, the walls of their first house together, how one had caught fire when it discovered an old, hot wire hidden in the wall.

Cheryl had taken care of the breeding and he the business, a steady flow of easy revenue. It was the last time he'd felt like he'd had a real partner. How simple it was to let the rabbits do the work, creating something beautiful as if from nothing, and how he and Cheryl were young then, happy.

Champion was an animal too; they all were.

33.

DENISE MADE HER WAY ALONG A NARROW PATH IN THE RED LIGHT OF THE NIGHT SKY.

She looked at the photograph on her phone, tried to match what she saw to what she was seeing as she walked. Thick, overgrown vines wove over the cement path into the detritus of night visitors—empty liquor bottles, take-out containers, crushed beer cans. She shined the light from her phone in front of her and nearly stumbled on a gnarled stroller that had been carrying a pumpkin, now shattered and half-eaten by squirrels and skunks.

She heard whispering ahead and stopped. She looked again at the photo and she was no longer afraid—she walked quickly, quietly, walked with purpose through the vines, unruly and thick with garbage, clinging to her ankles, groping at her calves, scratching her skin with thorns like claws.

She heard them whispering.

She was thirteen, riding her bicycle on the trails behind the mall. Her mother had forbidden her to go because of the boys who rode their bikes there too, and the threat of the bad men lurking under bridges or in the tunnels beneath the mall parking lot. She went anyway, for the thrill of danger and to disobey, the boys hiding in the darkness less a threat than a challenge.

She was stronger than them, smarter and faster, and when she saw them ahead ducking into the growth, she thought: *cowards*.

"Hello," she called to them. "I'm just passing through. I don't care what you're doing out here." It sounded like a lie.

These were the same boys she saw at school huddled together at lunch, snickering like cartoon coyotes, afraid to be alone, afraid to be anything but synchronized and single-brained, useless and cruel. She wasn't afraid to be alone—she preferred it; with no one to share her lunch she would sit at the end of a table away from everyone, small and hunched, lost even then in her phone.

With Bryce she had loped along old rail beds, reclaimed by spindly trees pushing up through the gravel, reaching for light. She could feel the pressure of her feet with each step and the smell of tar and old coal dust, still lingering decades after the last steam locomotive.

As dusk fell, so came the rain and together they hid beneath a bridge, kissing and fumbling at one another in the waning light, as much to stay warm as to celebrate the way each other's strange body felt, unfamiliar and new.

When they heard others coming toward them, they scrambled up the embankment to the road. Wet and enervated and suddenly hungry, they held hands and snuck back to where they'd parked the car.

She'd hidden with her bicycle to watch the boys without being seen, entranced by their nervous and insecure energy, watching them smoke and laugh, their fingers and faces and clothes smeared with dirt. They must have heard the movement of leaves and branches or her breathing and when they began to spread around her, surrounding her hiding spot, she panicked and rode away hard and fast; she heard them following behind her, begging her to stop, insisting they only wanted to talk, heard their pleas turn to jeers of laughter as she made it to the road.

What she was looking for in the park was evidence—evidence she'd been there before, with or without Bryce, evidence of the reality or unreality of the memories, now a tangible stain, only transparent.

The overgrown path felt like a sick enchanted forest, the vines yellow and wanting for light; everything seemed to be begging for something, pushing in every direction, needy and searching.

She lay awake at night and thought about the boys, wondered what they did there, all alone, wondered who they were, why they'd stopped what they were doing to chase her. She would go back again, she thought, repelled by the feeling of their eyes, but also yearning for something.

She felt the eyes in the undergrowth, hiding but not hiding, the boys betrayed by their smoky breath, the musk of hot bodies.

"I know you're in there," she said.

When she returned, she let them ambush her, let them surround her on the path. She held a pocketknife in her hand, the blade open, the body of the knife tight in her fist.

"I'm not afraid of you," she said.

They cackled: inhuman in their awkwardness, not yet aware of their own bodies and what harm could become them. She could see the details of their gaunt faces, their acne scars, their big ears, dirty hair. Their arms were bruised and thin, barely there, connected to wiry bodies, wisps in dirty shirts. She could smell them molding beneath thin layers of deodorant, smell their fecund breath. One of them wheezed and sucked on an inhaler.

"Don't be afraid."

The path narrowed and wound up to the crest of a low hill beyond which she could see the river red in the strange light. She could still smell the men in the woods, hear their voices following her, maybe, or simply moving with her, watching, trying to figure out what she wanted, why she was there again.

A spidery heron perched in a burnt tree and turned its mechanical neck, its eyes seeming to flash as if it was photographing her progress.

When they took a tentative step forward, she was aware of her power over them—none of them knew what to do. She could pick up her bike and escape, but that's not what she wanted, not why she'd come.

"You've been watching me," she said. "You've been mean to other girls before."

When they closed around her, when they lifted their little hands, her body went fluid.

A metallic taste in her throat—the poison she'd inhaled. Forever now, always present.

She remembered a blissful spring day years ago, lounging in bed, a very particular light, warm and antique, cast over their naked entwined bodies.

She remembered the convoluted drives they took on Sunday afternoons, looking for new places, new things. Once getting stuck on a car ferry across a river, sitting there for hours, waiting for somebody to show up to repair the barge engine, another time finding themselves eating sandwiches in wax paper on a bench outside a country store, a goat begging for a bite of their lunch.

Remembered visiting an antique store full of old medical equipment: crutches and walkers, archaic machines like torture devices with strange clamps and straps, old tubes hanging on wheeled metal racks. They'd found a thing like a wooden electric chair in a section with the other chairs heaped on top of one another. They pulled the electric chair from the pile and arranged it in the aisle, stood and considered it as if they wanted to add it to their home. Each took a turn sitting, imagining what it would like to be executed; they made their faces into the faces of the condemned, inhabiting for a moment a last electric moment.

Remembered a bicycle ride, getting lost on some country road, a thunderstorm, lightning striking a transformer on a utility pole above them, how her heart had stopped at the sound like a gunshot directly above.

She remembered how they edged toward her, how she vibrated. Their faces full of fleeting menace and fear—no idea what to do, only that they were about to do something, anything to dissipate the charge building inside them. She unfolded the knife in her hand, held it unsteadily in front of her, the thin metal visibly meager, barely a threat. She showed them her teeth.

The blue sky, the light of the sun broken by the thin tree branches above. The boys looking at one another, laughing, coming toward her.

She held the knife, lunged forward, grazed the t-shirt of the boy in front of her, tearing it. He stopped, took a step back, the others following. One of them said something, something pleading, something explaining they were just fooling around. They meant no harm, they said, but it was too late. They were too close again.

She saw their energy discharge and lunged again, felt the knife pierce his belly; he took a step back, scrambling to hide behind his friends. He fell on the ground, his dirty white t-shirt blooming red. She closed the blade and dropped the knife.

She tried to remember the name of the boy she'd stabbed, but there was only Bryce. She'd only done it to protect them.

She remembered—walking through a silent house, calling Bryce's name, chemical lemon stinging her nose and eyes and tongue. The bloody boy, crying on the path, afraid to look at her. They never said a thing and when she saw them at school, they avoided her gaze, walked the other way.

She remembered the bench, saw the bench in front of her like it was in the picture. The bench at the edge of a neglected field ringed by an asphalt path, the sound of the high river lapping at the bank, the aromatic wind extending its reach, threatening the land. She looked for Bryce knowing she would find nothing except for reassurance, knowing this place was real.

She could see him sitting, writing in his notebook. She imagined the memory of taking his photograph and could feel the weight of the camera in her hands. She heard the shutter click and click and felt the rain of that day. It poured hard; she heard the men rustling in the brush, running for shelter.

She curled her fingers around the weight of the knife gently pulled from the mud. She'd never been so happy.

⁞

34.

THEY GATHERED IN THE DAYTIME DARKNESS ON THE FENCED-IN FIELD near the hangar where they'd built the airship; it was the blackest day any of them could remember. Angie held a clipboard securing a sheaf of blank paper; they all wore safety goggles for no good reason and lab coats to show they were experts. They'd kept the thing covered to avoid the drones but it was so large and unruly, like a newly born elephant, big and clumsy, still learning to use its body.

One of Angie's coworkers stood too close to her, let the back of his hand graze her hand. She took a step to her left; he took a step, too, and when he touched her hand again, she slapped him away, dropped her foot heavy and hard onto his, then pretended to look at something on her clipboard.

The ominous blank page. *Report Dan*, she wrote at the top of the sheet, underlining it for effect, grateful for something to write down on this momentous occasion. She followed the note with a series of meaningless numbers: *9, 18, 4, 337, 16*.

They'd been working on the thing for months and there it was, floating slightly off the ground in front of them, ready to be raised. She stepped forward, impatient for somebody to start the celebration.

The size of the switch for the lighting ceremony was deliberate—the kind of plunger used to explode dynamite in old movies; they wanted the silent horde to see that what they were going to see would be *explosive*.

Though it was not literally meant to be one, an explosion was a strong possibility. Angie was worried about that, whether they'd really tested everything thoroughly. She had never never sure if any of them knew what they were doing enough to unleash such a thing. They were well paid, and they were engineers according to their degrees and job titles, but that did not mean they were experts. She knew she herself had slept through many of her classes, barely graduated—but here she was in goggles and a lab coat, charged with holding the clipboard.

Let's get on with it.

She imagined the thing igniting in a great ball of white fire, all fury and rage, raining metal and glass shrapnel down on all of them. It would be terrible, she knew, but at least she wouldn't have to go back to work.

The sky was especially gray, the thick, dark clouds tipped with burgundy, illuminated by occasional distant yellow lightning. Wind whipped around them, pulling the sun ship tight against its tethers.

Was it time? Who would announce when it was time? She waited for the fanfare.

35.

TAMMERS SAT ON A BENCH OUTSIDE THE BON-TON at the mall and held her blender, still in the box, like a baby. She lifted her Julius, touched the straw to her lips and sucked; she imagined making one at home and could taste the future treat, just as delicious as the one she now drank, refreshing and familiar. She'd wanted another, just as she had begun to enjoy this one. She put her cup back down on the bench, tapped the top of the box as if to comfort her new appliance, and looked for Cheryl.

Her favorite bench, *this* bench, afforded a view of the best stores, all nearly empty at this early hour. The few shoppers there hurried toward or away from their errands, none of them lingering to consider all that there was before them, the seemingly endless options of things arranged neatly, compartmentalized.

Tammers had no reason to hurry; the hours of the day were hers to do with as she pleased. She moved the blender from her lap to sit next to her on the bench like a friend. She leaned back and looked up at the skylights above like the arcades of Paris on a rainy day, the light indistinct and gray. She turned, reached to touch one of the dying ferns in the mall garden behind her, plucked an empty liquor bottle from the spindly foliage and tossed it farther back into the weeds.

So much to see, so much for which to be grateful.

Cheryl had not come with her to the mall. Tammers had texted her to ask if she wanted to join her, to help her pick out a blender, but for some reason Cheryl hadn't returned her message.

She moved a little closer to the blender, took a sip of her drink. She watched, waited, and looked at her phone. A mostly elderly group of mall walkers speed-walked toward her; they appeared to Tammers to be moving in slow motion, the apparent effort of their athletic gate insufficient to carry them faster than a shuffle.

When they finally neared, Cheryl sat up straighter, pushed the blender to the side, and admired the walkers' dedication to their longevity, their silver tracksuits, their sport shades. They looked like they had come from the future.

She could join them, leave her blender for a lap or two around the mall, maybe meet somebody new. She could invite them all back to her apartment to break in the blender: Juliuses, daiquiris, protein shakes—whatever they wanted. She'd put on some music and then they'd gather on the roof and catch raindrops on their tongues.

She extended her leg to trip one of them, but they outmaneuvered her, shifting their positions with graceful precision, like a school of slow fish, to thwart her.

One of them smiled at her and winked. She ignored the walker; she talked to the blender.

"I am never lonely," she said to the blender.

Maybe it was time to leave this mall; maybe she'd check out the other mall, the old mall, and see what that was like. Maybe Cheryl would meet her there.

"You'd like Cheryl," she said.

Her friends were unreliable; she couldn't count on them when she really needed them: this blender, this decision, one she would have preferred to make with the candid help of a confidant.

"Are you the right blender?" she asked.

Though plural in her mind, her friends were singular: just one friend. She looked at her phone, looked for a message from her friend, but there was nothing.

36.

DENISE FOLLOWED THE CLUES SHE'D FOUND: a person named Dale, mysteriously dead, who had worked under Champion on the same special project that Bryce had worked on. Two deaths among many: Cam, dead in their cube, Howard, face down in a puddle on the roof, an intern named George, backed over by his own car, somehow, on a Sunday morning in the parking garage. Two Mikes, a John, another Denise. Champion had supervised them all in some way or another, and after each death, their timesheets went blank, marked "on vacation" or "out sick." None of them took vacations or called in sick for fear of being fired. Champion in particular seemed lazy and incompetent, so she knew he would not risk giving anybody under him any time off.

"I need to talk to you." She spoke, finally, firmly. She was not used to being the first to speak to a person. Always spoken to, spoken at, spoken over, never spoken with.

He alt-tabbed away from what he was doing, spun around in his chair, smiled a huge, yellow grin.

"Yes," he said. He rubbed his hands together like a villain and chuckled, his voice loud and false. "What can I do for you?"

"I know what you're doing," she said. "I know what you've done. Dale. Bryce. Others. A lot of others."

The office floor had become quiet and shadowy. The ambient hum of the office swelled.

She wasn't afraid. She remembered the boys in the woods, the bike trail, remembered how she'd made them see her when she finally decided to be seen.

"I've emailed human resources." She'd scream if she had too.

"We don't have human resources."

He was right about that; he had her. She took a step back. "I've emailed, Carl, too."

He only laughed and stood, curling his fingers into fists. She looked hard at him, curled her own fingers, too, but she could see something different in his eyes, something off.

"My hands are gentle," he said.

"Your what?" she asked.

"I don't know what you're talking about. I don't care what you say to the Boss. I don't even know why they keep you around." He turned away from her to his computer screen and fumbled at the keys. A rack of vials stood in a line next to his keyboard. The ones she'd opened and inhaled prominent.

The scent rose in her throat. A tightness in her chest. The groan of the office air drumming in her ear. She felt lightheaded and distracted by all the things she thought—memories of Bryce inventing themselves, taking over only to be pushed away by the adrenaline of the moment. Standing together in the mall, waiting for him to pick out a shirt; at a pool party, somebody screaming because a dog was drowning in the water and nobody knew what to do; waiting out a ground delay at the airport watching lightning on the tarmac. The feeling of his sweaty hand in hers, pulling her forward toward some thing she couldn't remember. The taste of his mouth, his sour breath. A speck of something on the edge of his ear—wax or dirt, something too big not to notice, not to remember.

Champion was Bryce, standing in front of her, his hands spiral fists, his body leaning forward. He planted one foot behind him, turned to the side, drew his hand back as if to prepare to hit her. She couldn't remember why he was so angry—she could never remember the whole scene, only glimpses.

She wished she'd never met him, never fallen in love, never invested the time.

She wished she'd never inhaled the scent, angry he'd poisoned her, taken control of her mind and invaded her memories.

Here he was, all body and rage, then suddenly Champion again.

"I don't know what you want from me."

She didn't know what she wanted from him or what to say, only that she wanted him to know that she knew what he was doing and what he had done

He whispered: "Gentle, gentle, gentle."

Running away from Bryce, running out of the building, leaving him there. Locking the door to her apartment even though she knew he had not followed. She could see him from the point-of-view of the hole in the ceiling above his cube, see him reaching up into the cavity, cutting the network cabling, pulling it down. She could see him wrapping the wire around his neck. She could see his eyes, cold and dry, hungry for something.

This isn't what I'd meant to happen; this isn't how it was meant to end.

"There's been a misunderstanding," he said. Champion moved his fingers through his long, thin hair. "I didn't know Bryce. Dale drowned. I didn't have anything to do with that."

He took a step closer; he wasn't particularly tall, but managed to make himself huge, his hair wild and dry, the shadows of his face dark, pronounced, as if he was carved from stone.

"I'm watching you," she said. "Whatever you're doing, it's got to stop."

She had nothing more to say, so turned and walked as fast as she could to the elevator where she hoped she would not have to wait, where she would escape to the outside, disappear in the fog and rain. She would go to her apartment, keep the lights low, and lock the doors.

He didn't follow. His hands *were* gentle, he thought. He sat, turned to his computer, brought up Bryce's record, then Denise's, then Carl's and Carl's wife, Cheryl. Finally, he looked at his own Concordance entry; he hadn't looked for years, could not bear to see what was there—his face, his sad, slow life recorded, rewound, and replayed in photographs he did not take and did not want to see.

"Soon, I'll the Boss," he said. A small comfort.

Gentle, he thought. He would delete them all.

He began the process of erasure.

Part Three

37.

CHAMPION FELT THE VIAL IN HIS POCKET.

He'd worked late and taken the long way, winding through the narrow, twisted streets of Old Town, backtracking, circling, retreating, and repeating his course. He delayed for no particular reason except for the conversation he'd had with that woman at work and the unsettling feeling that things were about to get very bad for him. He walked slowly, extending time to delay whatever it was—if only he could walk forever and all but stop the inevitable.

When he'd finally come home, the front door was open. He looked around—nothing out of place. Maybe he'd forgotten to close it.

Maybe the cat had returned.

Jellybeans had forgone his chance for freedom and was perched on the dining-room chandelier. He was bent low, his beak opening and closing, gurgling *pretty boy* in a guttural skronk as if to warn Champion that something wasn't right.

"Hi Boss, hi boss, hi boss," he squawked, bobbing left and right, feebly pointing to Champion's study with his left claw.

Instead of heeding the bird's warning, Champion loudly told the bird to shut the fuck up.

"Cakes and steaks!" Jellybeans shrieked.

"I don't know what you're talking about."

He found out when they surrounded him—asking him questions he didn't know how to answer. Jellybeans flapped his violent wings and feathers fell like snow, drifting around the room like an exploded pillow. "We know what you're doing, and we know what your company's making," was the jist of it.

"Making? My company makes flavors. Perfume. The cheese dust on snack chips."

"We know what you've been really making." They hadn't identified themselves.

He'd erased himself. He was nobody now.

"Who are you? What do you want?"

"We don't need to talk about that right now. We just need to know how you're doing it."

"I'm not doing anything. Are you the police? Disney? Who do you work for?" Maybe Denise had reported him. Maybe this was the end.

Jellybeans fell onto the dining room table and pretended to die,

"Just. One. Cracker."

"Don't believe everything you see on television. We don't have to identify ourselves. All that matters is that we outnumber you here."

These were the people who had been looking for the zoo.

"Why would I tell you anything if you don't have to show me that you're cops? What if you're corporate spies trying to steal my company's secrets?"

One of the women spoke. "We work for an agency you've never heard of. It's a long story as to why we're investigating your company, but here's something." She handed him a badge.

He held it in his hands—it was heavy, authentic-feeling, and inscribed: United States Forest Service, Special Investigator.

"You're Forest Service police?" Champion asked as best he could without sounding disrespectful. The badges looked like they'd found them on the Internet somewhere. "I don't understand."

"We haven't been an official agency since the government stopped giving a shit about the forests. There aren't any real trees now anyway, so we're our own unit now. We do our own thing."

"You don't need to tell him that. All you need to know is we know what you're doing and we want to know why."

Nothing Champion had done was against the law, he thought, unless he really had killed Dale, Bryce, and the others. Murder was probably still illegal, yes, but the Concordance—that belonged to the people. That's what Carl had said. He'd warned him that erasing people would have consequences.

The woman spoke. "Do you see how we broke into your house? Do you see how we followed you? We're not afraid to use force. We almost killed your bird."

"That would have been a huge favor." Champion looked at Jellybeans to see if he had understood him. Champion turned his back.

"Try telling the real police that you were tortured by U.S. Forest Police. They'll never believe it."

"You haven't tortured me."

"Not yet."

Champion couldn't tell if they were joking or not. It seemed like a joke. "Sooo, you couldn't find the zoo."

"What are you talking about?"

Champion conjured peaceful thoughts: groves, water gardens, symmetric monuments to past disasters.

They *could* do anything, and as angry as they made him, he couldn't attack them—they looked like people who worked out all day because they had nothing else to do. They probably harbored angry fires deep inside, too. But what if they were corporate spies? They would find his formula and Carl would be furious.

He asked if they wanted refreshments, if they wanted to sit down. He could make a snack, though he didn't have much because he wasn't expecting guests. *I will kill them with kindness*, he thought. Or he'd poison their drinks.

He was happy when they declined snacks but accepted glasses of water. That was something like progress.

Three of them sat. Jellybeans strutted around the table like a pretty boy.

The last woman who spoke remained standing and crossed her arms. She clearly didn't like the direction this was going, sitting them all down like that in his living room.

When he returned with a tray with water glasses for everybody, he sat with them and waited for them to drink.

"So, what do you want to know?"

"Why are you making mustard gas?"

"That's not my department."

"Did you put something in this water? It smells odd."

"I don't think so. Why do you ask?"

"I can't drink this. Don't drink the water."

"What are you doing with the Concordance?"

"Just posting articles. Stuff people like to click on and read. There's nothing wrong with the water. Why would I do something to the water?" Champion lifted a glass to his lips, unsure of which glass he'd left formula-free. He pretended to drink. "See, the water's fine."

"Who writes the articles?"

"He definitely put something in the water."

"We have consultants. I'm a manager, so I don't do any actual work. I coordinate." He was lying; he managed no one, coordinated nothing.

"The water's not fine. We're not idiots."

"What are you posting to the Concordance?"

"Just stuff. Stuff we know about. Fragrances. You can look all of this up. The water's super chlorinated now. That's probably what you smell. The chlorine makes it safe."

He took a long drink, a real drink, and winced as the formula burned his throat. He had made a mistake.

His hands trembled. He bounced his knee furiously as if to pump the potion quickly through his system. His stomach burned; his head pounded.

"We know what you're really doing."

"You do?" His throat swelled.

"The federal government knows everything you do."

"I don't understand, if you know what's in the messages, then . . ." he paused to cough, Bryce's formula coming back up his throat ". . . you know what we're doing. It's not illegal. There's nothing in the law protecting. . . ."

He closed his mouth and eyes, took another drink of water to show them it was fine.

"Maybe this is off the record."

"Maybe this isn't about the Concordance."

As the tone of their voices changed, Champion felt them moving closer to him, moving in around him. He had surely ruined something. He needed clean water badly, but all that he had was the tainted glass.

The humming in the house stopped and was replaced by a long silence. The passing moment made the Forest Service police all the more menacing.

"Why don't you just explain what it is you want? Maybe I'm not understanding."

"We don't have to explain anything to you."

"Why are you making mustard gas?" One of the men spoke.

"I don't know. Are we really doing that? I don't know anything about mustard gas. That sounds terrible."

"We're very angry, Champion. You shouldn't mess with us."

"You shouldn't have poisoned the water."

"What are you going to do to me?" Champion hoped they *would* beat him up if only to distract him from the strange and awful things that were happening inside of him.

"You think we don't have any juice. You think, *Oh, defunct Forest Service cops, why should we be afraid of them?*"

His organs pulsed, his spleen and kidneys shredded and were surely bleeding.

"One thing you should know: we see everything you do, on the Internet, the Concordance, email, text messages, your Googles, all of it."

"We still can't see in your head, so that's why we're here."

"We're not inadequate," one of them said. "That had nothing to do with the dissolution of our department."

One of them lit a cigarette. Champion opened his mouth; he was so offended and surprised that somebody would smoke inside a stranger's apartment. "I don't allow that in my house."

"We can do whatever we want! You poisoned our drinks when we thought you were being polite."

When Champion tried to move toward the kitchen to find fresh water, the agent dropped her cigarette on the carpet and let it burn for a moment before grinding it out with her shoe.

Now would have been a fine time to become enraged, he thought, but he was only frightened and ill. Jellybeans was laughing at him, he was sure, from the safety of the chandelier.

"Please, I don't know anything more. I just follow instructions."

"What were the instructions?"

"I already told you. Stuff. VPNs, the dark web. I don't understand it."

"What have you changed? What's different?"

"Some stuff about Franklin Pierce."

"Who's Franklin Pierce?"

"He was the 14th President. I'm really not feeling well."

"I'm tired of your bullshit."

"We can make you talk."

"I am talking. I think I need to go to the emergency room. Do you have a car?"

"Please stop talking." The agent lit another cigarette, took a long drag, and smothered it against the dining room table, a table that had belonged to his mother but he now despised. Maybe now he could get rid of it without guilt.

"Should I get a lawyer?"

"Shut up."

"I need a doctor." He felt at once as if he might vomit and like he was collapsing from the inside.

He took another drink seeking relief. "Shit," he said, though it was not so bad the third time.

"You're not under arrest. You're not even a person of interest. You're boring. We just need you to tell us what we want to hear."

Champion couldn't move. They pressed their bodies against his as he struggled to find a way to get beyond them; they were huge, bigger than they had been somehow. When he thought he'd gotten free, when the air was cool again, and he couldn't feel their bodies against his, somebody put a black cloth bag over his head and pulled a rope around the opening to tighten it around his chest.

38.

STEEL AND GLASS AND A CLEAR BRIGHT SKY neither of them could remember ever seeing before. The sun was so warm they could feel it reflecting off the glass buildings, blue and new. The city had erupted before them like sudden massive crystals pushing up from the ground in every direction.

On the train a man with a German accent shouted a story about how he'd been stopped between cars by a federal agent, and that he was under arrest for impersonating a veteran when it happened.

Bryce gave him a dime.

Denise looked up from her phone. Her screen had gone dark from inactivity.

There was no such thing as a dime. She had seen them in a museum exhibit about old currency, but had never seen one in public, had never had any change at all. Surely they'd never been to war with Germany, either; such an exemplary country.

She wanted to know what was happening to her, when it would end, if she would be driven to do what Bryce had done.

She was unsure of how long she had been away. A technician walked by with his eyes on his clipboard; he looked at her, winked, paused a moment too long. The office smelled like burnt toast and brisket, infuriating her because she hadn't had anything to eat. It was far too early to waste her precious lunch hour. She found an old bag of unsalted almonds in her desk and pushed a handful into her mouth, then returned to the screen.

They emerged from the train station. Bryce had wanted to see something there, something he'd found in the Concordance, a mystery, he'd said, a new place; the particular *something* escaped Denise—she experienced these visions in a way that seemed like she was always just waking up trying to grasp the last bits of a dream.

A place nobody had seen before, he told her, even though she knew that was impossible: *everything* had been seen. That's why they were sad, he told her, because everything had been written about and photographed. They had to make their own adventures, find their own newness.

Why was it important that there be new things? She asked him because she had never wanted new things before.

The lobby of the building smelled like plywood and carpet glue. The doors were unlocked, even though they saw nobody inside, and the interior was still an unfinished shell. They touched every surface—the rough red carpet, the intricate patterns of the wrought-metal elevator doors, and the wooden walls, so authentic they smelled like real pine. They pressed their faces against the mirrors in the elevator and smudged the glass and went as high as it would go. When they emerged, they were in a new lobby with flowers on pedestals and animal pelts on the floor. They ran down the hallway past each numbered door, not knowing where they were going but drawn in that direction nonetheless. They opened two double doors and inside was an enormous natatorium, the biggest swimming pool they'd ever seen, and a domed ceiling so high and blue it could have been the sky.

Bryce was right, she thought; here they would be naked in the warm indoor water. She could feel herself floating, remembered the quiet lapping of water, the amplified echo of every sound. The blue sky above them, a true memory of what the sky *must* have looked like when she was young. Bryce, next to her, extended his hand, the tips of his fingers touching her own.

She clicked on the screen to see another photograph and an error she'd never seen before appeared: *entry not found*. She backed up to Bryce's main entry and saw the same thing: *entry not found*. Every search for Bryce resulted in the same thing: *entry not found. No results found. No such user. No such person. Nobody.* She looked at her phone and found the same—Bryce gone—as if he had never existed.

39.

BRYCE AND ANGIE JOINED THE MASSES on their way to the park where a row of makeshift market stalls had been built around the path to the railroad tracks.

"This is weird." Bryce didn't understand where the stalls had come from, why they were selling so many pies, why everybody seemed to be dressed like a colonist.

"We're creating a world here. It helps us cope with the stress of living, to imagine a simpler time."

"I thought this was just about a train."

"It's about so much more than the train. The train is like the cherry on the sundae. Don't you ever come to the park on weekends? We're almost always down here."

They passed a couple of clowns giving away balloons twisted into strange shapes. A woman on stilts leaned forward to pass out bits of cheese. Children in britches pushed metal hoops with sticks, laughing like they'd been paid.

"When do we get to see the train?"

"Soon. I think somebody will probably ring a big bell."

Angie led Bryce into one of the tents to look at leather bags hanging from a rope draped across the ceiling of the stall. Bryce picked up a wallet from a table and held it to his nose.

"This isn't real," he told the man selling the wallets.

"Of course it's real. I order the leather special. It's organic. It'll hold all your cards."

The man took the wallet from Bryce, put it away behind the table, and handed him a different wallet. Bryce held the new wallet to his nose and shook his head.

"It's definitely not leather."

"It's totally leather," he said. "Everything here is natural. From nature. It's the skin of a cow. I promise. Cruelty-free, no-antibiotic, all-natural, organic cow. Guaranteed." He pointed up at a sign that said the same: Guaranteed all-natural cow.

"Are you sure?"

"It's best not to think about it too hard. Just buy it."

Bryce held the wallet to his nose, still skeptical, and bought it.

The man winked. "You're a man who knows quality when he sees it," he said.

Outside, the crowd grew. They feigned palpable glee, cheering and whooping in a way that seemed spontaneous, but was as forced as their costumes. He had never seen so many stovepipe hats.

"How's your work girlfriend?" Angie asked.

Bryce blushed. "I sent her an email I shouldn't have sent."

"Bryce."

"Not interested," he said. "But there's chemistry. She almost came home with me even, but nothing happened."

"That doesn't sound like chemistry," Angie said, pointing to a tent. "Let's go in here."

Inside, an aquarium housed one of the zoo's famous parthenogenic sharks, born of a virgin mother, the Famous Miracle of the Sea on special display for the occasion. A small crowd huddled around the Miracle, touching the aquarium glass, weeping at the lone bamboo shark resting on the sandy bottom, its stony eyes frigid and empty, staring back at them as if it too might begin to weep. A golden goose egg rested next to the shark as a reminder of the holy mystery.

"What will the light look like?" Bryce asked. He pushed closer to the aquarium for a better view, blocked by the circle of people pressed against the glass. "The sun ships you told me about."

They made their way toward the tracks where the train would emerge, the back of their hands grazing each other as they walked. The sky was black and blue and the air billowed with mist. He missed the light.

"I don't want to talk about it, I told you."

"I'm just curious about the blimps, that's all. We could use some sun today."

"They're not blimps."

"What are they, then?"

She shrugged. "What about you? Tell me about artificial fragrances."

"There's not much to say you don't already know, except that I'm certain that guy's leather goods aren't made from leather. I'm very good at detecting artificial smells."

"Then why'd you buy it?"

"He told me to. I don't know."

"Why do we need artificial scents?"

"We need them because there aren't as many real smells as there used to be."

"I don't think that's true."

"I create new smells we didn't even know we needed. People get bored, so there's a demand for new stimulations. Like artificial banana. We can make very convincing banana scents and tastes, but people like the one that really only suggest bananas. I've seen entire bananas made from hydrocarbons in the lab."

"Isn't it easier to just grow a banana?"

"That's not the point."

"What about your project, the smell of memory?"

"I don't know. I guess I'm working on it, but it's not really a thing I can do."

"The ambrosia of nostalgia," she said. "The wistful odor. The plaintive whiff."

"I think I've figured something out," he said. "It has to do with Denise."

"You should probably leave her alone, right?"

"I can't," he said. "Chemistry."

"The sentimental scent. The fetor of regret."

"Please stop."

"I can't believe those bags weren't leather."

"At least they're cruelty-free."

"When's the last time you saw a cow?"

"They had cows at the zoo."

"They died."

A bell rang.

"I think it's time for the train."

⋮

40.

CHERYL, GONE FROM THE CONCORDANCE, felt white-hot death radiating from her core like a virus, fast and fatal, a fever engulfing her body.

She shuddered and checked again. Maybe a glitch, maybe user-error. Gone.

A deep breath made things seem not so bad and this is what she did: she took a deep breath, and then another, and then she put on her coat and went outside, leaving her now useless phone on the dining room table.

Her hands shook. She rolled her sleeves, then unrolled them, looked in her bag for a piece of gum. She felt the back of her neck, sweaty and cold, and steadied her trembling hands in front of her.

How would she restore her photographs, the events she'd recorded there, the links to all the things in the world she liked? How would she know anything?

"Be cool," she said. She rolled her sleeves again.

Her phone vibrated in her pocket even though she'd left it at home, the specter of what-had-been.

She paused to look at brown leaves clinging to a dying tree. *All living things are dying*, she thought, and she imagined a new commune with nature only *she* could feel—she felt the dying tree as if she too were dying. She held its branch in her hands like the withered hand of a grandmother, squeezed a bit, not too tight, and held its fingers to her nose, trying to detect the smell of death. She looked at the leaves, nearly brittle and curled, looking for the enlightenment of new, previously ignored details—*pores*, she thought; *this leaf has pores, like a human*.

"I'm sorry," she said to the brittle bark, stroking the thin, gnarled trunk. "I'm so sorry."

She looked wistfully toward the red sky and conjured profundity.

Having communed with nature in this way made her hunger for more and she really hoped, for the first time ever, to encounter some sort of creature on her walk.

She breathed the blowing wind, began to imagine what could be. And then she thought of Carl, Carl who she had tolerated or liked or maybe even loved. She could no longer picture his face; instead, she remembered blue and bruises.

Carl had surely been the one to erase her; he loved revenge as much as he loved himself.

What had he looked like? Who had he been? *What was his name again?*

She focused.

Carl; they had been married. She had a friend named Tammers and she had a job where people respected her.

She had believed in artificial fragrances and she had believed in . . . what was his name?

She remembered a body sitting across from her, somewhere in Florida, the two of them about to enjoy an enormous steak. They weren't alone, but surrounded by others—men in suits with napkins tucked into their shirts. Their lips were beautiful and full and covered with grease and the juice of their meat. Her husband went from person to person and dabbed at their mouths with a moistened napkin.

She stepped into an intersection without looking both ways and was hit by an autonomous car; she felt as if she was floating through the air, and in the air she began to wonder: what would become of her?

She opened her eyes and was not, as she'd imagined, dead; she hadn't floated through the air. She hadn't been knocked over even, but she felt a sharp pain in the side of her knee and when she saw the car she realized it had barely bumped her and the passenger inside was flipping her off and yelling at her with the windows up. She would not apologize. Pedestrians had the right-of-way and yes, she'd stepped into traffic against a green light and probably looked suicidal, but his car should have stopped. The car inched forward, its passenger still inside, pounding on the window. She whispered through its grill: "You've been warned."

41.

THE LATE-NIGHT AIR SMELLED LIKE FABRIC SOFTENER as Denise walked between Bryce's house and the house next to it, to the small backyard where she'd figure out how to get inside.

She'd come on a night with no moon so she'd be able to take her time, but the sky was still dusky red, the darkness barely a cover at all.

The long grass grazed her ankles.

She remembered Bryce standing in the tall grass in front of some abandoned stone structure crumbled beyond identification. The sunlight in the photo was bright and came from behind the photographer, covering Bryce and the ruins with a yellow and washed gauze. The photo had been taken in the early morning—she remembered the dewy grass sparkling in the sunlight.

Bryce's eyes were nearly closed and his left arm was in motion as if raising it to block the light. *So strange,* she thought, *to waste a clear day by hiding from the sun*; if they had only known what was to come, they would have better embraced each beautiful day.

From the stone foundation behind him grew short gnarled trees with windblown branches twisted horizontally over the debris. She could see what looked like church pews among the thick growth behind him. Had she taken the photograph, had she been there, standing in the wet grass, she would have felt the freshness of the spring morning on her bare ankles.

She and Bryce had fought that morning about something inconsequential, fought because he'd misunderstood something she'd said. Instead of apologizing, he'd kept arguing with her as if she *had* actually said what he thought she'd said, only admitting later, in the car on the way to wherever they'd gone that she'd been right all along, and how, after so long in the car together, he had been truly sorry.

Before they'd found the old church, they'd walked along a narrow stream, the water moving quickly over rocks and rusted and misshapen industrial debris. They'd crossed the stream by stepping on a bridge of wooden shipping pallets thrown across the water. She remembered a thick, tightly wound spring beside the bridge, rust-orange and protruding from the water. They'd eaten blackberries and walked along railroad tracks. They'd whispered to one another and stood close when Bryce saw a bloody doe limping toward them.

She could make her memories into loss, mourning the real that never had been.

She searched for a hidden key in the darkness, looking for a pot or something under which to hide something. She ran her fingers along the top of the door frame, looked beneath the tattered mat on the patio, tried to open a window, locked.

She crept back between Bryce's house and the house next door and waited to make sure no cars were coming before she hurried onto the front porch. A dog began to bark, so she crouched behind the short brick wall around the porch edge and waited for silence.

She waited, but the dog still barked. And then another dog joined in, barking until a third and fourth dog answered them.

"Shut up!" Somebody yelled from a window. "For the love of god, shut those dogs up!"

The ceiling of the porch had been painted the color of the sky. A single light fixture with a yellow bulb hung in the center. Two chairs faced one another at angles and were so dusty she could not imagine Bryce and his mother ever sat in them together.

"Go fuck yourself!" Another voice from down the block, the dogs still barking.

Her knees ached as she knelt on the green plastic porch rug—so dated, so hideous and unpleasant to touch. If Bryce had chosen it, she knew she could never really have loved him, lucid again despite the burning in her throat. She both ached to make real the memories blooming in her head and to break from the spell of the poison.

This was a life she should not want, did not want, but still, she yearned for it even as the hideous carpet repelled her back to reality.

A black mailbox full of yellowed catalogs and flyers poking from the top hung from the brick wall next to the front door. She'd have to risk standing, but it was nearly three and all the houses on the street were dark despite the dogs and angry neighbors. She stood and took the mail, rolling it into a bundle, tossed it on the floor of the porch, and stretched so she could reach down into the deep mailbox, where she felt a key with the tips of her fingers. After pushing it along the bottom of the metal mailbox with her middle finger she was able to lift the edge and grab it between her thumb and finger.

She fumbled the key into the first of three keyholes in the front door, then the second, and finally the third before realizing she'd locked the first lock, and unlocked the other two.

A car appeared at the end of the block, driving too fast, then stopping abruptly in front of the house. She stood still, trying desperately to melt into the wooden door, hoping they wouldn't notice her. Bass rumbled out of the car and a cigarette lighter flicked on inside, lighting the teenager's faces.

The porch light flickered on above her, most surely on a timer. When they saw her standing on the porch, one of them threw a fast-food bag onto the lawn, French fries scattering into the long grass and weeds.

"Let us cruise!" One of them yelled before screeching away.

After some maneuvering, she was able to open the door and slide inside. The house reeked of mothballs and an old mother, bodily and medicinal. A clock ticked loudly in the dining room.

"Hello?" she called out. "I brought in the mail."

A stupid thing to say. She'd left the mail on the porch.

When nobody returned her greeting, she called out again. "Hello," she said. "I'm not here to hurt you. I'm just here for a visit."

Only the clock on the wall answered her with a single, bright, chime.

She looked around the room for a desk or bureau, something where somebody might tuck photographs. She risked turning on the tiny flashlight she'd brought, barely bright enough to illuminate her path.

Bryce had given her a tour of the house, but she remembered being so annoyed with him after their long night of commuting from the party back to his house that she only wanted to sleep. She also remembered getting off the train early, taking a car service home, feeling lucky to have avoided going home with Bryce. She had been in the house or hadn't been in the house—still, she remembered it, had vague knowledge of its layout, the old furniture upstairs covered in sheets, how Bryce seemed to own nothing but what had belonged to his mother.

She looked in the drawers of the dining room credenza, finding only the good silver (tarnished), yellow linen, and countless candles. In the cabinets below, she found stacks of china wrapped in newspapers, bags of potato chips and pretzels, the crockpot.

The memories of almost hooking up, or hooking up, or going home were there—she knew one had happened, or now, all of them. The strange love she now felt for him made it almost as if the Bryce she constructed wasn't the real Bryce at all. Her Bryce would never live here. Her Bryce was a cooler, smarter, more beautiful Bryce. A Bryce who wouldn't store chips in the dining room credenza.

Her Bryce was great in bed, she knew, even though she couldn't remember actually fucking him in any of her new memories, only watching him, walking with him, arguing with him. Barely touching. Her Bryce drove a black car with a bike rack, always ready for adventure. Her Bryce knew all the good music the young people liked and knew how to dance.

She had no understanding of the depth of her hallucination, whether they would grow, deepen, and solidify, or fade away like real memories. She remembered riding a bike, driving to the mountains, spotlighting deer at night for some reason.

She could fight the images, or not—maybe she needed to sculpt the memories instead of yielding to them.

Bryce's mother's room felt untouched and preserved. The rocking chair in the corner, next to the bed, was covered with a white sheet. Bryce had draped a plastic tarp over the dresser, too. She lifted the tarp and opened the top drawer and pushed her hand through Bryce's mother's underwear looking for something hidden there: a folder, or an envelope. When she found nothing, she moved to the second drawer, then the third. After the dresser, she looked under the bed, where long, empty, plastic bins, newly dusted, were pushed into a neat row.

She looked into Bryce's bedroom.

She heard something outside. From the window, she could see somebody start a car across the street and drive away. The dogs were still going, their voices growing hoarse.

She shined her light into the room. Stacks of papers and magazines and books formed little islands around the floor. Open cardboard boxes covered the bed. It was as if he were packing to move, or still organizing his mother's things after so much time since her death. She sat on the floor and fanned through the papers—no photographs, only old tax returns, insurance records, and receipts.

She found a clipboard with a white sheet of paper on it and fifteen dates written neatly in bold block letters. Bryce had circled some of them, and below the top sheet were other sheets labeled with each date, with notes below, but Bryce's handwriting was terrible and in the bad light she couldn't read them.

After searching through the rest of the piles, she looked into the third bedroom, full of more paper stacks, magazines, newspapers, books. Bryce had removed any furniture that had been there; only a folding table pushed against the windowless wall remained. On the table was a plastic freezer bag stuffed full of hair—long, light-brown and gray hair, curled into a nest.

Maybe Bryce had been a serial killer.

She set the hair aside and looked at one of the piles of paper on the floor—Bryce's mother's papers: yellowing receipts, invoices, bills. She found a cardboard box full of costume jewelry and scarves, and another with scraps of fabric.

The door downstairs opened and closed. The sound of someone moving inside.

Heat flowed to Denise's cheeks and her hands shook. She turned off her light, slid it into the pocket of her jeans, and walked to the edge of the staircase to listen. No sound came up the stairs; she waited.

She heard things—strange things and footfalls and somebody coughing.

She opened the bedroom window, looked down, and considered a jump.

42.

THEY FOLLOWED THE CROWD, THICK WITH WOMEN IN BONNETS AND MEN IN HIGH PANTS. A fop on a unicycle pedaled after a woman on a penny-farthing bike swerving around bowties and neckerchiefs, walking sticks, and mongrel dogs circling them all.

A flock of waxwing drones flitted above, their tiny cameras squirming toward the ground like snail antennae, groping for some invisible stimulation.

"The train!" A man barked through a cone. "The train!"

They shouted and gathered around the railroad tracks and held their phones high above their heads to photograph what was about to happen. Those in back pushed to get a better look, the crowd growing into a single mass of moving bodies.

A thick plume of smoke appeared above the trees before the train emerged from the forest, chugging slowly toward the crowd. They stretched their necks and pushed, the earth shaking beneath their feet.

Bryce hummed to himself, trying to cover the sound of the burning coal infecting the air with its bluster and groan. He felt the crowd behind them, his arms pressed against his chest and the back of a man in front of him. Angie looked as if she was being swallowed between bodies, as more and more merged from the forest, the tents up the hill, and from the meadow behind them.

The hot bodies rustled feebly, then cried out.

"Isn't it exciting?" Angie asked; the swash of sweat and adrenaline fomented, rising inside of Bryce, filling him. The sound overtook her words, enveloping and drowning them.

Bryce looked at Angie's hair, twisted on top of her head. When he was close enough to catch a note of Angie in the air, the sound crashed against the bodies pressed against him; the collision happened again and again, pulsing in fast swells punctuated with explosive, metallic lacerations.

"Aren't you excited?" Angie took his hand, led him closer.

The crowd shouted and cheered, whistled and screeched; the train had appeared before them as they had hoped: an iron bear, laboring and heaving after so many dormant years.

"I thought it would be bigger," he said. He held his head up and looked down over his nose, through the crowd. He took short, quick breaths, pulling in the clearest air he could through the grinding of expectant bodies, too close and loud.

"I think it's pretty big," Angie said, stretching to see. "It's a big train."

Bryce saw the black steel of the miniature locomotive. The smoke, thick and white, plumed above the crowd and thrilled them, the exhaust rising above, blending into the heavy sky. The train was there at last and they began to work their way forward where there was no more room. Together they leaned into the crowd, compressing their friends and neighbors closer and closer until somebody screamed.

The sound of the scream was real, cutting through the noise of sweat and smoke. "Something's wrong."

Angie and Bryce had succumbed to the crowd, the people behind them falling forward onto their backs. Together, they toppled.

"Are you having fun?" Angie asked in a way that sounded like she wasn't having fun anymore. She struggled to help him to his feet.

Another scream came from ahead of them and the slow squeal of the engine coming to a stop.

Someone yelled out at the front of the crowd for help. "We need an ambulance," they shouted, though nobody seemed to call, only reaching their phones above their heads to photograph whatever was happening as they moved away.

Whomever the train had hit made no sound. Instead, the accident silenced them.

"Horrible," Angie whispered.

The subtle scent of the boy's blood touched the air and was lifted, fusing with the reek of bodies and smoke, the smell of the old railroad, rust and coal dust, all screaming of the boy, bloody and headless, before them.

They pushed closer.

The train engineer sat on the ground in front of the locomotive, away from the body and head.

Bryce had heard nothing like it, the coalescing chord thunderous and dark, piercing him from inside. First, trembling hands and an ache, an old wound opening and swallowing him; next, the sweep of weakness.

"Bryce, let's go," Angie said. She took Bryce's arm and pulled him, but he could not move, his body filled with the deafening fetor of adrenaline and death.

Bryce saw his mother, frail and fading, sitting in her chair in the house, Bryce sitting across the room from her. Her body had begun to retract as if swallowing itself, her skin collapsed around the bones of her face. He saw Angie, standing by him, trying to move him. He saw Denise with her hair combed straight in front of her face, the silence almost something he could touch.

"Bryce?" she asked. "Are you there?"

43.

DENISE OPENED THE CLOSET, the clothes inside bulging out from the open door. She was able to slide between the coats and shirts and push herself behind them. The fabric against her cheeks and the smell of Bryce's mother still on the coats reminded her of childhood, hiding in the closet, hiding from her mother at the department store at the mall—sliding into the middle of a clothes rack, tucking herself behind stacks of jeans on a low shelf.

She escaped into another world and in the back of the closet she waited, feeling as if she could stay there indefinitely. She leaned forward and rested her face and arms on the clothes hanging there. Maybe she would sleep until whoever was inside had gone.

She remembered the things she'd done and had not done, emerging inside the echo of the dark night. Camping with Bryce in the desert—he'd driven away for food after a raven had stolen theirs. Alone and hungry, she sipped from a water bottle, staring at the dotted sky, listening to distant rustling in the brush, the chirp of insects, the buzz of a vehicle off in the hills, and an unknown rumble, looking at her cell phone to see if she'd caught a signal.

She opened her eyes again. At the bottom of a steep slope, her ankle twisted and swollen, Bryce's body a few yards from hers, a coil of rope twisted around his neck. She stood and limped toward him and was hovering above, watching him lower himself down the steep slope with a rope, calling out to her. She stood near his cubicle, the office dark, watched him reach into the ceiling with a utility knife, watched him hack through the bundle of network cable, watched him twist the rope around his neck, shouting to her from the edge of the slope to let go.

She awoke next to him, the smell of the bed sheets murky and medicinal. She looked for Bryce's hand, but he had gotten up in the night, moved to some other part of the house. She listened for him, appeared in the doorway, pale, emaciated. She remembered meeting him at work, how there was something in the way they looked at one another when they'd met, a kind of energy she'd never felt before, how they'd found each other in the dark corner of the office holiday party and gone home together without a word, as if it's what they'd been meant to do.

She'd grown cold, waiting for him to return with food; she felt stranded, the distant rumbling coming closer, animals seemingly all around her, so close she felt them on her, their tongues and hot breath.

She saw the headlights of his car, finally, hours later than she'd thought.

When the bedroom light went on and the closet door opened, she closed her eyes against the intruder and waited.

"What are you doing in there? Denise?"

Bryce's voice came through the clothes, but it wasn't Bryce's voice—this voice was deep and thick, less watery, taller.

She remembered how he'd sounded telling her he'd gotten lost, telling her it was too much, the sounds, how he couldn't live like this. Telling her he had loved her the moment he'd first seen her, before she'd even looked at him.

She opened her eyes and realized she was not nearly as concealed as she'd imagined.

"Hiding?" she asked. She suspected that answer would not be good enough. Something wasn't right with Bryce—his voice, his eyes.

"From what? What are you doing in here?"

Denise pushed through the coats.

"What are *you* doing here?"

The Bryce before her was both Bryce and not Bryce at all—a Bryce, more robust, but not the real Bryce. His hair was thick and his skin was not so much like a hide. His dress shirt was crisp and fit him. He wore nice jeans, fashionable sneakers. The cool Bryce, the Bryce of her dreams.

"I thought you were a burglar."

"A burglar? I waited for you at the restaurant for an hour. I texted you, called."

She looked at her phone—three missed calls, texts.

"I didn't get these. They just showed up on my phone. I forgot. Where were we going to go to dinner? It's really late."

This reality pulled her forward.

"It's nine o'clock. We were supposed to meet at eight. The buffet. Our place."

"I hate that place."

"You love that place. You picked it. The pudding?"

She looked at the room, their room, transformed. New furniture, hardwood floors, tasteful lighting, bigger. A painting of a tiger on the wall.

"Are you sure there's nothing wrong? Nothing you want to talk about?"

Maybe she hadn't been feeling well lately, maybe she'd been having strange dreams.

Bryce's things neatly arranged on top of the dresser, a photograph of the two of them on a sailboat on the bedside table. Bright, blue skies.

"Whose hair is in the bag, Bryce? I found the bag of hair." She'd caught him.

"What? Is that why you're in the closet?"

"Yes," she said.

A stuffed animal she'd had as a child, a two-headed calf, clean and new, resting on her pillow.

"I don't know anything about a bag of hair."

"Don't fuck with me Bryce, I found a bag of hair."

"Why would I keep a bag of hair, Denise? Why? That's why you stood me up? That's why you've been acting like you barely know me."

"I don't know what's happening." She curled her hands into fists.

"I didn't kill anybody, if that's what you think."

"That's not what I'm suggesting."

"Why else would I have a bag of hair? Do you think I'm weird?"

"I didn't say you were weird," she said. "I was just asking about the hair."

"I'm not weird, Denise."

"Then why do you have the hair?"

"There's no hair. I don't know what you're talking about."

She pulled one of Bryce's mother's coats from a hangar and wrapped herself in it.

It was *her* coat; she remembered buying it—she couldn't decide if she'd like it or not. She found her wallet in the front pocket, her keys, her phone.

"It's like you're not even here sometimes, Denise. It's like I'm not even here."

"You're not, most of the time. You're always working. You can't even tell me what you're working on really, even though work's all you talk about."

"I told you, it's secret. Everything I do is a secret."

The tops of his shoes were scuffed. One of his socks was black, the other blue. Behind him she noticed a crack running from the top corner of a window to the ceiling.

"Where were we going to dinner?"

"The buffet place. Where we always go. I just told you that."

"I hate that place."

"You picked it. The pudding?"

"I hate pudding. Everybody hates pudding."

"I don't know what's going on with you."

The front door opened and closed. Bryce turned, suddenly frantic, and ran downstairs.

She waited and heard nothing. "Bryce? Are you coming back?"

A woman stood at the bottom of the stairs.

"Where did Bryce go?" She regretted the question. She knew where Bryce had gone.

"Bryce is dead."

"I know that."

"I know who you are. You're Denise."

"Who are you?"

"Anger. Angie. Bryce's friend. I saw the light in the bedroom."

Denise looked back into the bedroom—the crack had vanished and the salmon carpet had grown back in the sick yellow light.

"Bryce and I were in love."

⋮

44.

BRYCE SAT AT A TABLE IN THE FOOD COURT, nursing a pretzel and Julius; the smell of the train, the dead boy, and the sweat and adrenalin of so many excited bodies still resonated inside him, his body hot and spent. He hadn't eaten for days, so here he sat with Angie waiting to pick up his photographs, picking at a pretzel with napkins stuffed in his nose, cataloging old smells, trying to focus on something else.

He remembered the smell of the old mall, sitting on the wooden train while other kids climbed over the top of the locomotive, burying his face in a basket of yarn at the knitting store. The smell of silk-screened prints, crisp and new on t-shirts at the custom printer.

He remembered the stale popcorn in the air drifting from the discount department store, remembered the taste of the hard candy his mother would buy for him for a dime outside Sears. The smell of food court, of shoe leather, of the chlorinated water in the fountains.

The notes still came to him, clear and real; if he focused, the hum of the decapitated boy still vibrating inside him would stop, overtaken by the sounds he conjured from memory.

He remembered the bookstore where the owners kept a monkey that sat on the thick black bars of his cage and squawked at customers. He remembered the odd smell of magazine paper and newsprint and the monkey shit at the bottom of its cage, on the counter near the cash register, on the tops of the bookshelves.

He remembered his mother browsing the fiction aisle. She would leave him in front of the long racks of magazines where he'd look at comic books and the porn, fascinated by the faces of the women on the covers, mysterious behind brown-paper wrappers. He could feel the monkey behind him, watching, and felt both fascinated and ashamed, shuffling away from the magazines to hide among the greeting cards where the monkey could not judge him.

The smell of grease and sweat and pizzas cooking across the concourse. The darkened steak house, stale beer, the smoke curling from the kitchen. He remembered being old enough to be left alone in the video-game arcade where his mother warned him to never go at night because of riff-raff. He'd learned the dangers of krabkake at school, so heeded her warning carefully, balancing a sense of wonder and menace inside the dark arcade.

The smell of teenagers, of cigarette smoke, of weed, of fortified fruit wine in paper bags hidden under their shirts.

His mother would give him five dollars—twenty games—and he'd trade it for singles from the old man on a stool who watched over the place. From machines he'd get tokens with his dollars and play the old games as long as he could.

The kids in the arcade carried a particular smell, a kind of dampness that moved across the space in slow waves, reaching his ears in crests synchronized with his breathing, like the pulsing of sonar from movie submarines.

He looked up from his pretzel at the skylights above them in the food court, through the broken glass into the red sky. Angie was watching the teenagers while he tried to navigate his memories, unable to remember what his mother had looked like standing at the entrance to the arcade shrouded in light.

"My mother," he said, "I saved a bag of her hair."

"What?" Angie looked up from her phone.

"I saved my mother's hair."

"Why would you do that?"

"I don't know."

He took a bite of pretzel, dry and salty, felt it move down his throat into the hole of his stomach. Bright spots obstructed his vision and bathed Angie in sparks like tiny halos.

"Gross."

"If I inhale it, it silences almost everything."

"Does this have something to do with what you're working on?"

"It's comforting. It helps with my condition."

"It's disgusting."

"Denise's hair, it does the same thing."

Angie's face looked like she had just solved a crime "So you've got her hair, too."

"A little bit. I collect it from her cubicle at night after she's gone home."

"That makes you a psychopath."

"I don't know what else to do. I need her. Or a part of her. I can't live like this."

"Like her hand?" she asked. "Do you want to wear her severed hand around your neck?"

"This isn't a joke."

"I wasn't joking."

"It's just hair. I cut my mother's hair when she died."

"Do you have other pieces of her? Buried in the crawl space?"

"I know you're trying to be funny, but I don't think it's funny."

"I'm not trying to be funny. You're the one that's acting like a serial killer."

"You don't understand what it's like."

She took a bite of his pretzel, took a sip of his Julius. "Let's go."

In the parking lot they sat in the car while kids lit another bonfire near the mall entrance to an incomprehensibly loud song played through a PA system they'd set up. Bryce thumbed through the photographs, growing gradually more upset as each new print failed to produce an image of his mother as he'd hoped. Instead, he found photographs of the old zoo, photographs of the neighborhood train before it had been shut down.

He found photographs of old parties with strangers' faces gathered in the living room, watching something on television. In some of the photographs, the strangers were naked, wearing only masks.

"I like those train photographs," Angie said.

"Where are the selfies?" Bryce opened another envelope; he set the orgy photos aside, face down, on the dashboard.

The photos seemed faded already, the colors dull and less vibrant than he imagined them to be. He looked out of the car, across the parking lot and imagined that the faded images, decades old, were really the color of the world, and that the saturated colors of digital photographs were an enhancement that had trained their imaginations to be brighter and more vivid.

Heavy rain fell. The teenagers abandoned their bonfire and ran into the mall. Bryce turned on the car. The wipers struggled against the sudden weather.

He handed the photographs to Angie and began to drive slowly home.

"Is this your mom?"

Bryce looked across at her, squinted, and took the photo, holding it at the right distance from his face. The photograph was out-of-focus, overexposed.

"Yes, that's her," he said.

45.

"I'M CALLING THE POLICE."

"What? Why?" Denise put her hands into her jumper pockets, took a step back.

"Keep your hands where I can see them."

"I'm not going to shoot you," Denise said. She removed her hands from her pockets, opened her hands. "Empty, see?"

"You weren't in love with him. Why are you here?"

"I'm looking for photographs."

"Bryce has plenty of photos in the Concordance."

"His Concordance page is gone. Vanished. No more photographs."

"That's impossible."

"It's not, you should check."

Denise looked over Angie's shoulder for Bryce.

"Why do you care?" Angie said.

"I think I was poisoned. Sort of."

"Weren't you the one that found him?"

"Yes, I found him. Are you in love with Bryce, too?"

"No, Bryce and I were friends. Did you kill Bryce? I don't think he killed himself. He wasn't that intense. I'm not sure I believe he's even really dead. He's still alive in the Concordance."

"Bryce didn't have any friends."

"You didn't answer my question."

"No, I didn't kill him." Maybe she had killed him.

"We were friends. Why do you give a shit about photos of Bryce?"

"Something happened when I found him dead."

"So, you broke into his house."

"So did you."

"The door was unlocked."

"I still want to look around. I can't explain it, but I really need to find photographs."

"How do you know there are real photographs?"

"Have you seen anything strange over here?"

"Just you breaking in. I water the plant once in a while. In case he comes back."

"Bryce talked about photographs. Please, I really want to see them."

"I'm going to call the police."

"Can you give me, maybe fifteen minutes? Then call the police? I just need to look in the attic."

"He was saving your hair, you know. Collecting it for some reason."

"What? Why would he do that?"

"It has something to do with silence."

"The hair in that bag, that's not my hair."

"There's a box," Angie said. She looked exhausted. She led her back upstairs to the bedroom. "He was weird."

"I know." Denise touched her hair, held it to her nose. She washed her hair, but for some reason it always smelled like garbage.

"What I'm saying is, what I'm going to show you, it's weird, like the bag of hair."

"Why was he saving people's hair?"

"He was a psychopath," she laughed. "I told you—it had something to do with silence."

They walked upstairs and Angie led Denise into Bryce's mother's bedroom. Now that there were two of them, they were less careful and turned lights on as they went. It was as if they were in their own house.

From under the bed, Angie found a shoebox-sized plastic case inside one of the long clear boxes Denise had seen earlier. She snapped open the lid and showed Denise what was inside. Everything was wrapped in layers of plastic covered in thick dust. "I think you're going to need to take the whole thing."

"It's really dirty."

"It's dust Bryce collected. Something disgusting about skin. He thought the dust was his mother, like the hair."

Denise felt angry and a little ashamed she'd missed this discovery during her initial search.

"I don't know what you want with him. He's dead. Let him be dead."

"I can't," she said.

Denise wouldn't touch what was inside. Angie shook the plastic sheet a little bit so they could see the photo album inside, which was covered in plastic, but also immersed in the gray dust—compacted and felted—that surrounded the package.

Denise snapped the lid back. "I'll just take it."

46.

CARL SPUN CIRCLES IN HIS DESK CHAIR trying to kill the day. He held his phone in his hand and paged through the Concordance.

"Who gives a shit about Franklin Pierce?" he asked the empty room. "Who cares about Alan Alda?"

When he tried to turn to his own entry and found himself missing, he knew who was to blame. His sudden absence was alarming—where were the photographs? He did not want to forget the lops, did not want to forget Cheryl. He made an attempt—slight and effortless, but an attempt—to conjure them but could not. All he saw were Cheryl's lips hovering in darkness like a cruel joke.

He texted the Consultant for an appointment and tossed his phone aside, waited a moment for it to buzz with her reply, then picked it up again. Nothing.

He spun and looked at the clock. He was in charge, could leave at any moment. He opened the center drawer of his desk and looked for the vials that had been found on Bryce's desk after his death. He held one up. Probably harmless he thought, but maybe not.

"The smell of memory," he said, shaking the tube.

He looked for himself on his phone again: still gone and nothing from the Consultant. Maybe death was fine. Maybe Bryce's work had succeeded; maybe this was the answer, this captured cloud, milky in its capsule. Maybe he was fine with dying.

He gave it a shot. He broke the seal, held the vial to his nose, and inhaled something that was not quite anything at all: a floral vein, the whiff of musk, a kind of misty something familiar and not.

He winced as burnt hair bloomed in his sinuses.

He stood, walked to the window, looked out at the churning river, the drones flying in circles like vultures over an island of floating trash. The scent flooded him, a pleasant burning like an awakening, and the vision of the lips grew into a face he once knew. He removed the belt from his pants, unbuttoned his shirt, and began to beat himself.

With the familiar sting, he heard somebody enter the room. "Who's there?" he asked, continuing to lash himself over his shoulder.

Then the feeling of somebody sliding a bag over his head.

Yes, he thought. "Hello, my love."

Then silence, then darkness.

47.

TRASH STEWED IN THE SLOW CURRENT of thick brown water like churning sewage. Cheryl knew from science the river water wasn't really brown, but only reflected the brown sky, but the water was disgusting. Shit river.

She missed scrolling, how her eyes could just look into the abyss of the screen for hours that seemed like days, how boredom had made life seem so long, but now she was free: free from the phantom in her pocket, free to observe all the things in the world she'd missed.

She watched a couple walking, consumed by the window of the screen, and felt an almost crushing sense of superiority modulated by trembling, frantic, pocket checking.

She was sad she would have to miss the launch of the sun ships, the project she'd overseen for so many years. At least the project had been finished, her life's work done in the moments preceding her death.

She missed Tammers, maybe the only person she'd ever truly loved —the evolution of their relationship was not yet done, and now she no longer existed. She missed Orange Juliuses and she missed the mall.

She checked her pocket. Still nothing.

Here she was: walking along the thick water, the strange light, the frozen pellets clicking and bouncing on the wet walkway.

She ate sushi at a small restaurant at a table with a view of the disgusting river. The gritty fish was briny and crumbled as she chewed as if she'd put clumps of dirt in her mouth.

Outside, her stomach felt like an inescapable void, a black hole enveloping the rest of her body. She held onto herself and groaned, workers on their breaks parting as they passed, ignoring her.

A group of children had gathered at the edge of the river and were looking into the water. One of them poked at their discovery with a long stick heavy with dead and brown plant matter and algae. The children laughed and cooed.

What had they found? She approached, because here, before her, the spell of her smartphone broken, she was about to have an encounter!

She could feel the bad fish moving through her body like a virus. She should not have eaten the sushi.

The children poked at a half-submerged shopping cart draped in braids of algae and garbage. Inside the basket of the cage, an enormous bird had built an elaborate nest of branches, snack wrappers, colorful strands of network cabling, old and frayed power lines, burnt rope. The wet and oil-soaked bird bobbed in the water, protected by the cage of the cart as the children jabbed its gnarly body. The bird, some kind of pelican—she didn't know anything about birds—opened its long beak and spat algae-wrapped fish spines at them.

The children seemed to be trying to free the bird without getting their feet wet. *What a good toy for them*, she thought. She approached and offered her arms, long and adult, to try to reach the cart. The children gleefully accepted her help.

As she leaned forward, she felt like a hero. She reached out, was able to touch it, but wasn't able to get a grip.

"Children, hold onto my hand," she said, reaching back with her left hand.

The children took hold and leaned back to steady her as she closed her hand around the metal cage; she pulled and the cart moved, but the bottom must have been thick with sludge and so would not easily move.

"That's the spirit," she said. "Hold on now, children! I've almost got it!"

She leaned forward to get a better grip and the child behind her, a boy, somewhat older than the rest, let her arm slip out of his and she fell into the cold river water. She flailed and tried to find her footing.

"Fuck you, lady," the boy said.

The children didn't laugh or help. Instead, they watched her struggling, poking at her with their sticks like they had poked the bird.

The water was only waist-deep, but when she found the bottom of the river with her feet, she sunk into the thick mud and detritus and became stuck as she stood upright.

This is what the end feels like.

Her body was heavy with river sludge and every smell was new and complex and disgusting. She could feel every inch of her body, a feeling that exhilarated her while her humiliation deepened. She felt her wet clothes clinging to her body, exposing her shape to the children.

The bird was free. It perched on top of the shopping cart, stretched its enormous wings and poked at her with its beak. She swatted at the thing, but it jabbed her, breaking the skin on her arm, and then her face. She couldn't move her legs. The children laughed as the bird squawked and stabbed, opening new wounds, serious and deep. Her stomach still burned.

48.

CHAMPION RECOGNIZED THE SMELL OF INSTITUTION, like sanitizer-lemon and sadness, before he opened his eyes.

There he was, in a dark dormitory. Rare moonlight shown through the vertical blinds of their narrow window while two others bundled in blankets slept in their bunks.

His head ached; he felt a bump on the back of his head where they must have hit him. The last thing he remembered was the Forest Service knocking him around. At least they hadn't killed him and dumped him in the river or buried him alive beneath a dead tree somewhere. He hoped it would be like every other time he'd been incarcerated. If he said the right thing and swallowed his pills and sang the songs with gentle glee, he'd be out before he knew it. If he praised the silence of sleep and the gentle memories of childhood, if he held the hands of the others instead of hitting them, they would see he was not so bad, not violent at all; he'd soon be home.

He looked at the ceiling panels—just like the ones at the office—and he had another thought: perhaps he wouldn't be here long, after all, as he considered another escape.

He looked at his roommates quiet in their beds and imagined smothering them with their pillows, whispering *sweet death* to them at the moment of their last breath, reveling in being alone once again.

"My hands are gentle," he said. He looked at his hands, saw them holding the pillow above their heads. He saw his fingers wrapped around their necks, squeezing their throats, waiting for them to stop their horrible breath. "My hands are not harbingers."

He looked again at the ceiling panels.

He remembered the roof, walking away and back to work like it was nothing. He could do it again, just leave, if he wanted; he could just walk home and forget this place. But he'd be back the next time his gentle hands failed him.

He didn't know what time it was—his body felt like it was morning, but the night was still and dark and his roommates slept soundly.

He ran his gentle finger along the seam of the cinder-block wall.

"I guess it's good to be home," he said.

He imagined lots of people felt that way about jail or rehab, especially if what they returned to was a nondescript house, an unruly parrot, and an office cubicle. Here, he had no responsibilities—no Concordance, no network, no cooking, no cleaning, no work. No cleaning up bodies. Just gentle non-competitive checkers, group therapy, and so much television he would begin to imagine he was part of the shows.

Imprisoned again, he felt like he had either woken from or returned to a dream. He felt wrenched from the rest of the world as if he belonged nowhere. It felt like death. Faced with the reality of his incarceration, he thought again of the ceiling.

Out of bed, he went to the narrow window with a view of the other wing across the empty courtyard and a slice of the sky above. On the floor near the window were what looked like a pair of claws, the kind of claws an amputee would wear—crude, dangerous-looking prosthetic claws like knives. They were 19th century claws.

Mike. He must have finally gotten rid of his hands.

Champion smiled. *Good old Mike,* he thought.

Mike's body rumbled with angry sleep. Champion hoped that at least while awake, his amputations had brought him peace

The room was spacious and pleasant—he'd never stayed in a triple before—carpeted with three little individual areas, each with a desk, slim closet, and bulletin board with peaceful pamphlets tacked to the cork.

"Mike, it's Champion," he whispered.

Mike grumbled and rubbed his eyes with two scarred stubs.

Champion looked at his face to be sure; it was Mike. He'd shaved his head and though it had not been very long since they'd last seen one another, Mike looked old and bristled, his face and head covered with thick gray stubble.

"What time is it?"

"Remember me? We were in here together. Remember that guy Sab? We helped you try to cut your hands off. I'm back!"

Mike looked at his hands and shook his head as if realizing for the first time his hands were gone. "That could be a lot of people."

"With a paper cutter. You drank schnapps and smoked krabkake."

"Schnapps? I'm sorry, I don't remember you. Don't take it personally."

Champion took it personally. It hadn't been that long; they'd had a significant night together: the night Mike had decided to get rid of his hands. It hadn't been just any old night-at-the-bar. Champion would never forget it.

"We partied together."

"I'm going back to sleep."

"We got blotto."

Champion examined the other sleeping body. Carl.

Something was very wrong if Carl was here, too. His throat burned with mystery and emptiness—he might never be able to leave.

The door was locked. He breathed intentionally and calmed himself and whispered; "Gentle, gentle, gentle hands."

"Carl. Wake up. We're at Gentle Hands."

Carl mumbled something and opened his eyes.

"Carl, we're in Gentle Hands. Together. We're fucked. I think we're fucked."

His heavy eyes, Champion thought.

"Did we fuck?" Carl looked confused.

"No, we didn't fuck. It's me, Champion."

"My head hurts."

His woozy speech. He'd been drugged.

"We have to get out of here."

"Cheryl? I smell roses. And mustard? Where are we?"

Carl looked hungrily at Champion's lips.

"I'm Champion. You're my boss. Remember me, Boss?"

"Boss? Cheryl?"

"There's no Cheryl, Carl."

"But you're Cheryl. Blurry Cheryl."

"I erased her, remember? From the Concordance. Cheryl's gone forever."

"Oh. I'm so sorry; I love you." He closed his eyes again. "I really love you."

"There's no such thing as love, Carl."

"No, I feel it. I miss you."

"You're drugged, Carl. You don't miss me." Champion shook Carl's shoulder. This was no way for him to live. "It's time to get up. Shake it off. I'm not your wife. It's Champion."

Carl raised his body. "Kiss me, Cheryl, I've missed you."

"You're dreaming, Carl. I'm Champion"

"Maybe later you can slap me around a little?" Carl winked, turned away from Champion, lucid for a moment, and then suddenly asleep again.

Champion sat at his desk, spinning his chair in circles. When it was clear that Carl was out, he stood on his desk and pushed up one of the ceiling tiles. Inside he could hear the hum coming from the old blue cabling—not Scentsate's new thing, but it was connected. He was so sure he could smell it.

⋮

The sound of their door automatically unlocking roused Mike. They introduced themselves, again.

"Something's not right with Carl," Champion said.

"Can you help me with my pants?" Mike pointed at a pair of orange pants draped over his desk chair.

After helping him into his pants and prosthetics, the two of them headed down to the cafeteria for breakfast.

In the hall, Mike apologized for not remembering Champion. He'd had many late nights that ended with attempts to cut off his hands.

"Paper cutters, hacksaws," Mike said. "You name it, I tried it. Miter saw. Circular saw. Box cutter. Razor blade. Chef's knife. Lots of different knives."

"Knives?"

"A corkscrew. Spinning ceiling fan. Spinning ceiling fan with razor blades attached."

"Really?"

"I tried it all."

"How'd you finally do it?"

"It's a long story, Champ, but I'll tell you," Mike said.

⋮

49.

THE SUN SHIP SWAYED IN THE WIND, jerking its tethers tight, whipped by the heavy storm. Angie and the others wrapped themselves in ponchos to protect themselves from the storm blowing into their shelter. They huddled together in the middle beneath the metal roof and each wondered privately if they should call off the launch.

Angie had drawn the short straw and was honored to push the plunger to launch the ship—she was a sucker for ceremony and was happy to do it despite the danger. If this sun ship worked they'd launch dozens more, sending them on missions to quench those who missed the sun. "Do you think this is the big one? The storm?" Angie asked. She stepped forward, readying herself to run into the rain to hit the plunger to release the tethers.

One of her coworkers sighed. "I've seen worse." With each major storm somebody would declare it was the *worst* storm and then the rain would slow and water would lap back. But the water groped, with every storm taking a little more land, never quite receding to where it had been.

Angie ran into the rain, the water hitting her poncho like tiny bullets. The red-black clouds moved fast above her, groaning and twisting, dropping water in thick ribbons. She pushed the plunger and the tethers flailed for a moment in the torrent and then dropped to the ground. The sun ship's autopilot kicked in, the drone of its propellers awakening, joining the chorus of the storm. The ship teetered for a moment, as if it were going to fall, but quickly stabilized—rising into the air—its first position before the pilots in the command tower would execute the next program.

The small crowd of scientists huddled beneath the shelter cheered as Angie ran back to them and the dirigible hovered over them, slowly rising into the storm. When the control tower sent the signal, the sun ship's light arrays began to activate row by row—illuminating the airfield, the tower, the shelter—and seemed to evaporate the rain, the heat from the lamps fogging the wet asphalt.

Fully lit the ship ascended like a minor star, the light brighter than any of them had imagined, brighter even than the sun they thought they remembered. As the light broke through the clouds, parting the red-black darkness, it felt like a new day, the sun ship's program sending it off to test the new light.

50. THE ROOM WAS LIKE CARL'S BEDROOM AT HOME—here, plainly, was his bed—but it was also not like his room at home. The view of the garden had changed, as if somebody had smudged the scene with an eraser—and the room smelled odd to him, like something masquerading as lemon. He didn't remember that smell at home, but then many of the things in the room were unfamiliar—the lamp, for example. The lamp on his desk had changed. And the desk at home had been in its own room, he was sure of it. He was a powerful man, powerful enough to have a desk with its own room and leatherbound books nobody read.

He looked toward the window, small and barred, and the unfamiliar light coming through it. When he moved to stand and look, he felt a sharp pain in his neck, his stiff legs. He looked at the desk. Something about the desk? He could see the books on the shelves in the office, smell the wood and the cleaner somebody used to dust—lemon masking the smell of imitation wood—that's what this room smelled like, his favorite lemon-scented dusting chemical. Of course he was home in the freshly cleaned library, surrounded by his things.

On the desk was his computer. He'd want to check in with the Concordance later, maybe his email, see if Cheryl had gotten in touch with him—she'd been gone for a few days, maybe a week. He'd dreamt of her, dreamt of her hovering over him, dreamt of trying to kiss her, but that was all—she was always just out of reach.

Maybe there had always been three twin beds in his bedroom, maybe he'd always had three desks. Maybe there had never been books. In the bathroom he looked for his toothbrush and there he found it with his favorite brand of paste, his floss, and the solution in which he could put his contact lenses. He couldn't remember how to find the kitchen. He tried the doors, opening closets where he found his suits—orange jumpsuits, soft shoes. Where were his ties?

In the hall, he tried to make his legs work in the way he remembered his legs working, but he had difficulty lifting them as high as he'd been able to lift them, so he shuffled forward, sniffing the air for some sign of food. He was battered and sore. He bent to feel the bumps on his shins, feel the dull pain of old bruises.

The hall wasn't like a hall in a house—there were many doors and soft, gentle light reflected off the low sheen of the tiled floor.

51.

TAMMERS IN HER TOWER LOOKED DOWN FROM THE PERCH OF HER PLYWOOD COUCH, her new dog silent and obedient sleeping at her feet. So small, everybody moving through the rain. *Like ants*, she thought, *or some other industrious insect.* She paused to consider her profundity, looked around her bare apartment, cold and concrete. *If only we could all have* this.

She stroked the cold dog, got up from the plywood couch, her body sore from sitting so long on the hard wood, and in the kitchen, she poured the last of her Julius from the blender through a strainer to catch the bits of eggshell. She took a sip and let it linger in her mouth. Something wasn't right. Too sweet, or not sweet enough. She would try again tomorrow.

She had been without a refrigerator since discovering that hers was a prop. Only after sickening herself from eating spoiled food did she begin to store her food in a cooler full of ice she had delivered daily. Her stove and the dishwasher were fake, too, but she didn't care—the blender was real, and as long as food could be pulverized into a smoothie, she would be fine.

She held the Orange Julius to her nose and had a vague memory of the mall and a friend—*Cheryl*, she thought—when had she last seen her?

Her life of leisure afforded her many trips to the mall, not to shop, but to wander and watch; most often she opted to sit on the hard couch gazing into the middle space between her high-rise and the high rise across the street or down on the diligent people below braving the weather to go to their jobs.

Good, productive souls, she thought. She liked to take their pictures from above, to zoom in as far as she could to try to see the details of their faces and sometimes, she could—hard faces, pale and fallen.

Right now, these good people are going to office buildings where they make things that we need. Like this camera! Or my blender!

She got so excited she thought she heard the dog bark. She stood at the window, looked down through the rain, and spied a tiny man in a red scarf scampering along the sidewalk.

His name is Harold and he works in an office where they invent custom sandwiches for people. When he gets home from work, he likes to take a long bath with the dog, drink Orange Juliuses, and stare out the window at people on the street.

She could go on and on, inventing lives for these people.

Had something made a sound? She looked at the silent dog. No, nothing had made a sound.

She couldn't remember the last time she'd been to the mall. Her desire for it had faded for unclear reasons—she'd had a friend, she was sure, a best friend, her absence now more vivid than any memory of her presence.

Oh, yes. She'd been to the mall three days ago, an uneventful trip. She'd ordered a Julius, sat on a bench, waited for something to happen.

She looked at her phone, tried to find Cheryl in it, but couldn't. *Cheryl.* She tried to conjure Cheryl's face in her mind's eye but her mind's eye conjured instead a doughy blob where a face should have been. *Cheryl.*

Because her days were mostly the same—at the mall, at home staring and stroking the new dog—she had trouble with time. She had seen Cheryl, yes, but was it yesterday? A week ago? A year? Was Cheryl somebody she had seen on T.V. or a person on the street she had only imagined was her friend?

She had no idea how to make friends. She was many years into the period of adulthood where forging new relationships was so much work.

Cheryl was definitely a character on a television show. Yes. Or a person she'd seen on the street.

Or the art museum! She had surely been to the museum.

She pretended to turn on the television and nearly knocked it over. From the couch she pretended to flip through channels.

A dull pain took root in her temples and made its way slowly across the front of her skull and she wondered why she couldn't feel the thoughts banging around in her brain in the same way she could feel food in her stomach after she'd eaten it.

She lifted her glass to her lips and tasted the froth, exactly as she imagined it would be.

"Ah" she said. "Refreshing."

She pretended to turn off the television, sighing as she hit the imaginary switch because the new shows were *not* as good as the old shows.

She looked at the dog, still nameless.

"Cheryl," she said, trying it out on the dog. No response. *"Cheryl."*

She was pretty sure the dog looked up at her that time. Maybe Cheryl was the dog.

She heard the doorbell ring, but had never heard the doorbell ring before so did nothing, not registering it as a doorbell, or anything but a thing in space that was suddenly something and again, just as quickly as it had become, nothing.

Maybe she would take a nap; it seemed like nap time—the gray light had parted and afternoon sun appeared in the cavern between high-rises, warming the living room.

Again, the bell. Then a knock. Somebody at the door requesting her attention.

She looked through the hole in the door—outside a man holding a box looking at his phone.

"I'm here to fix your drain, ma'am," he said, looking up when she opened the door. He showed her his toolbox, like a toy, small and plastic, impossible for it to contain drain-fixing tools. A hammer hung from a loop attached to his pant leg.

"My drain's fine," she said.

"Are you sure? Somebody called it in. Said your drain's stuck. I'm here to service it. Plunge it, snake it. Whatever it takes."

"I know how to take care of my own drain. I don't need you to service it."

"Are you sure? I have special tools." He held up his tiny toolbox. His shirt was tight over the hard bulges of his muscular body. "It's probably clogged up with hair and food. Maybe broken glass, even. You wouldn't believe what I find in people's drains."

She looked at him. He wasn't unattractive, but he didn't look like somebody who knew his way around a drain. His nails were smooth, manicured. Some subtle cologne drifted from his skin.

"Once a squirrel had crawled up from the sewer and died right in a woman's disposal. Its head had come off. A real mess."

"There're no squirrel heads in my drain. I keep it clear. I don't need your tools."

"You probably have a squirrel. I'd bet money on it."

"I live on the 25th floor; there's no squirrel."

"Have you noticed any strange smells? Like something rotting?"

"Is this a joke?"

A woman walked through the open door of her condo, pushing past the plumber and Tammers. She wore a gold jacket with an elaborate crest patched onto the breast.

"Excuse me, can I help you?"

While she talked to the new intruder, the plumber took his tools to the kitchen and got to work on the drain.

"Hey, I told you I don't need your help, okay?"

The plumber ignored her.

"I'm sorry, do you live here?" the woman said. "I'm supposed to show this unit."

"Yes, this is my condo."

The plumber had his hand down the drain, fishing around for something.

"I have this listed as a model."

She wanted to turn on the garbage disposal; she was suddenly hot, imagining the plumber naked and semi-erect, his hand grinding in the maw, screaming in a way that could be either pleasure or pain.

"Yes, it's a model condo, that's why I bought it. The best." She turned to the plumber. "How is it in there? Clean, right?"

"But, on my list here, it says this is an empty unit."

"I think I found your problem," the plumber shouted, smiling and dumb. He was sweating through the back of his shirt. "You mind if I take my shirt off? It's so hot in here."

"I'm not paying you. I told you I didn't need your help."

"Take a look at my list," the woman said. "See? Vacant."

"No, that's wrong. I live here."

The woman looked around the apartment, looked oddly at Tammers. "Are you sure? This unit doesn't even have a real refrigerator."

"Oh, I've got that figured out."

"How long have you lived here? Is that your husband?"

"We're not married," he said, smiling. "Yet."

"That's not funny," Tammers said.

He pulled something out of the disposal like a rotted braid of grass. He had taken his shirt off even though she hadn't given him permission, but he was not unpleasant standing there holding the rotted debris like a fresh kill, his skin glistening in the afternoon light.

She didn't know, maybe she would marry him.

"You put that there," she said. "That wasn't there!"

"Definitely the problem," he said. "Or one of them. I'm still feeling a blockage down there. I'll have to go deep."

"Will you please go? There's no blockage," she said, wanting him to put his hand down the drain again. Maybe the blades could take his fingers.

"Hey, what's wrong with your dog?" the plumber asked.

"Nothing's wrong with the dog." She turned to the woman. "I

bought this condo with money from my app."

"I don't have any record of this condo being anything but a model."

"It's mine."

"Is that dog stuffed?" The woman turned to the couch and approached.

"Oh, that's just my friend Cheryl," Tammers laughed. "Can I make you an Orange Julius?"

"Can I pet her?"

"I'd rather you didn't."

"Hey little guy," the woman said, reaching toward the dog's unflinching mouth.

"Please don't. He's not for you to touch."

A couple, young, thin, and eager, appeared in the doorway.

"**Wow,**" the young woman said to her partner. "This is *amazing*. Tom, isn't it amazing?"

"This is Tom and this is Alice," the woman said. "They're buyers."

"But this is my condo."

"Isn't Alice cute? Just look at that dress," the woman said. "Polka dots!"

"We love it," Tom said, nodding in approval, pulling a finger across the wall. "Great light. What's wrong with the dog?"

"That's it. That's the ticket." The plumber was in elbow deep, moaning a little.

Alice fished in her purse and found a tape measure, stretching the metal tongue the length of the window. "Too bad there's no balcony."

Tom agreed. He hovered close behind the plumber, resting his hand on the counter next to him as the plumber pushed his arm farther into the drain. Tom looked at his wife. "He's really going at it!"

"Can we knock down this wall?" Alice pressed her body against the wall between the living room and bedroom, spreading her arms and legs like a crushed insect. "I can really feel the space in there, wanting to be free."

An elderly man standing in the doorway cleared his throat. "May I speak to the man of the house?"

"That's me," the plumber answered. Tom looked hurt.

The woman answered. "There's no man of the house. This is a model unit."

"I need to talk to the man of the house," he said, holding up a piece of long paper, like a scroll. He unfurled it, tapped it with his fingers. "I have very important news."

"There's no man," Tammers said. "I own this condo. I bought it with money from my app, and I'd like you all to leave."

Everybody paused, looked at Tammers, saddened by her force.

"Who are you?" she asked the man holding the scroll.

"The inspector," he said.

"What's your important news?"

"I can only tell the man of the house. It says so right on the scroll."

"Do you think we can paint the ceiling like the sky?" Alice twirled around the living room. "It's so airy in here."

The plumber held up the wet, headless body of a squirrel. "See, your drain needed me after all!"

The woman found a tape measure in her gold coat and pulled it across the kitchen wall, then tried to measure from the floor to the ceiling, but the flimsy tape measure collapsed. She dropped the tape measure, then turned to the plumber, took the hammer from its loop on his pant leg, and took a hard swing at the wall.

"I love it," Tom said, crossing his arms, proud of his wife's great idea. "We'll paint the ceiling like the sky!"

Tammers remembered Cheryl—her face, her eyes, her lips. She sat on the couch, stroking the cold dog, and watched these diligent people in her home, the energy of their movement a kind excitement. She looked out the window, the heat of the sun an array of lights on an airship floating across the skyline, fading behind the tower across the street. When it was gone, the red-gray sky returned and dropped hail and the hot sidewalks below disappeared in a cloud of steam.

52.

AT BREAKFAST, MIKE WAS IN THE MIDDLE OF A STORY and Champion had lost interest, focused instead on escape.

"Are you even listening?" Mike said.

The cereal was dry, a combination of oat clusters and bran, bland and chewy, but something. Champion could not remember a more satisfying meal. "Yes, I'm sorry. Where did you finally get rid of your hands?"

"That's what I was telling you."

"Sorry, had you gotten to the good part yet?"

"No, not yet. I was just telling you about how when I'd gotten out of here the last time, my report was pretty bad—I'd tried everything to get rid of my hands, my arms were scarred. They told me I was crazy, that I probably needed real doctors. But you know, the people in here, they don't give a shit."

"Why'd you come back?"

"I'll get to that. So they let me out. I was staying in a halfway house with a couple ex-cons and we were all working as brine-shrimp fisherman in Utah."

"What do they use brine shrimp for?"

"As a thickener. Plus, other stuff."

"Like what?"

"Flamingoes eat them."

"You were fishing for them to feed to flamingos?"

"I told you they're used as a thickener, you stupid shit. They have all kinds of industrial uses, too. Gasoline additive, insect repellent, deodorizer. Lots of stuff."

"What kind of thickener?"

"Look it up. That's not the point."

Champion stared at him and waited.

"Toothpaste and peanut butter, mostly. And paint."

Champion was satisfied by the answer.

"So, we were fishing for brine shrimp—we'd ride out onto the Salt Lake every day on jet skis with our nets and we'd net the little guys and then once our nets were full, we'd ride back to shore. It was easy money, and I'll tell you there's nothing like riding a jet ski on the Great Salt Lake at dawn, the sun burning down on you, the briny air in your face, tiny black flies feeding on your exposed skin. We were all being paid pretty well, and for the first time ever I was saving some money and I didn't feel like my hands were my enemy. Now my hands *did* something—everybody needs brine shrimp, and I was doing my small part."

Champion saw Carl at the other end of the cafeteria shuffling toward the serving line. Even from across the room, he looked confused and prematurely aged.

Mike gnawed the end of an untoasted bagel. "At night, we were having a really great time, really hitting it off. We'd drink a few beers, smoke a little krabake if somebody had some. Sometimes we'd get laid, or sometimes we'd just finish each other off if we were feeling lazy. Everything was cool because the future looked good—I was going to save up, maybe come back East, find somebody to marry—the future, for once, seemed bright."

"Sometimes we'd stay up too late and it'd be tough to get on the jet-ski in the morning, but I never missed a shift."

"Then one night one of the guys who'd done some real time—Tiny—we all had nicknames, except they mostly just called me Mike. Tiny says he's got this big idea."

Champion was bored, but he did want to know how Mike finally got rid of his hands.

Carl looked like he'd figured out how to get a tray of food and was wandering around the cafeteria, perhaps looking for friendly faces. Something about him had changed—he shuffled, but had withered too, his skin looser on his skeleton, his head hung lower. He looked lost.

"Can you hold on a sec, I'm worried about my friend."

"But I haven't finished my story."

"Just hold on." Champion stood and waved across the room to Carl. Maybe they'd tortured him. It was strange and a little sad to see Carl like this, confused and vulnerable. His presence made the world of Gentle Hands feel a little less strange though, a little more like the outside.

With every return, Champion started to think that this was the real world and everything else was just some strange dream he got to visit once in a while. He thought of the red sky, the rain. His parrot, his walk home. Even if he escaped, they'd just keep bringing him back. He didn't belong anywhere.

He looked up at the ceiling. The network offered him another kind of escape, maybe a permanent one. He could climb up—nobody would even notice—and make his way into the ducts to find the network cables—his network cables. He could almost hear them calling to him.

". . . So, we just started shooting." Mike was still talking.

Champion was relieved to have missed the middle of the story. He propped his head up with his hand to look like he was still paying attention.

"We'd done it; we had the money, but at what cost?"

"What'd you do with all the money?" Champion had long ago learned how to make it seem as if he'd been listening the whole time even when he hadn't.

Carl had found them and before he sat down, he leaned over and kissed Champion on the lips. "Hey, guys."

"Mike, this is Carl. He's our roommate."

"Hi, Carl."

"Mike was just telling me about cutting off his hands."

Carl raised his eyebrows and looked at Champion as if he could not believe what he was hearing.

"It may seem unbelievable to you, that I was able to saw through both of my own arms, but I did."

"That's some story, Mike." Champion meant it.

"How long will you stay here?" Carl asked.

"Until I'm really cured."

"Aren't you cured now? Your hands are gone."

"That's the whole point of the story! My hands weren't the problem, all along. It's Gentle Hands."

"What's Gentle Hands?" Carl asked. He looked confused.

"The problem is with our minds."

Champion took Carl's hand. He knew to be gentle. "It's a place where we'll get better, Carl. We've been violent, and here, we'll learn to be gentle. How does that sound for once? Gentle?"

"Gentle? I don't want to be gentle. I want to go home."

"This is home," Champion said. "This is your home." Champion could feel the pull of the network. How easy it would be to remove a panel, climb into a duct, and crawl away to where they could never find him.

Carl nodded as if he understood. His eyes were vast and empty, like somebody who would not begin to understand for a long time.

53. EVEN IF HE WASN'T HOME, IT SEEMED LIKE HOME.

The room had been big and strange and full of people, but when he sat, he was again in his dining room, oaken and dark, with Cheryl next to him about to break into a soft-boiled egg.

A stranger was eating with them.

He remembered that Cheryl's brother had come to stay with them for a few days once. Cheryl seemed to know him, maybe even she liked him.

The man deftly fed himself a bagel.

Cheryl was just a little bigger and maybe a little balder than he remembered—he'd had a dream that she'd left him—only a dream, a dream from which he'd awakened, finally.

She seemed distant and far away, like somebody he'd known and then not known, like somebody he'd only be looking at in pictures. Maybe they'd make love later that day, after lunch when the sunlight would warm the house and they'd want to take a nap.

"Who are you?" he asked, looking at the man. "How do you know Cheryl?"

"Mike," he said. "We're roommates. I don't know Cheryl, I'm sorry."

Carl looked at Cheryl—*why was this man in their dining room?*

"If you'll excuse me, I have group therapy."

Cheryl said they should go too, since they'd only just gotten there. Show they were making a go of it.

Carl was confused again; when he took her hand she pulled away from him.

"I'm not your wife, Carl," she said.

"Don't be silly. I know you were angry." He wasn't sure if he'd gone anywhere or not. Maybe he *had* been gone? Where had he gone? Had he had his own apartment? "I don't really know what happened."

"I don't either. But I'm not Cheryl."

Carl nodded to agree with her. It wasn't worth arguing.

"I'm Champion. You're my boss. Don't you remember?"

Carl looked at Cheryl and really tried—something about her eyes, her face. But her lips. He knew her lips; he would never forget.

"I'd like to walk in the garden."

"I don't think we can do that. There's no garden here."

Carl didn't know why they wouldn't be able to walk in the garden, but he wasn't going to question her, not like this. "Is it raining?"

"Yes," she said. "It's raining. We can't walk in the garden when it's raining. Maybe we could just watch some television? Go to the library to read a book?"

"A book. That might be nice. Can't we do something else? Is it Saturday?"

"I don't know what day it is."

"Shouldn't I be at work? I need to get dressed for work. What time is it?"

"You took a few vacation days, okay? Just relax. Think gentle thoughts."

Carl's head felt like it had been filled with glue. Thinking had never been an *effort*, but when he thought hard about what he was trying to think about, thoughts indeed came:

He remembered being hit on the head. He'd been sitting in his office late going through what Bryce had left on his desk when some people in suits appeared in his doorway. He'd been startled, but not frightened—after all, they were wearing suits. Big Wigs, he'd thought, there to commend him on all he'd done and accomplished.

Then they'd beaten him until he'd gone black—not the kind of beating he enjoyed, but a painful, involuntary assault.

When he'd woken, that all felt strange to him, like he'd dreamt it or imagined it. A fragrance he'd inhaled, something Bryce was working on, something mustardy and floral, lingered in the back of his throat.

"Did I hit my head?"

"Yes, you probably hit your head," Cheryl said. They were walking down a long corridor again. Carl noticed the hospital beds. "Am I in the hospital?"

"No, you're not in the hospital. It's like rehab. Do you know about rehab?"

"Rehab? Am I addicted to something?"

"Sort of."

The lines of each thing they walked past were sharp and geometrical as if a pencil outline of what he was seeing was laid over everything he saw.

"I'm having trouble seeing."

Carl felt as if he might fall forward, down the length of the hall, and into the void.

"I love you, Cheryl."

Cheryl sighed. She was looking down at him from above from inside the ceiling.

"I love you, too, Carl."

54.

SOMETIMES A RINGING, SOMETIMES A WHISPER, sometimes the siren of so many bodies: the scream of sweat and skin and shit, the shrill reverberation of the boy, blood, and death, the echo of every scent bouncing and rebounding, repeating, and multiplying.

Bryce held the strands of her hair in his trembling hand, held them to his nose, inhaled and listened to the whisper, so close to perfect silence.

At night he tweezed—Denise's chair, the tight weave of the carpet around her desk, her brush, the walls of her cubicle. He'd woven strands of Denise's hair into his mother's hair, liquefied it while working on the other projects: compost, saliva, a new kind of banana.

The sounds twisted into tight knots behind his ears, his head full of furious noise: the grinding and gnashing of molecule against molecule, synapses leaping across the regions of his brain like lightning.

He'd used every scent he could remember in different combinations, suffered the noise of them still ringing in his ears. The hair he hid in an enveloped in the back of his desk drawer and inspected the vials arrayed on his desk, the final result, liquid silence.

Goat's rue, the musk of an African civet, rye fungus. Bitter lemon, a teaspoon of his mother's dust.

He looked at a blurry photograph of her, taken from before he was born, and prepared to meditate.

The sound of death, heavy and low, pulsed as if the sound came from within, pushing against his eardrums, trying to escape.

He uncapped a vial, held it to his nose, and inhaled, moved the vial to his other nostril, and breathed again.

The silence came like a fist, the absence he longed for like a suffocating mask growing as the stench spread through his nose and throat. The fragrance was without sound, merely a scent, merely a taste, bitter and awful but now with a promise.

He heard the low hum of the air conditioning system, the creak of his chair. He could hear something moving above in the ceiling, somewhere beyond the dropped panels. He heard soft music from somewhere at the other end of the floor, coming from somebody's office, heard the sound of his heart, he thought, the blood crawling through his veins.

He looked at the photograph and was consumed by memories of his mother: the touch of her hand, the crevices of her face, her nose. He could see every pore, feel her hand in his. He was overcome by the silence and the sadness of longing as he felt the thing he had made expanding, forcing itself into his stomach, his veins, his heart.

The sound began again like a kind of migraine. The dim light of the office wrapped around him, covering his pupils with a thick gray cloud. The rain pounded the windows from outside, then inside, as if the torrent were surrounding him. He longed for Denise, the smell of her hair, intact on her head.

He could focus on nothing, the pleasure of any past replaced with a pounding, relentless present.

He looked up, a dark figure at the entrance to his cube.

55.

CLOUDS COVERED THE SUN, but faint light showed the details of the wet, dirty street in front of Denise's apartment: the trash, the filth, a film across the scarred black pavement.

The old park across the street, verdant in Denise's memory, was instead a brown mess of long dead grass and thick yellow tendrils thriving despite the lack of light, climbing and twisting around the trunks of dead trees.

The alien vines crawled from between the iron fence posts and onto the parking lot. Denise didn't drive often and sometimes had to pull them from the cracks between the door and body of her parked car. She opened her trunk and removed the box she'd been given at Bryce's house.

Inside her apartment she put the box on the coffee table in front of the couch and carefully lifted the lid. Inside, grey soot covered a twisted clump of long hair and a book of photographs of Bryce and a woman Denise guessed was his mother.

She slid her index finger through the dust, leaving a trail where her fingertip cleared away the dirt. She remembered the bruise arced across Bryce's neck, his body limp against the cube wall, the feeling that Bryce might simply be sleeping, the yearning that took hold of her after she'd found him.

She lifted first the hair, and then carefully removed the wrapped photo album from the box and set it on the table. She pulled the tape holding the plastic wrap protecting the photos and unwrapped the book like a body, Bryce's heart or his brain or all of those things bound in the book.

This dust, these photographs, the last of him.

The photographs on the first page, placed carefully between a layer of cellophane and the sticky board of the album, were overexposed and gauzy, but clearly of Bryce as a boy with his mother.

The long steel necks of heavy and rusted construction equipment, resting and limp like the necks of feeding dinosaurs, surrounded the old playground. She remembered following Bryce, chasing him. Remembered the metallic taste of the water from the fountain, the feeling of cold, rough metal in her hands as she climbed the swingset after Bryce.

Sweat and thirst, the exhaustion at the moment before sleep, too hot in her bed despite the dark summer night.

They orbited around one another beneath the enormous maple trees hunched over the park. They ran to the edge of the river and back before his mother had seen them, took turns climbing into an empty dumpster, climbed to the top of a mountain of gravel behind the ancient bulldozers.

She remembered her favorite toy, a doll, the figure of a woman, naked and featureless, without emotion or a companion. With the doll she played on the surface of stiff dead grass, while Bryce, only feet away from her, pushed a toy dump truck over the hills toward some imagined construction site.

He had made fun of her doll—he'd asked her why it had no clothes or eyes and she'd cried, asked where her mother had gone. He pushed her, threw handfuls of dirt at her until she'd run to the other end of the playground where she'd hidden in the canopy of a dead willow.

"Denise," Bryce called to her from the other room. "What are you doing?"

"Nothing," she replied. She didn't want him to see her looking through the photographs.

"What are you doing? Why are you here?"

Only silence came from the second bedroom. She didn't know he'd come home.

She looked out the window of her apartment, looked at her car in the parking lot; already the vines had climbed over her tires, into the wheel wells, pushed into the space between the body and door.

She had no second bedroom, no back room, no extra space at all besides her own small bedroom, her living room, her galley kitchen, a cage in the basement where she piled all the equipment for sports and hobbies she'd once begun and abandoned.

The voice had stretched the apartment, opening up new space, and then let it contract.

"Is everything okay?" she asked. "Are you there?"

She walked to where she'd heard the voice, the room she'd imagined now no longer there. She took the silence to mean contentment, whatever ghost she had conjured suddenly gone. She touched the wall, tapped on it, listened for the echo of hidden space.

She sat down again, opened a page in the album and remembered.

Friends had rented a boat and together on a brutally hot August day taken them down the river, away from the city, away from the heat radiating from the concrete and asphalt surfaces to a shaded grove where they dropped the anchor and swam in the calm, murky water.

She could not remember the friends—how they knew them, their names, or their faces—only their boat, its beige surfaces, the pattern of the plastic diving platform at the back. She remembered the cloud of brown-green algae in the water, how it felt on her legs, swimming in the water so hot it brought no relief from the air. She remembered filling the boat with gas, maneuvering into the slip at the end of the day, the drive to the little bar where, sun-tired from the long day, they ate hamburgers and hoped to soon be home. The bar was famous—politicians had gathered to make an important decision though nobody ever remembered what that decision was or what it had meant. A commemorative plaque on the wall of the building let them know so they could feel the aura of the once-important thing that had happened there.

They saw another plaque on a historic building, on another day, in another neighborhood. A famous writer had lived there, or died there. Or slept there. They'd walked from there to the writer's grave beneath a grove of dead trees, the grave clearly marked with a stone bigger than the others in a circle of markers surrounding a long-dry and crumbling fountain. She couldn't remember the name of the writer; she was certain she didn't know who he or she was, anyway. Just another name.

Bryce had held her hand. She remembered a fight they'd fought on the boardwalk of some dry and dusty coastline, the weeds coming up through the sand and the boards of the walk and the beach a long stretch of debris: the dead tendrils of monstrous sea plants, pelicans, seals, and crustaceans dying, writhing and breathing their last breaths on the blood and oil-stained sand.

They'd wondered why they'd come there, why the reviews in the Concordance didn't emphasize the terrible insect problem, why they'd forgotten protection from the sun, why so many dead birds.

She heard him drop a book in the second bedroom. Something fell from a shelf in the hall closet. A noise in the kitchen, a scratching at the front door. Something burning in the oven.

"Bryce, is that you?"

They'd been fighting, again; he'd walked toward her, larger than he'd been before. Something was off about his smell—something dark and cold, something medicinal. His face was serpentine, his eyes small and close.

He'd told her he'd wished she was dead. She could still hear him saying it, would always remember.

Maybe he'd gone somewhere for the night—a bar or back to the office where he'd sit at his desk and lose himself in the Concordance.

"Are you home, Bryce? Are you angry?"

She opened her eyes in the bathroom, her hands on the vanity, her face in the mirror the same as always—swollen and gray.

She looked in the closet and found only her things—none of his clothes or shoes, no space where they might have once been.

She remembered sitting together on a rainy, empty beach. They'd taken the day off. The sun was unusually bright and a cold breeze blew through sparse blades of rain falling from a single black cloud. They chased each other in the choppy water and fell asleep wrapped in towels, in their chairs, under the shelter of their beach umbrella. They ate crab cakes and drank warm beers at a gas station diner on the way back, the only customers, sitting in the dark dining room, the sun now covered in clouds. The rain returned in force.

She looked at the photos and touched them and tried to imagine Bryce's light reflecting onto the film, that same light now reflecting off of the image, dying in her eyes.

"Denise," he shouted from downstairs. "Denise!"

She ignored him, waited.

"I need you," he yelled again. "Come here."

She hated his commands, hated his shrill, angry voice screaming from downstairs.

"Right now," he yelled. "I need you."

She was frightened; what frightened her was not his voice or what he said, but the stairs, the stairs that had appeared next to the second bedroom that had appeared, then shifted, then disappeared.

There they were: the stairs descending into the dark basement where Bryce went at night to watch television without her.

She stood at the top and called out, afraid to walk into the darkness not because she was afraid of what she would find, but because she was afraid the house would shift back into an apartment, leaving her in the limbo.

"What do you want?"

When he didn't answer, she turned, was in Bryce's house again.

She remembered.

He'd hurt his knee. He'd fallen down the stairs, and she'd wanted to take him to the emergency room, but he insisted it would be fine. He'd hit his head on the low door to the walk-in closet in the back bedroom and complained of headaches for days. They'd fought at work, something they promised never to do. They avoided each other for a week.

He'd argued with her about the Concordance, how they couldn't hide it from their coworkers—they needed to update their entries before they'd been updated automatically. He'd been arguing with somebody named Champion, somebody she knew nothing about, asking him about trying to alter the Concordance, to do something she didn't understand. He wanted to add things to his mother's entry, things that weren't true, though she didn't know what; he wanted to make her into something more than she was, more than she would ever be.

She held a handful of hair to her nose and inhaled the dust, the remnants of Bryce or his mother or both of them. She sneezed.

She missed him more than she could have possibly imagined.

Denise woke in her apartment and remembered dinner with Bryce the night before. They'd been arguing because his difficult nose made mealtime a challenge: anything too exciting, anything with a complex odor profile, made meals painful. She was tired of bland meals; she missed *real* food and though she ate alone a day or two a week, she wanted to have a meal with him they both could enjoy, that perhaps he could work a little less, that he could step back from so much testing throughout the day—it wasn't his job anyway—and save his concentration for a really good dinner with Denise.

Exhausted, they'd gone to bed angry with one another, and despite Denise's fatigue, she'd lain awake, rolling their argument over and over again in her head until she realized the argument wasn't real, that Bryce wasn't there, that she ate all of her meals alone. Still, she could not sleep and when she turned toward where Bryce should have been, she shuddered.

She tried to remember if she'd actually cooked something with Bryce, if she'd eaten his portion, too. She rolled over and looked for Bryce and confirmed he wasn't there, but when she put her hand on his pillow, she felt the warmth of his head, could smell the scent of his skin in the impression he'd left.

The next day, he'd made up for their fight by leaving work early to make an elaborate, fragrant dinner for both of them—a roast something, she couldn't exactly remember the meal, only that he'd made it and that it smelled amazing like so many onions and lemons and garlic.

She'd seen him leave early and imagined he was up to something, but was still surprised by dinner. When he walked by her cube for the last time, she remembered how she used to feel about him, felt annoyed, again, at his presence. A part of her still loathed him and—late at night when she was most sure that he was dead, that all of what she thought and felt for him was an illusion—a sober voice somewhere inside her knew how much she hated him, knew how much she didn't want to think about him anymore, didn't want to be in love at all, if there was such a thing, didn't want these memories. *That* part of her would tell her *she was glad he was dead* and that all of this, all this *feeling* was just a distraction, that if she could only get rid of it, if she could cut away the part of her brain still diseased by whatever drug, whatever *thing* Bryce had invented, she would return to normal, return to going through her days like they were just days.

After dinner, they sat on the couch and watched television and checked the Concordance on their phones. When she looked at him, she noticed that he looked worn out, his face gray and waxen.

They'd had such a nice dinner.

He was quickly asleep on the couch, his breath heavy and loud.

When she felt herself breathing, she felt the burning in her throat, musky and thick, ever-present.

She remembered going to the park. It was fall and though summer had been cool, the days were still long and the air, though crisp, was not unpleasant. The rain had abated and they were going to spend some hiking along the creek. He was particularly excited at the prospect of seeing deer and she imagined they'd probably see a few. He worried, too, about coyotes. They should have bought pepper spray, but instead they made walking sticks with which they imagined beating the coyotes, if it came to that. They packed snacks and water and put on their boots and took Bryce's mother's old car—they'd have to walk too far to take the Metro—and consulted the Concordance's maps for directions.

There they parked and gathered their things and walked to the trailhead. Theirs was the only car in the lot. They'd taken a day off, Denise remembered, or it was a Sunday. Maybe there were a few cars in the parking lot, but she knew she'd commented to Bryce that she would have thought there'd be more people out on such a mild day, a day without rain or excessive heat. He'd told her he thought people were afraid of the vast park, more like a dead enchanted forest in the middle of the city, and that people mostly used it on weekends. *It must have been a weekday*, she thought, *but could they both have taken the same day off?* Maybe she'd called in sick, she thought. It didn't matter.

The Bryce-that-was, was neither the Bryce she'd known, the real Bryce, nor the Bryce she'd seen in her apartment; this new Bryce was a menacing Bryce, larger and hostile.

They began their hike beneath dry skies, walking briskly downhill into the woods.

She stood at the top of the dark staircase, about to descend into the basement to answer his call.

They passed only a single cyclist meandering along the twisted path, and then no one as the skies darkened and the air grew cool.

She could see his little eyes in the darkness, the indistinct shape of his body.

"I'm not going to hurt you," he said. "I just want to talk."

They paused to consider the sky, but decided to continue their hike; they'd gone far enough that if it started to rain or hail, they'd be stuck in it for a while, anyway, and they'd brought ponchos.

A noise in the kitchen. Something outside. When she turned back to the basement, Bryce was gone; the stairs were a steep, rocky slope, the darkness of the basement the darkness of night.

They passed abandoned shopping carts in an orange, rust-stained pool, a heap of tires in a clearing, and could see a row of six concrete cylinders, like bunkers, whose purpose wasn't noted in the Concordance; the debris marked the way.

Bryce shouted to her not from the basement, but from the kitchen.

"Where are you?" he yelled.

They'd had some purpose, some destination, now forgotten.

She asked Bryce to check the map on his phone, too, which he did. They were going the right way; he insisted, pointing to a pile of railroad ties, a split in the path in the map, a faded blue mark on a tree.

"Where are you?" he yelled as she stumbled down the rocky path into the basement cave.

If she looked back, she would have seen him about to descend after her.

They just had to follow the wide path, a path of dirt and roots compacted to cement-hardness by decades of hikers and cyclists that wound through the sparse forest along an oily stream. They occasionally crossed the water over worn and wobbly bridges only to cross back later.

Bryce held his nose against the stench of some dead thing.

"Are you okay?" she asked.

He described horrible sounds—long, loud scraping and scratching tapering off slowly into high-pitched squeals, a feedback thrum punctuated by deep, bass warbles, or the slurping of licking lips.

Sometimes she thought he was making it all up, even when he seemed genuinely distressed. He was the worst when his mind was adrift; focused, he seemed okay, able to push away the sounds.

She could hear him behind her. The ceiling of the basement was wet, water dripping from old pipes, twisted wires, old bent nails from the joists. Roots and stone grew from the floorboards above and consumed the ceiling; the cement floor became mud as her passage narrowed.

And they walked and descended: a deep valley, a cut in the park, up steep slopes and over soft hills. Street bridges shadowed them from above. The sky darkened.

"You can't run," he said. His voice was on top of her, inside her head.

She breathed the thin air—lemon and pine, earth and mold. She squeezed herself into the narrow passage, pushed her body like ooze into the crevices.

They should have turned back. Bryce said they had plenty of time; they hadn't yet gone where they wanted to go.

The heat of his body moved through the darkness as she pressed herself into the scant spaces. She was a child again, a meager slip; she risked folding her fingers into fists as she willed her body to melt away.

He reminded her they'd brought their ponchos, so everything would be fine.

She became the crevices, folding herself into nothing, his monstrous shadow blanketing her.

Where had they wanted to go?

His breath became the air and devoured the chill; his body took the light and in darkness she felt his hands slipping into the cracks of the wall around her wrists, scratching and pulling. She willed herself liquid, slid from his hands, slid down the walls onto the ground, and sloped away.

She often thought of the night of the holiday party, thought about why it was she *had* gone home with him, *if* she had gone home with him. She had fallen asleep on the train, but then?—her memory was double.

"Where are you?" he said. "Denise?"

Sometimes when she remembered the party she remembered an intense night—something fun, a magical beginning.

"Nowhere," she said. She felt a rivulet of cool water on her chest, joined it, following its flow. "I'm nothing."

Sometimes that night was by design; she had *wanted* him and seduced *him*.

Her throat was the earthy ground, the smell deep and gravelly, cold and bitter.

Sometimes she remembered lucidly: she was drunk and bored and believed, in her inebriation, that fucking him would somehow hurt him, that after he slept with her, he would be so devastated by her further rejections he would be so humiliated he would leave her alone, only intoxication and fatigue and the long commute had interfered.

She conjured blossoms, floral, dewy, celestial. Somewhere a pleasant memory: a hidden lake, the darkness of the movie theater, an early-morning market. Bryce's hands slithered around her and she slipped away only for him to find her again, pulling at her ankles, pulling himself toward her.

She looked up: the dark office, a single light shining from Bryce's cube, the air dry and quiet, filling with something floral and musky, then moldy and foul.

Her new memories were narrated to her by a voice neither hers nor Bryce's, like a voice whispering in her ear.

"Why are you doing this?"

Her new memories were transplants, shaky things.

She conjured spring, lush meadows, garden parties. Solitary bicycle rides on the trails behind the mall, filled with menace and the tinge of freedom.

The night she'd gone home with Bryce.

Maybe she'd gone to the holiday party, maybe she'd stayed at home. Maybe Bryce didn't exist at all.

She had only her memories to follow.

His arms like vines, his body erupting around her, enfolding her.

She sat up in bed. Something outside scraped the window. She felt as if she were sleeping in a stranger's bed, and then as if she were back at Bryce's house, in his mother's bed that night anticipating a hangover. Then she saw her dresser, her bare, white walls.

She walked into her dark apartment, found the photographs

arrayed on the coffee table.

They walked and it began to rain. He opened his backpack beneath a tree, removed a poncho, unfolded it, and gave it to Denise before unfolding his.

"Torrential," he said, as they ran with their heads down. The cold rain cascaded around her face. Bryce pointed to a bridge ahead of them and so they ran to it, knowing it would provide them shelter.

She would let him surround her, thrust outward, destroy him from inside.

The clouds were furious bruises. When they reached the bridge, they stood in the middle beneath it, staying barely dry. Cars drove over the bridge above them pushing water over the edges like waterfalls on either side of them.

His body and the walls around her amalgamated into crystalline thew.

They stood beneath the bridge and waited. The rain thickened hitting the ground like blades. Bryce took a picture of her in her poncho with his phone.

She conceded, felt herself dropping a photograph onto the ground.

They zipped their ponchos and continued their walk.

"Where are we going?"

Maybe they should turn back.

She could not leave him even if she'd wanted to.

He had sealed her into the stone, into stone.

She remembered the smell of the valley after the rain, like something wet and earthen. The path was no longer paved; instead, they walked on thick, pungent moss and as they hiked she began, gradually, to feel like the path had disappeared beneath them.

The sky turned red and coyotes howling in the distance.

Her feet sunk into the damp earth, the ground swallowing them; when she looked at Bryce's feet, he had sunken in to his ankles.

"What do you want?"

She could barely move, her lips and mouth only barely free.

She said something to him about the coyotes and he told her not to worry.

The earth will protect us. He told her they could build a fire in a nearby cave and wait until morning to go back.

All she could see was the plane of the wide, moss-covered forest tilting toward them, wild animals breathing from the dark woods, the distant noise of the city hundreds of feet up on the long bridges spanning the scar of the park.

She awoke at her desk. She stood and looked around at the other cubes. It was late, the office was empty, and when she looked out the window, she could see that it was still gray.

She and Bryce ran; they'd heard the animals in the distance. They bit at their feet, their hot breath on the backs of their wet calves.

She tried to maneuver her body, to push him away, his hands like claws; she slid away, free for a moment, then caught again.

The rain filled the valley around them, the ground finally too saturated to absorb any more water, the space between the trunks of trees, rivers of water from every direction.

She looked through Bryce's photographs: a photo of a dog, a moss-covered forest floor, thick dark pine trees, no moon, only water. She could smell the pine, feel the needles below her feet, and hear the coyotes in the distance.

The earth swallowed their ankles, their calves, their knees, but still they walked.

He grasped. She tried to escape again, but couldn't—his hands, the water, the things surrounding them.

Bryce said he'd lead them to a cave he knew, where they'd be safe. The mouth at the bottom of a sinkhole.

"Won't it be full of water? We should be going up?" she asked, still following him.

He didn't answer.

"Where are we going?" she asked.

"I'm taking you away," he said.

The cave of the basement was a stone enclosure. She pushed forward and dragged him with her, feeling the crack closing.

She inhaled, the smell of the rotting earth so strong it became a scream.

She strained to remember what he'd said. She could no longer hear him.

She had no memory of a cave.

They stopped. The floor sloped down and away from them in every direction and she wanted to skip ahead to the part where they were warm, safe, and silent.

She put her hands in front of her and searched for something real: her desk, the office window, the pillow on the bed next to her, but there was nothing.

Bryce climbed onto his desk, opened the panel above him, cut through the network cabling, and wound it around his neck in the early morning, the office a blue dawn.

"What are you doing?" she asked.

She felt only the rain and the water, the mud sucking at her legs. She felt his hands reaching through the darkness, wrapping the cable around his neck, wrapping his hands around her, around her neck.

Sunlight above: the shadow of an airship arrayed with light cut through the rain, burned away a cloud, and washed the forest floor in steam.

The water rose. She felt the heat of the lamps on her face.

"Where are we going?" she asked.

She put her arms around his neck, felt his hands around her wrists, begging her.

"I need to end this," she said.

He pulled the network cabling down, wrapped it around his neck. Her long red fingernails pushed into the skin of his throat.

The office lights came on, row by row. She heard whispering: *"gentle hands, gentle hands, gentle hands,"* as she squeezed, waiting for the memories to end.

56.

CHAMPION FELT THE NETWORK DEVOURING HIM, wrapping him in a womb of wire and plastic, every smell he had ever known filling his sinuses, his mouth, his lungs, taming any thoughts of returning to Gentle Hands as his experience of the real world was submerged in the intense focus of his current situation. He'd climbed up and followed the familiar vibrations—into the depths of Gentle Hands, down into the subterranean tunnels where information and sensation coalesced, back into the thrumming heart of Scentsate's new network alive with fragrance and memory.

The energy pulses had increased in duration and speed into a single stream of humming vitality pushing over and through him. He was inside a cable, feeling the life of the network as part of it. He felt at peace, here in this cage, a conduit for the endless flow of data in all its forms.

Maybe this is what he had always wanted.

Somebody unwrapped him, peeling layers of black plastic from around his body.

Now the light.

He closed his eyes and tried to move his hands over his face, but they were still bound in plastic. The room was intensely hot.

"Carl, is that you?" An earthen smell, like dung and soil, crept into the air, crawled up his nose. The smell of smoke and the sting in his eyes—he was in the crematorium, not back at Gentle Hands.

"I'm not Carl." The voice sounded like Raymond, his ex. Good old Cakes and Steaks. Or was it Steaks and Cake? "I'm just doing my job."

"Can you unwrap me? Let's go home."

"I'm afraid I can't do that. Once you're dead, you're dead. Gone from the Concordance, gone from payroll."

"Raymond, is that you? Why are you here?"

"We've let Raymond know. We'll give him your ashes, though I'm not sure why he'd even want them."

Champion struggled. "But I'm not dead."

"That's not really true. You're definitely dead. We found you in a tunnel above the office. Already rotten. Face eaten by rats."

Champion did not blame him—he would have done the same, following orders. After so many lifeless years, he felt suddenly alive. He twisted and writhed, felt himself screaming as if he was hearing somebody else.

"Please, your body, it's decomposing, you smell terrible. There's nothing left. Give up."

Champion felt the man push his finger into his decomposing body and swirl it around. "See?"

He could find no argument to counter this indisputable proof; he was already decomposing.

"Why are you doing this? Can you just let me go back to the network? Back to Gentle Hands, even?"

"Sorry, it's too late for that." He wrapped his arms around Champion's midsection and heaved him off the gurney and onto the floor. He began to drag him toward the furnace.

"You'll feel dead again soon, I promise."

57.

THE STALE OFFICE AIR AWAKENED, SUDDENLY VIBRANT and alive as the technicians opened their morning samples and released the aroma of artificial spearmint, honeysuckle, and rye. Something abrasive erupted—one of them, working on something like bleach, burned the air with their chemistry and corrupted all of their work.

The fragrances coalesced into a kind of chemical white noise, stinging their noses and throats and burning their eyes.

A collective sigh spread through the dying air from cubicle to cubicle, and they rose from their chairs and sought to complain and looked for the one they were to complain to, their name suddenly escaping them—D . . . something?

One of them went to look for them—a project manager, a woman—maybe? D or E . . . something. He looked and was sure he'd found their cube and it was empty—a whisper of an aura still, a kind of warmth—something in the fabric of the walls, or in the stained gray of the carpet, maybe. This was not just an empty cubicle—it still carried the air of somebody recently gone. He sat down in the chair and spun, trying to remember, looking for something tangible. He lifted the keyboard and looked behind the monitor and found a single empty glass vial. How strange, he thought, to miss this.

He lifted it to his nose and inhaled and smelled nothing. Then he remembered—oh yes, nobody had occupied this cube for years. He tossed the vial into the trash and returned again to work.

Acknowledgments

A huge thank you to PJ Carlisle and everybody at Texas Review Press who helped to make this a book. To PJ, especially: thank you for taking a chance and for making this novel so much more than it was. A huge thanks, too, to my writing group pals, Russ Brakefield and Aaron Burch who read this so many times and offered invaluable advice, encouragement, and friendship. Thank you to all who helped in some way at some point in this book's life, especially: Matt Bell, Lindsey Drager, Jacob Paul, Hilary Plum, Joanna Ruocco, and April Wilder. Thanks to all my former teachers, classmates, and students. Thanks to Eastern Michigan University for supporting this project with time and a warm office. Thank you to the best colleagues in the world: Rob Halpern, Carla Harryman, and Christine Hume. And thank you to the journals who published bits of this in various forms: *The Collagist*, *Juked*, *Five Chapters*, and *The Conium Review*.

And thank you infinitely to my partner in life and art, Susan McCarty, who makes everything possible, and to our daughter, Matilda, who fills every day with light and laughter.